PERPETUAL CARE: STORIES

ALSO BY JAMES NOLAN

POETRY

Why I Live in the Forest (Wesleyan University Press)

What Moves Is Not the Wind (Wesleyan University Press)

POETRY IN TRANSLATION

Pablo Neruda, Stones of the Sky (Copper Canyon Press)

Jaime Gil de Biedma, Longing: Selected Poems (City Lights Books)

CRITICISM

Poet-Chief: The Native American Poetics of Walt Whitman and Pablo Neruda (University of New Mexico Press)

ESSAYS

Fumadores en manos de un dios enfurecido: Ensayos a caballo entre varios mundos (Madrid: Enigma Editores)

{ WINNER OF THE **2007 JEFFERSON PRESS PRIZE** }

PERPETUAL CARE: STORIES

JAMES NOLAN

ISBN: 9780980016413
Library of Congress Control Number: 2008922047

Book and jacket design by AuthorSupport.com
Edited by Henry Oehmig
First Printing May 2008
Printed in the United States of America

Published by Jefferson Press

jefferson
press

808 Scenic Highway
Lookout Mountain, TN 37350

Publisher's Note

These stories are works of fiction. Names, characters, places, and institutions either are the product of the author's imagination or are used ficticiouly. Any resemblance to actual persons, living or dead, is coincidental.

in memory of my mother,
Helen Partee Nolan

Parce que le temps passe, je prie pour vous.

CONTENTS

I
THE OCCUPIED CROSS

THE IMMORTALIST

P eter Cordero tried to forget about the funeral as, chopsticks poised, he dove into the onion cake and spicy smoked ham at the Hunan on Sansome Street. At home in New Orleans he worked as a food spy, even though he enjoyed eating too much to send anything back, which is what he was paid to do. He was hired by restaurants to secretly evaluate waiters and cooks, but liked to think of himself as an incognito food critic. This was the first time he'd been back in San Francisco in two years, since he had written a gourmet column for one of those weekly consumer rags he still thought of as "underground." Unfortunately, he was here for another memorial service. This time it wasn't AIDS or breast cancer.

This time it was Limmel: shaggy, gold-rim-spectacled Limmel, as Peter always remembered him from the commune on Baker Street. Limmel, a.k.a. Sea Ananda, guru to the stars. Vegan and celibate, his herb-tea sipping friend had even more bottles of organic vitamins on his kitchen counter than Peter's mother had doctor's pills. Limmel Rock, another Immortalist dead as a doornail.

"What'd your little friend way out there die of?" Peter's mother had asked before he caught his flight yesterday afternoon. Even though he was forty-seven, she still called his friends "little." And the city where he had lived for sixteen years she referred to as "way out there."

"I don't know," he replied, curling the phone cord around his index finger. "Guess he starved himself to death. He called himself an Immortalist and believed you don't have to die if you eat the right food, don't smoke, drink, or have sex, and spend most of the day sunk in the tub. Something about how in water you escape the effects of gravity. It's one of those California ideas."

"So what'd he die of, immortality? Or a heart attack when he got his water bill?"

"Like I say, he wasn't eating much. Just a few nuts and pieces of fruit a day. He thought most food was poisoned."

"Poison! Lord, I wish I could stick to a diet like that. Me, I eat everything in sight. So what you think of that stuffed eggplant I made on Friday? It turned out a little on the mooshy side. Too much shrimp and crab meat and not enough Parmesan cheese and bread crumbs, don't you think?"

His mother's stuffed eggplant was perfect, and she knew it. At eighty-two, she was hobbling around her kitchen on swollen ankles with a hot casserole in hand, laughing raucously at her jokes and praising her own cooking. Her only last wish was that the family not eat at Mandina's across from the funeral parlor after her wake. There was too much butter in the meunière sauce, she insisted, and the string beans were canned.

Hours later, as Peter tore open the foil pack of airline peanuts with his teeth, he grimaced imagining Limmel's ten almonds-a-day diet. When a wispy voice phoned to tell him that Limmel Rock had "vacated his vessel," Peter had been chopping onions for a pot of red beans. Limmel left instructions that his oldest friend—Peter Cordero on Dante Street in New Orleans—was to scatter his ashes from Lands End. Peter jotted down the time and place of the memorial service on the back of a restaurant invoice. Then he rocked all afternoon on the gallery in a weepy daze while the beans burned.

Under the jet wing, rose-tinged clouds were spread out in every direction like a comforter. *Way out there*, he sang to himself, *I'm going way out there*. No angels were strumming harps up here, but he could make out the sunken eyes of Limmel's meditating Buddha skull in a dark formation on the western horizon. When he blinked, the only face staring back at him from the oval porthole was his own—bearded, pink, and ripe.

After lunch at the Hunan, Peter Cordero strolled through North Beach toward Stockton Street, where he could catch a bus, then transfer to the N-Judah car to take him to the Immortalist Center in the Outer Sunset. Compared to the sticky armpit of Louisiana, the June weather here was perfect—sunny, crisply cool—with angular views of almost edible pastel Victorians framed by brilliant blue.

Actually, this incessant pleasantness annoyed him to no end, like the goateed lawyers with cell phones glued to their pierced ears, slurping decaf, low-fat lattes next to bulbous muffins at cafés along Columbus Avenue. A regular theme park of bohemia. Cookies and milk, the only vices left out here were cookies and milk, he thought, flicking his cigarette butt into the gutter. He'd much rather live in the ruins of the Confederacy than in the ruins of the sixties. There, at least, it was no skin off his lost dreams.

With relief, he shoved his way onto Stockton, toward the crowded fish stalls and vegetable stands of Chinatown. For years now this was the only place in San Francisco where he felt real. Here the cornucopia of California overflowed in a delirium of sqawking Cantonese merchants and rotting mango perfume. He walked past double-parked trucks disgorging barrels of live fish and whole hog carcasses, elbowed his way past cages of live frogs and chickens, tubs of languid turtles and scrambling crabs, disheveled mountains of bok choy, dried mushrooms, and papayas.

How the hell could Limmel starve to death in the middle of all this?

Nearby was the Basque Hotel, where he and Limmel had shared a room that summer before the commune. Broke, at night they scavenged French bread and flowers from the trash in front of Italian restaurants and filled the room with patchouli incense while drinking Burgundy from gallon jugs. Limmel had long blond hair down to his waist, as satiny and wavy as a Breck commercial, and Peter's Mediterranean 'fro frizzed out into a pubic halo that bounced as he walked. Often they had made love to their girlfriends at the same time on the big bed that creaked in counterpoint to two rhythms. The four of them would then fall asleep in a tangle of braceleted limbs and ringed fingers, listening to cable cars clang by.

After the summer of cheap wine and week-old roses, Peter and Limmel had settled into a strict routine at the Boddhisattva commune in the Haight, lured by free rent and homemade LSD. The commune was run by a middle-aged writer named Arnold Goldstein who had published one famous novel in the sixties, then moved to San Francisco on a petroleum trust fund to save the planet with collectivism, vegetarianism, and herbal enemas. With his Louisiana accent and irreverent humor, Peter was soon banished from the Sunflower Room to the compost heap. Limmel's ethereal looks and Pennsylvania Dutch business sense earned him a place as altar boy in the Sunflower Room and as bookkeeper for the commune's health food shop, the Hungry Organ.

Years later, Peter had realized this was the point when the hippie movement first began to harden into an ideology. Limmel bought it and thrived. But Peter, brandishing a hoe and declaring himself a Spanish anarchist in a showdown with Arnold in the vegetable patch, didn't buy it and left, wandering back to the rumpled corduroys and smudged mimeos of North Beach. Not only did Peter refuse to squirt sage water up his butt in purification rites, but he didn't want to be told what to eat, who to sleep with, or how long to meditate in the Sunflower Room. The last straw was when Arnold made Limmel raid other communes' refrigerators, sniffing for meat. If he found any, the sinners were cut out of the Hungry Organ's food co-op.

Peter chuckled out loud at the bus stop, recalling the meat raids, and how he had screamed at Limmel that he wasn't really a spiritual revolutionary but just another Lutheran cop. Limmel had risen to become heir-apparent to the Sunflower Throne, and after Arnold was busted for his acid lab, he began to market Arnold's whole bag of tricks as "spirit cleansing workshops." He attracted his own followers, mostly divorced women who had moved to California and changed their names to Maya or Shanti. Then David Bowie's ex-wife in Beverly Hills took him up, and he became guru to the stars. Peter had a snapshot of him from that era: glamorous in round, black sunglasses and an Afghani lamb's wool coat, emerging from a white BMW on his first day back after three months in an ashram in Poona, India. He had sat in on some of Limmel's workshops and complimented him as the ultimate con man. Sea Ananda, as he now called himself, had even shared some of his kurta-clad Mayas and Shantis with Baba Pete, for old times' sake, at his temple hot tub in the Marin redwoods.

They lost touch during the eighties, when Peter was studying at the Cordon Bleu in Paris and living in a postage-stamp-sized attic apartment in the thirteenth arrondissement with a Spanish girlfriend who sang *sevillanas* as she hung wash on their narrow terrace. Years later in San Francisco, when they had finally arranged to meet again at a tapas bar in the Mission that Peter was reviewing, Limmel just ordered a bottle of mineral water.

Peter, now pudgy and short-haired but manic as ever, wouldn't have recognized his old friend. Limmel was gaunt, shaved bald, dressed in black, with a severely serene expression. His only conversation was about what he wasn't eating, smoking, or screwing, which was nothing and no one. He nixed the idea of smoking a number on the patio before dinner, wouldn't touch the wine or beer, and when the *gambas al ajillo* arrived, looked like he was in mortal pain.

"Feel sorry for the shrimp?" Peter asked, spearing one with a toothpick, Andalusian style.

"I feel the pain of all sentient beings, and I don't care to have dead animals rotting in my stomach. I don't eat any cooked food at all. I'm centering my eternal self."

"Don't you think rotting along with the funky shrimp," Peter said, angling his toothpick at a particularly large one, "is sharing in the suffering of all living things with Christ on the cross?"

"We Immortalists don't believe in the occupied cross, only the empty one." Limmel's eyes flashed. "The resurrection of the perfect diamond body in this life."

"You're still the same Lutheran choir boy I've always known. Listen, I didn't believe in that ugly cruifix either," Peter said, biting off a shrimp tail, "until I realized I was just another blob of flesh nailed to it." He crossed his legs to hide a protruding gut, and tried not to chew on the molar that needed a root canal.

So while Peter ate, sopping up garlic sauce with hunks of crusty bread, and threw back half a bottle of Rioja, he listened to Limmel explain the Immortalist Center. From what he could gather, the Immortalists spent most of their time bobbing in a lotus pool in the back yard, or cultivating the few fruit and nut trees they ate from. The trees were fertilized with Tibetan yak ca-ca blessed by someone in Berkeley who guaranteed eternal life to anyone who bought his shit. The Immortalists made a living as computer programmers, and Limmel went on and on about the Immortalist website.

"Any foxy Immortalist babes in the commune?" Peter asked, trying to change the subject.

Limmel stared intently at a shrimp tail in the middle of the table, then shot Peter an empty look.

"I mean why do you want to live forever, for Christ's sake, if you can't enjoy anything?"

"Enjoy?" Limmel pronounced the word as if he'd just bitten into a rotten pear.

Peter poured himself another glass of wine and pushed back from the table. "You're in one hell of a mid-life crisis, buddy. But look, if you can still say all this when you're one hundred twenty-five-years-old, you win. Only I won't be around to congratulate you."

Limmel had lost the argument at forty-eight, but Peter felt no vindication as he boarded a 30-Stockton packed with elderly Chinese balancing pink plastic sacks of food. A damp paper bag on the lap of the old woman seated next to him was rustling with life. With two wizened fingers she skillfully removed a blue crab, which she turned over to inspect, its claws waving frantically in Peter's face. Peter waved back. Then she dropped the fat female back in her bag with a satisfied smile as the bus entered the Stockton Tunnel.

The Pacific Ocean really began at 19th Avenue, Peter decided as he whizzed along on the empty N-Judah car through the chill underwater mirage of the Outer Sunset. Tufts of fog swirled up the planetary street, blurring the shapes of squat storefronts and row houses that seemed stranded in the dunes of a mournful sea. Staring out the window, Peter felt as though he were peering into an aquarium where all the fish had died.

The Immortalist Center was on 41st Avenue, across from the West Sunset Playground. Shivering in his seersucker sportcoat, Peter trudged along with shoulders hunched against the gusty wind, smoking a cigarette. He doubted you could light up in the Immortalist Center. For a moment he lingered in front of the International UFO Museum and Alien T-Shirt Shop, scanning an urgent Xerox taped to the window about the takeover of the government from outer space. The shop was closed on Wednesdays.

He found the address, a 1950s two-story stucco painted lavender with black trim. A stone-faced woman seemed to be frisking people as they entered.

"I smell tobacco," she announced as Peter approached.

"Well, Fee Fie Fo Fum to you too, lady. I just put it out, okay? Look, Limmel Rock was my best friend for a long time, and I've come all the way from New Orleans to scatter his ashes."

"This center is also a fragrance-free zone. Some of us suffer from severe allergies, environmental illness, or multiple chemical sensitivity. I will have to monitor you for deodorants or colognes before you enter our safe area."

Then this wiry woman with the fuzzy gray scalp-cut began to sniff Peter like a Rottweiler, opening his jacket and almost sticking her snout into his pits. It turned him on.

She wrinkled her pointy nose. "I can't smell anything but garlic." And then she brightened. "Garlic is a natural antibiotic."

"Yeah, I like my Tetracycline stir-fired with smoked ham. Did you know Limmel?"

"Yes, of course. He'd been with us for several years." Her puckered mouth was twitching at the corners, trying to smile. "You may go in."

Peter stepped inside as though walking into a tax audit. The floors and walls were bare and spotless, and a diamond-shaped fixture suspended from the ceiling was spinning like a disco ball, casting amethyst facets of light against the white walls. Woozy New Age music was gurgling from a lone speaker in the corner, and in the center of the room, on a low silver altar, stood a square urn of ashes and a photo of Limmel. Peter inched over to study it. Limmel had never looked worse. His face was emaciated, lost in its own shadows. In front of the picture sat a brass bowl of almonds and a few wilted white chrysanthemums.

Several neuter Immortalists with skeletal ribcages were practicing their breathing on meditation cushions scattered across the floor. A group of overweight ladies, who once might have been named Maya or Shanti, were milling around in their multicultural muumuus admiring one another's interesting earrings. California was no place to grow old, Peter thought. No wonder Limmel moved in here to finish himself off. The Immortalist Center was a fucking suicide club for aging hippies.

Suddenly someone grabbed his ass with both hands. Peter spun around into the arms of Leah, as long and boney as when he and Limmel both had bounced her on that big Basque bed.

"Let me look at you, sweetheart! I haven't seen you in fifteen years," Peter shouted as the Immortalists looked up sourly. "What are you now, queen of grunge?"

She was dressed in frayed denim and flannel, and informed him her new name was something he couldn't remember that began with a Z. She let him know in her customary machine-gun delivery that she wasn't a confused Jewish princess anymore but was now a lesbian animal-rights activist who lived in Berkeley with a girlfriend suffering from environmental illness. And she had a joint in her pocket.

"Leah, I'm sorry to hear about all this," Peter responded, dragging her by the hand past the Rottweiler at the door, "except for the chicks and the joint. That I can relate to."

For an hour they sat hunched over on the hood of her old Volvo, catching up, rehashing old times, doing what middle-aged people do at funerals. Peter was sorry there was only a Korean grocery across the street and not a Mandina's, where they could reminisce over bad meunière sauce and canned green beans.

"And so I was near the Basque Hotel just yesterday, picketing the Chinese stores on Stockton for animal cruelty. You should see how they clobber those frogs and turtles, then tear their guts out."

"Honey, leave the Chinese alone. They know what they're doing. They been at it for five thousand years. Back where I come from, it's considered a good night if just the frogs get hit over the head. Come on, you don't like frog legs with lemon and butter?" he drawled in disbelief.

"Give me a break," she groaned, sticking her finger down her throat in a vulgarity leftover from the eighties. "So yesterday this store owner walks out to disrupt our rally, and I'm like, 'I hope you come back as a frog in your next lifetime.' And he goes, 'And I hope you come back as a fly. Then I eat you.'"

They both found it hard to talk about Limmel, who had withdrawn from the eternal struggle between flies, frogs, and Chinese butchers in the last few years. Leah approved of his diet, although she thought he had needed a supplementary starch. Peter said he thought he'd needed an oyster po'boy, a roll in the hay, and a one-way ticket out of San Francisco.

They were buzzed by the time they approached the Immortalist Center. The Rottweiler woman met them at the door, informing them they had missed the ceremony that channeled Limmel's reconstituted body to the eternal diamond sphere. Then, as if putting out the garbage, she held out the urn of ashes to be scattered off Lands End. It was seven o'clock and almost the Immortalist bedtime. They were going to meditate in the lotus pool.

"Immortalists must get pretty depressed at their own funerals," Peter commented, walking down the steps.

"Limmel probably fucking died of pneumonia," Leah snorted as they scooted into her car, where Peter balanced the ashes on his lap. "Did you get a look at that so-called lotus pool? It's a slimy tank where those skinny assholes sit like frogs eight hours a day up to their necks in algae. Out here in the fog? The neighbors are suing them because the drain split and is leaking into their yard. And the Immortalists are suing the swimming pool company that put it in. I never want to set foot in there again. Besides, it's racist, sexist, and homophobic."

"I can't imagine RuPaul wanting to join up, if that's what you mean," Peter mumbled, twisting a radio dial that didn't work.

Ponderous with the prospect of scattering Limmel Rock to the wind, they drove along the beach as all the light in the world was about to be swallowed by the Pacific. This was it, Peter thought, as if he were a pallbearer for the last citizen of Byzantium: the end of an era that had brought unimaginable freedom and joy before it turned, like everything before it, into caricature and real estate. He felt like rolling down the car window and shouting at the horizon, GOODBYE, CALIFORNIA!

But California kept shifting fast as the horizon, and he was tired of chasing it, reinventing himself every five years, remodeling his dreams, running after an imaginary meridian that, like youth, was gone. Like Limmel, simply gone. He looked over at Leah in her latest incarnation, dear beat-up, buzz-cut old Leah. Tears were running down her cheeks, too.

Peter tapped the metal box in his lap, the missing piece of the puzzle. So the end of the line was a stucco house in the Outer Sunset, last stop before America vanished, where a bunch of ex-revolutionaries sat scared shitless in a frog pond in the fog, worrying themselves sick about death.

Now the big secret was out. And the repressive stuff they'd rebelled against had clanked back into place with a vengeance because—this was why it was there in the first place—you gonna die, motherfucker.

Peter thought of his old man at eighty-four, back by the barbecue pit last week with that dumb apron on, drinking his bourbon highball and reading the paper. Call it bravery or stupidity but after the Battle of the Bulge, his father knew how much this rotting piece of meat was worth. By the pound. By the ounce.

They swerved past the Cliff House restaurant, where he'd brought his parents when they visited, and his mother had raved about the scallops while his father made a drunken pass at the waitress. Then they pulled into a dirt parking lot.

Leah took off her distressed-leather jacket and draped it around Peter's shoulders. The wind howling in their ears, they wobbled up a path smelling of fennel and salt air, along a barrier of dwarfed conifers hunched over by the force of the ocean, like the fingers of drowning men hanging on to the last ledge of land.

Soon they were standing on a sheer promontory in front of a concrete bench under a canopy of dead limbs, staring below onto a thrashing metropolis of granite and foam, trying to take Limmel out of his can.

"Here, can you get this open?" Peter asked, handing the urn to Leah and fumbling to button the jacket collar around his neck. They were both windblown and freezing by the time they finally dipped their hands inside, shocked by the gravelly texture of the remains.

"Say something, Peter." Leah shouted to be heard over the wind. "Say words. Limmel needs words."

"*Libera me, Domine, de morte aeterna, in die illa tremenda: Quando caeli movendi sunt et terra,*" Peter sang in a choirboy tenor as they both threw handfuls of ash into the air. "*Requiem aeternam dona eis, Domine: et lux perpetua luceat eis.*"

As Peter opened wide to sing the "Kyrie, eleison, Christie, eleison," the wind whipped a handful of ashes back into his face, filling his mouth with charcoal pebbles.

He gagged.

Sputtering, he spun around wild-eyed to Leah, spitting bits of Limmel to the ground. Then he screamed like someone who didn't expect to be heard. His spindly legs took off, racing back down the fennel path as if pursued.

In the parking lot at the end of the open road, Peter fell to his knees and vomited. Onion cakes. Rice. Smoked ham. Between dry heaves, one decade after another came up in a spasm, the sixties and seventies, then the eighties and nineties. He crouched under the lone streetlight, his neck stretched forward as though awaiting a blow from on high. Ashes drooled down his chin and through his beard, the ashes of everyone he had ever loved mixed with everything he had ever eaten, the Pacific pounding inside his head against the Western Gate.

Looking up, he saw Leah moving toward him through the mist, her silhouette as serene as a figure in a Tang Dynasty painting. Running his tongue along the inside of his teeth, he knew he would never get that taste out of his mouth, whoever he might kiss, no matter how beautiful or how young.

PERPETUAL CARE

The Easter Sunday that Miss Estelle Arceneaux heard someone singing inside the tomb was the first time she'd been back to the cemetery since All Saints Day, and everything was a real mess. With a grimace, she emptied dried cockroaches from a glass vase and turned on the spigot full force, careful not to splash the white crochet handbag hanging from her elbow. Algae caked around the rim was the hardest to clean, and the paper towel turned to mush between her fingers. This part of the ritual was for the men of the family, but they were all either in the crypt waiting for their gladiolas or way out in California playing in some kind of band.

As the last of the Arceneaux women who could both walk and see, she took her family duties seriously. Opalescent plastic earrings marked the formality of the occasion. It was a shame, she thought as she spun the spigot shut, how fast things went to ruin if you let them.

She squinted in the overexposed New Orleans sunlight reflected off the whitewashed tombs, noticing for the first time the profusion of day-old wreaths piled around the corner crypt. Shielding her eyes from the glare, she could barely make out the name: Famille Lemoine. The Lemoines. She knew them. One had married a Lanoux and lived on North Miro near Esplanade back before the war. The last Lemoine buried there was in 1975, and the family hadn't engraved the marble slab yet with the recently deceased's name. Wedging the vase under one arm and securing her pocketbook under the other, she turned to walk on when she heard an echo from somewhere inside the tomb, a tinny, rasping wail.

At first she thought it might be the previous coffin moved from the shelf inside settling to the bottom of that pit—or whatever they have down there—the endless darkness she had tried not to peer down into during a lifetime of burials. Once she had dreamed it was filled with giant crawfish clattering their claws against coffins, trying to open us up for a change. When she was a little girl she had asked her Pepère if it led to China, and he told her no, chère, back to France, an answer that satisfied her until she had made her second communion. There was nothing about underground funerary passages to France in her catechism, and one of the Abadie boys had told her that down there was where the devil went to the rest room.

Stepping through spongy grass in her oxfords, she mounted the first marble step and stuck her silver perm into the alcove of the plastered brick bread-oven of a tomb styled like a little Greek Revival house. Immediately she was blasted by a crescendo of horns and a roll of drums. She jumped back, almost knocking over an enormous basket of Easter lilies with a ribbon marked "From the Senior Class, McMain High School."

She could swear a Negro was inside singing, "I been loooving you toooo looong to stop noooow. . . ."

"You are tiiired and you wanna be freeee," he was moaning in falsetto. "My looove's growing strooonger as you become a habit to meee." She had eaten a banana this morning, and bananas made her dizzy. That was it. She had forgotten to take the potassium Dr. Schumaker prescribed. She would put the white gladiolas in the clean vase, pray for the souls of her family kneeling on the steps of their tomb, sweep around it, get back in the car, drive carefully home, and lie down on the daybed in the back room with the blinds closed.

A brass cascade of pleading followed her as she scurried away. "Don't make me stop nooow oh puhlease don't make me stop, don't make me stop nooow. . . ."

"Papa," she murmured to herself, "I can't do this all alone any more."

God knows he had done everything he could for the boy. So Easter morning found Dr. Lemoine speeding in a pearl-blue Cadillac DeVille toward Bay St. Louis, where he hoped to console himself over the black-jack tables of the Casino Magic Inn at the $29-a-night suckers' rate. And the getaway would do a world of good for Sybil, who hadn't spoken a word all morning. His wife sat sphinx-like with her flipped shoulder-length hair, staring straight ahead into the morning traffic, tapping an enameled fingernail against the cream vinyl seat-bucket to a medley on the Easy Listening station. Her debutante-ball mask had gotten her through the autopsy, funeral, and burial. And now Dr. Lemoine could picture her floating in a turquoise pool, hair fanned out in a nimbus around her face, that taut mask dissolving into tears like a lump of sugar.

No one could reach them at the Casino, not the hospital, insurance company, police, or well-meaning friends and family. None of the psychiatrists blamed either of them, of course. The hospital, well, just hadn't worked out, but it was the only choice left after all of those . . . shenanigans the boy pulled. Running away from home to go live in the Tremé. Brass bands. Drugs. He could have gotten shot. Yes, he had musical talent, but that shouldn't lead him into the middle of a black neighborhood and—whatever in the world was that place called?—the Little People's Club!

"You took the wrong exit," his wife announced.

"I'm going to take the scenic route, along the coast." He turned his bearded, marmot-like bulk toward her, stunned at the first words she had uttered all day. She looked back at him as if that was the saddest thing anyone had ever told her. The scenic route—the day after they buried their only son who jumped out of the window of the Rosary Three ward at St. Vincent DePaul Hospital on Holy Thursday.

Why couldn't Jay have become a normal gutter-punk? Dr. Lemoine had often wondered, with green hair and a shirt-stud in his tongue to click against his front teeth for attention. Those kids at least had a reasonable cure rate. A little therapy. Extra spending money. And an upscale party college. But what could you do with a boy from a good French Catholic family who thought he was black?

As the Cadillac swerved onto the coastal highway, his wife gasped at the first raucous screech, bracing her vermilion fingernail extensions against the padded dashboard as if the seagulls were about to nosedive through the windshield.

The devil was busy beating his wife over the clapboard office of St. Louis No. 3 Cemetery on Esplanade Avenue. Despite tentative morning sunlight, a persistant drizzle had driven the director inside, where Mr. Broussard felt comfortably alone with his sinuses and hemorrhoid. He was just biting into his second McKenzie doughnut when Miss Arceneaux stomped up the steps in a no-nonsense stride. He wasn't in the mood to talk about Perpetual Care.

"Mr. Broussard," she informed him, "there are colored people singing inside the Lemoine tomb."

"Where they at?"

"I said I hear the voices of Negroes coming out of the Lemoine family tomb. You must do something."

"Miss Arceneaux, always a pleasure to see you. Set yourself down right here next to one of these glazed doughnuts I got over by McKenzie. They nice and fresh."

"I had breakfast early, thank you. I couldn't sleep a wink last night. I kept thinking about what I heard here yesterday, inside the Lemoine tomb, when I brought a bunch of glads to my poor papa, who had a hard time of it, let me tell you."

Mr. Broussard nodded sympathetically and nibbled on his doughnut, pushing the box toward her. "They good."

"I don't care for doughnuts, Mr. Broussard. They raise my blood-sugar. So I came back this morning and heard puh-lenty more. What I'm trying to say is there's some . . . dis-TUR-bance," she said, enunciating the word like the retired public school teacher she was, "at the Lemoine tomb."

Remembering her mention of colored people, at "disturbance" Mr. Broussard jumped up as if for a fire drill, closing the box of doughnuts and grabbing his massive ring of keys.

"There's clapping, singing . . . and a trumpet," she continued, like a student trying to remember her lesson, "and then a man's voice saying something over and over about . . . ."

Holding the office door open, Mr. Broussard fidgeted while she finished her report.

". . . the fun butt bar, or funky butter. You better go see."

"We'll get to the bottom of this," he assured her, as they walked out into the middle of a busload of wet German tourists pointing cameras at each other in front of marble angels, the day after Easter, in the rain.

"Hello, WWOZ, New Orleans' jazz and heritage station. Travis Refuge on the air. Do you have a request?" Travis cradled the receiver between ear and shoulder as he began to line up CDs for his Afro-Caribbean program.

"You hear WWOZ coming out where? Out what tomb? . . . No, we don't have no transmitters down in there. What you talking about, man? . . . In his teeth? No, I never heard nothing about that, Mr. Broussard . . . Yeah, I'd like to hear that for my own self. Maybe Marie Laveau down there at St. Louis doing her some hoodoo. I'm on the air. Catch you later."

Travis hung up, swiveling his chair back to the mike to bleed his voice over the final percussion of a souk song. "And those are Les Poivres Rouges from Martinique, with 'Moucher Ma Bouche,' here on Afro-Caribbean rhythms this rainy Monday morning, at WWOZ, your jazz and heritage station, in La *Nou*vel Orle*ans*." Travis went on to give another plug to the Tremé Brass Band playing this evening at the Funky Butt Bar and Vietnamese Vegetarian Restaurant on North Rampart Street. Then he spun around and shut off the mike.

"Man from the cemetery call up," he blurted out to Shantrell Cousin, a Creole administrator tiptoeing through the sound studio with a file under her arm, "to say WWOZ being broadcast from a *tomb*. Say he sit there on the stoop of that tomb and hear me talking and the music I playing. Say he think the silver filling in this boy teeth they bury yesterday picking up the radio signals or something. I been working here for seven years and *that*," he said, shaking his beaded dreadlocks until they rattled, "is the *weirdest motherfucker* ever called up this station, and they been some. It give me the willie to think my voice coming out some white kid tomb."

Shantrell lowered her tinted John Lennon frames to peer out at Travis with a "what you been smoking?" inquisitive bugeye. As she rummaged through a drawer, her back to him, she winced at what he intoned into the mike with a dungeon tremelo.

"This is Travis Refuge, the voice from *beyooond*, on WWOZ, live from the (*crrreaak*) *crypt.* . . ."

. . .

Nine hundred seventy-two pairs of wet Nikes squeaked down the freshly waxed corridors of Eleanor McMain High School on the day after Easter vacation. As the first homeroom bell sliced through the banging of lockers, the stampede up the granite staircases left a group in the corner of the girls' gym, in front of the windows on Nashville Avenue. With looseleaf binders joined at their hips, the students were speaking in whispers and shrieks that echoed up to the exposed pipes on the ceiling.

"It was so gross. On Saturday I walk up to his mother at Schoen to go like how sorry I was, and she goes, 'Who are *you*? You didn't love him.' And I go like, '*Wait a minute*, Mrs. Lemoine, Jay was my boyfriend since eleventh grade and like what do you know about who he was? You the one made him leave NOCCA and stop playing the trumpet and then put him in that insane asylum.' And she like completely loses it right there. Goes ballistic and orders me out of Schoen, but there were so many people from McMain with us I just ducked into another viewing room where these Cajuns from Breau Bridge are having a wake with an accordion. And suddenly I'm dancing a two-step with this fat man who's crying to beat the band about his mama."

"Cool," the listeners murmured in unison.

"When they called me up on Holy Friday to tell me about Jay," chimed in Andrea, blowing wisps of frosted mane from her face with puffs of air, "I was like no way. I felt so bummed for you, Lynnette. And the next thing I know, I'm in Mass at Holy Redeemer with the statues all covered in purple and staring up at the crucifix obsessing on Lynnette and Jay, Jay and Lynnette. I was sniffling and my mawmaw goes, 'Finally you got religion, girl.'"

"I swear to God I don't know what come over me," Lynnette Terramina burst out, her Sicilian features taking on tragic ancestral proportions uncommon to a seventeen-year-old with a nose ring and fuchsia highlights. "After Mrs. Lemoine ran me out into the wake with those coonasses, I grabbed this tiny clock radio I keep in my purse so I can take naps in my car when I cut, maxed out the volume, set it to WWOZ for midnight on the dot, when Jay and I were usually doing it on Saturday night, ran back into the Lemoine wake like—*excuussse* me, I have to say good-bye to my boyfriend, if you don't mind—and threw myself over the open casket, carrying on like a banshee from hell. It took Dr. Lemoine and two security guards to carry me out that fucking place, but not before I jammed that radio as far as I could down into the closed half of the casket."

Giggles all around, followed by the hyena laugh of Chaz, a tall thin black kid who squatted down to beat his palms in a staccato rhythm on the gym floor, chanting "yeah (*boom*), yeah (*boom*) yeah (*boom*)!" Thumbs shot up around a smiling circle.

"So when was, you know, the burial?"

"The bitch goes don't you dare show up for the burial at three o'clock, but I followed the procession to the cemetery, my car radio blaring Clarence 'Gatemoth' Brown all the way."

"And did your radio like go off at midnight?"

"I don't know." Lynnette was sobbing as the second homeroom bell sounded and the girls' gym teacher bounded toward them, a volleyball under her arm, pointing at the staircase with the mock severity of someone who had just spent a week in a bikini across the lake, far from the crumbling gray building on Nashville Avenue.

Mr. Broussard rearranged the pillow on his office chair, took a bracing whiff from his inhaler, and hunched forward like a chief of staff manning a battle station. Word had come down that morning from the Archdiocese lawyer on Carrollton Avenue that under no circumstances was St. Louis Cemetery authorized to enter a tomb without the consent of its owners, even though X-rays confirmed an electrical device inside the coffin, presumably a portable radio. The petition to disinter the burial in the Lemoine tomb "due to unusual circumstances affecting the security of cemetery property" was denied. And he had already left three messages on Dr. Lemoine's home answering machine that had not been returned.

No one at Mercy knew where he was. The obstetrics nurse he spoke with explained that the doctor had taken a two-week bereavement leave. Where were those assholes? he wondered. If they wanted their boy to have some company in there, why didn't they toss in a teddy bear or a half-dead hooker from the Airline Highway?

The Archdiocese lawyer had been adamant, breaking off his legalese to thunder into the phone with a Chalmette accent that "we can't dig up some guy's dead kid even if they got the whole filly-monia orchestra in there. They can turn around and sue the pants off the Church. You get them people to sign on the dotted line, or we wait till them batries go dead, hear? Jeez, we got enough going on here with that priest in Houma diddling them altar boys."

But by Wednesday, the batteries hadn't gone dead. It seemed the radio was getting louder, broadcasting from an infernal echo chamber, the marble slab vibrating with jazz. Whole carloads of high school students dressed in black had started turning up in the afternoons, sitting in a semicircle around the tomb hung with yellowing wreaths of white roses, chain-smoking cigarettes and passing skinny joints. They said they were from McMain and the performing arts high school, where the dead boy had gone. Only his mama, they said, made him quit the artsy place on account of some monkey business in Tremé. The girlfriend had pink hair, and if you asked Mr. Broussard, looked like a little dago slut.

The telephone was ringing off the hook ever since that "Blues from the Tomb" article had come out in the "Living" section of *The Times-Picayune*. The place was a nuthouse. Gator Holiday had called to add three busloads of tourists a day to their contract, CNN was threatening to send someone to New Orleans, and WWOZ was in an executive meeting with the Board of Directors of the Jazz and Heritage Foundation. Mr. Broussard was secretly tuning into the station from a radio he kept in the bottom drawer of a file cabinet, and he knew the DJs were addressing comments to the kids around the tomb, clapping and hooting. Jay Lemoine was mentioned frequently, along with some guys named Jim Morrison and James Booker, who he assumed were dead, although he was sure they weren't buried in St. Louis No. 3.

His only ray of hope was the article had mentioned that this Jay Lemoine character committed suicide. Catholic cemetery bylaws prohibited the burial of a suicide on consecrated ground. The Archdiocese lawyer advised that to exhume a suicide required permission from the Vatican, no less, so Mr. Broussard was writing a letter to His Holiness, Pope John Paul II, over in Rome, Italy. He was stuck on the salutation. He had already scratched out "Your Holiness (and Mine), John Paul II" and "My Dear Pope."

Pushing the letter aside, Mr. Broussard glanced out the Venetian blinds. A Lucky Dog hot dog vendor had set up his cart outside of the cemetery gate, in front of two parked Gator Holiday buses disgorging stout ladies with sun visors and fanny packs. Gangly goth teenagers, wiggling to spectral rhythms from iPods, were slouched against the fence, handing pieces of paper to tourists. And two black kids had put out a cardboard box top and were squatting on the sidewalk, adjusting the taps on their running shoes.

He dialed the Archdiocese for the fifth time that day to ask if the Pope had a fax.

It took all afternoon to decide, but the project was a go.

The Executive Board of the Jazz and Heritage Foundation, meeting at their offices on North Rampart Street, felt it would be a unique way to kick off the Jazz Fest. The bone of contention was whether it would be "appropriate," a soothing word from California where people had transcended right and wrong. But they had just taken Marvin, a city councilman's cousin and the Fest's marketing consultant from Los Angeles, to a three-hour lunch at Dooky Chase, and he had convinced them to "go for it."

"What we got here is a tomb with a view," Marvin enthused over over crab claws with greens. "The damn thing sits but five yards from the fence that's right next to the Fair Grounds, where it all gonna happen. It's got all the classic New Orleans themes. Death. Cemeteries. Music. Sex."

"Where the sex come in?" Travis asked, sucking on a claw without looking up.

"Here's the pitch. It's Romeo and Juliet, man. He's a trumpet player, imprisoned in a tower, then driven to suicide by his high-tone folks who don't understand him. She's a seventeen-year-old gutter-punk from the wrong side of the tracks, devoted to her man and his music. She waits in front of his tomb all day, listening to all these beautiful sounds coming right from the spot where her love lies rotting. That swing, or what?"

"I don't know," said Shantrell, clearing her throat. "It doesn't seem appropriate to broadcast our program from a cemetery. This is a really Catholic city. It'll offend people."

"Where we at? Some French fishing village?" Marvin sneered. "Or the City That Care Forgot?"

When the vote was taken later at Jazz Fest headquarters, it was decided to broadcast, on the second Thursday after Easter, the day before the first Friday of the Festival, a special "Live from the Crypt" program of WWOZ. The master of ceremonies would stand before the tomb, where he would introduce the Rebirth Brass Band. Lynnette Terramina would talk about her boyfriend, and specially orchestrated acoustic effects would transmit the echo from the tomb to a hundred and fifty thousand listeners. The public was invited.

The mayor expressed his doubts. But when he learned that the local Romanian radio commentator with a Transylvanian accent would step in as the celebrity emcee, and the famous Gothic romance writer would lend her presence as a tie-in with the "Save Our Cemeteries" campaign and her new novel, he was sold. Reluctantly, he placed a call to his old friend the Archbishop. When he got him on the line and met some resistance, the mayor of New Orleans snapped his plaid suspenders, grabbed his crotch, and reminded the Archbishop of New Orleans of promises a then-simple parish priest had made during the 1960s to a little Negro altar boy at St. Rose de Lima Church.

In the meantime, Mr. Broussard had already sent his fax addressed TO: His Most Holy See, Leader of the Christian World; FROM: Dewey P. Broussard, Jr., Director, St. Louis Cemetery No. 3, 3421 Esplanade Avenue, New Orleans, Louisiana 70119, U.S.A.

Tuesday before the live broadcast, the ten o'clock news on WDSU. A spot with Thadeus Ribbit, the celebrated reincarnation of Louis Armstrong. "Jazz Fest kicks off on a solemn note this year" was the crisp lead-in voiced over a snazzy neon Jazz Fest logo, cutting to Ribbit, dressed in fedora and double-breasted suit, caressing his trumpet in front of a peeling shotgun in the Upper Ninth Ward.

"I don't know what to tell you all about him," he said sweetly, looking down at his trumpet. "He come in all the places we play. I see him by Little People, Vaughn, Funky Butt, tall white kid with a trumpet case standing in back the crowd every night, big old white T-shirt, smart-boy glasses, just looking, really digging it, but I mean in a quiet way, you know. He always there, sometime with a chick what got pink hair. One night late at Vaughn he let loose with his horn, when we was packing up our axe and barbecue, and he *goooood*, you know what I mean, just a kid, but he all right. Then he hanging with a crowd from NOCCA, and I think one day I gonna hear from this cat. Sorry to learn he passed, and I be there tomorrow at the cemetery to say good-bye before I play my ten o'clock gig at the House of Blues."

This was followed by a fade-out to the tomb, covered with bleached wreaths and surrounded by bleary-eyed teenagers, bleeding into a closeup of a petulant girl with pink hair, blowing fierce jets of smoke at the camera, backed by Aaron Neville singing "Mona Lisa" from a staticky transistor radio inside someplace that sounded like St. Louis Cathedral.

Minutes later, the Casino Magic house doctor was called from an evening consultation with a transvestite with silicone implants to administer a 20 cc. I.V. of Valium to a woman who had collapsed in hysterics off a high bar stool in front of the TV in the Wild Card Lounge. The cause of her attack was unknown, but her almost inaudible words before going under were something like "fuck the priest" and "even if I have to walk to New Orleans."

Miss Arceneaux stood at the edge of the crowd in a daisy-patterned sun hat, staring over the bony shoulders of a group of high school students in black tank tops who were circulating what looked like photocopies of a poem through the crowd. When they turned to look back at her, they did a collective double-take and began to chant "Oooh nooo, Miss Arceneaux, oooh nooo, Miss Arceneaux." Their retired English teacher stepped back to size up her former students, who seemed to have turned out even worse than she had imagined possible. Of course, they let them run wild as alley cats these days.

She was still in a state of shock from trying to maneuver her politely beeping Toyota through the Lucky Dog vendors and hot tamale wagons blocking the gate of St. Louis Cemetery. Scrambling between them were children with Styrofoam gumbo bowls Scotch-taped over their heads hawking beers and Cokes from ice-filled garbage pails resting in the shade of illegally parked vans. The wrought-iron fence was lined with scraggly Quarter-types selling handmade earrings stuck to red velveteen display cards. A mime playing an imaginary trumpet was walking through the crowd with a half-sad, half-happy face painted on, and a bald young man with elaborately tattooed biceps was distributing pamphlets about teen suicide from a card table.

Mr. Broussard, still waiting for a fax from the Pope and livid that the Archdiocese had authorized this display of bad taste, had hired an off-duty New Orleans policewoman as a security guard, confident that she could prevent any mayhem. Early that morning, he and his crew had stripped the Lemoine tomb of dead flowers, as stipulated in the Perpetual Care contract the family had purchased, and he had done as little as possible to cooperate with the radio people. Thick orange cables ran like writhing anacondas from their truck through the alleyways behind adjacent tombs to the front of the Lemoine tomb.

The news commentator with the Transylvanian accent was seated in the grass leafing through a copy of *Playboy* while technicians in African-print drawstring pants were taping special sound-sensitive mikes to the marble slab of the tomb. The arts high school Jazz Ensemble had assembled on the lawn, where the efficient blond principal was going over details with Travis Refuge. The Gothic romance novelist from uptown, a slight woman in a black cowl, was curled up on the stoop of a tomb with her arm draped over a plaster urn, gossiping with the grotesque writer from downtown, a tall woman dressed in billowy white, lounging on the steps of the next tomb. The visiting poet at Tulane was already drunk, and Babs Godoy, the beaming society columnist, was mingling like there was no tomorrow.

Then the Rebirth Brass Band blared in at full throttle down a broad

grassy avenue of the cemetery, playing "The Shiek of Araby." Those following along began to second-line, sashaying in and out of the narrow
alleys behind and between tombs, waving white handkerchiefs high in
the air and boisterously colliding with each other as they joined together
in a throng approaching the Lemoine tomb like a Southern Baptist vision
of the Day of Resurrection.

Travis raised his palm to silence the band and to still the bobbing
white handkerchiefs, then tapped his mike, sending an ear-splitting
electronic screech bouncing back from inside the tomb. Wild applause.
He gave a final signal for "on the air," and welcomed WWOZ listeners
to the "Live from the Crypt" kickoff of the Jazz and Heritage Festival,
broadcast from inside a tomb in the historic St. Louis Cemetery over-
looking the Festival site at the lovely Fair Grounds. He was introducing
the celebrity emcee from Transylvania when his voice suddenly turned
thin and sailed off, light as a paper plate, lost in the meringue clouds of a
cerulean April afternoon.

The echo had disappeared.

He tapped his mike.

Nothing.

A sepuchral silence was etched in the glare between row after row
of taciturn tombs, festivities poised in midair. "Shit," said Travis in a
stage whisper, staring at the pyramid of blinking equipment. "I guess
those batteries in there finally wore out."

At that moment Thadeus Ribbit lifted his horn, stepped in front
of the tomb, and in the lithest tones ever seduced from a trumpet,
began to play a taps rendition of "May the Circle Be Unbroken."
Lynnette Terramina collapsed. "Gone," she kept mumbling, "he's
really gone," as Andrea and Chaz wrapped their arms around her waist
and lumbered with her behind Thadeus, who was heading toward the
gate with his horn held high in the air, playing as slowly as a late after-

noon stroll through a New Orleans cemetery might inspire.

Everyone followed him out of the cemetery, walking arm-in-arm. Even plastic plates and go-cups trailed after him as if bewitched, swept along in a melancholic trance, and orange radio cables and studio trucks and disappointed high-school musicians who didn't get to play, holding their instruments over their shoulders like tired children. No one spoke a word until they were out of the gates, milling down Esplanade Avenue in the speckled sunlight under the shady arches of live oaks. And for weeks to come, many still didn't speak, afraid they would somehow find their own voices abruptly, irrevocably, gone.

Miss Arceneaux was the last to leave. She stooped to pick up the only piece of paper that hadn't sailed out of the cemetery in the wake of Thadeus Ribbit, one of the photocopied poems the students had been handing out. She fished reading glasses out of her purse and when she recognized what was scrawled there, her lizardy skin bunched into a broad smile. There it was, an unpunctuated, wildly misspelled rendering of the poem by Miss Emily Dickinson that she had required her tenth-grade English students to recite. "I died for Beauty—but was scarce / Adjusted in the Tomb," she declaimed, with chin up and chest out, as she had taught her students, "When One who died for Truth, was lain / In an adjoining Room—." Softly to herself, she spoke the final stanza from memory as she folded her glasses and this final homework from her teaching career into her crochet purse:

> *And so, as Kinsmen, met at Night—*
> *We talked between the Rooms—*
> *Until the Moss had reached our lips—*
> *And covered up—our names—*

. . .

By the time Dr. Lemoine made it through the bumper-to-bumper traffic on Esplanade, after having his wife admitted to St. Vincent DePaul Hospital on Henry Clay Avenue, it was almost four, and the massive iron cemetery gates were about to swing shut.

He braced himself as he approached his family tomb, but when he dashed out, leaving the car door ajar, he saw nothing and no one. He stood sweaty and disheveled, ready to be judged by ranks of seraphim and cherubim, by CNN and a waiting nation, by generations of pregnant mothers astride rows of tombs, by the only baby he had ever lost, his own. The mute marble slab remained as it had always been.

The stone had not been rolled away.

It bore the name of his father, Émile Eugéne Lemoine, buried in 1975, and stuck to the date was a sliver of silver duct tape. That was all. Next week, he promised, he would have his son's name sandblasted into the marble. He imagined it there already, followed by his own.

Weaving his way back to the car through the trellis of lengthening shadows, he passed behind an old lady in a sun bonnet kneeling in front of a tomb. She looked like she had been there a long time, and he shook his head at how absorbed she seemed in saying out loud prayers he remembered from childhood. "Holy Mary, Mother of God, pray for us sinners," he repeated with her under his breath, "now and at the hour of our death."

THE JEW
WHO FOUNDED MEMPHIS

I n belligerent silence, Jake pushed his mother's wheelchair up the
steep ramp to the cemetery office, her right leg sticking straight out
like the prow of a frigate. They were visiting Memphis to clean the
angel on her family plot, and as Mrs. Hokum had told her son on many
occasions, she intended to make sure the people who ran Oak Grove
Cemetery knew exactly who she was.

Three days before they left their fallow farm in Bossier, Louisiana,
an arthritic knee joint had frozen on her. Then she read in the Saturday
religion section of the *Shereveport Times* that fifty thousand black
Pentecostals would also be in Memphis for a Church of God in Christ
convocation. This, Jake had hoped, would do it, but she stuck to her
guns. He rolled his eyes as he wheeled her through the screen door into
the cramped office, dominated by a grandfather clock on one side and a
red Coca-Cola machine on the other.

Like an ostrich, Mrs. Hokum strained her wrinkled, pointy face to
the height of a long, curved neck, trying to see over the top of a paneled
counter. Finally she cleared her throat several times and chimed in a
cheerful singsong, "Guess who's here?"

A chinless head shaped like a white china doorknob rose over the counter, ice-blue eyes staring down at the plaid pant leg jutting out of the wheelchair. Holding up half of an egg-salad sandwich, the young woman had a full mouth and was trying hard to swallow.

"Hello. I'm Rebecca Berkow Hokum and my great-grandfather, Colonel Abraham Berkow, founded this cemetery in 1852."

The chinless woman managed to swallow. "Care for a Co'Cola?"

Jake's mother was undaunted. She removed a white glove and held out a claw-like hand. "This is one of Colonel Abraham Berkow's very own solid-gold cufflinks made into a signet ring. And here's the other cufflink," she said, tugging at the charm bracelet on her bony wrist that she couldn't get turned around.

Behind the wheelchair, Jake shifted his stooped shoulders, chuckling to himself. His mother had been rehearsing this speech for three years, ever since she'd begun receiving the Polaroids that her third-cousin Gloria in Memphis enclosed in Christmas cards of the "sadly deteriorating angel" at Oak Grove. He'd seen the life-sized statue only once, when he was a child. The fragile face was looking down at him shyly, bathed in a fairy-tale light. A mane of curls cascaded down her back, disappearing into a pair of crushed wings folded around the lower half of her body. Originally the statue had been covered by a glass dome, but an ice storm had shattered that decades ago. Now a fungus was eating it and had turned the angel pockmarked and black.

"And this is my son, Jacob Berkow Hokum," Mrs. Hokum said, pointing with her ungloved hand. "He's the artist in the family, and is going to clean our angel just as good as new. That statue was a memorial to my aunt Rachel, Colonel Berkow's granddaughter, who expired on her wedding day. It's marble. Genuine Italian marble."

"Too bad the director's at lunch," the woman said, feeding quarters into the Coke machine. "He's real historic."

The screen door creaked, and the shining dark face of a teenager in an ill-fitting black suit and stiff white shirt was framed in the doorway. His hair stood up in a three-inch wedge on top, the sides shaved close. Suddenly the office smelled of drugstore cologne. "Excuse me, but where Mrs. Wardell Ticker bury at? Her funeral this afternoon."

Mrs. Hokum flashed a stricken look at her son that he refused to acknowledge.

"Been no burial so far today," the chinless woman said, "but will be one in about ten minutes. It's the Ticker party, I reckon. So hold your horses till I ring the plantation bell when the hearse passes over the drawbridge."

"I'm Rebecca Berkow Hokum," Mrs. Hokum said, swerving the wheelchair around to aim her extended blue oxford at the young man's crotch. "My great-grandfather founded this cemetery."

"Yes, ma'am."

"Are you attending a burial?"

"Yes, ma'am." The young man was backing out of the door.

"I'm so sorry. Who is it, may I ask?"

"My mama. Ma'am."

"You mean to tell me your mother—"

Jake grabbed the handles of the chair and wheeled his mother out of harm's way, next to the Coca-Cola machine. This would have been the perfect moment to finally inform her about his brother Ed's brood of caramel-colored children that he and his wife Judy, a former Black Muslim, were raising on their pot farm in Northern California. That would have shut her up.

The chinless woman accompanied the young man to the porch, where she stood staring at her watch. At a certain moment, she bounded down the steps in spongy running shoes, and a bell tolled as a hearse, followed by a procession of cars, nosed its way over a frail wooden drawbridge. The young man stood by the side of the road, waving his arms at the second car.

Mrs. Hokum sat erect, half-closed eyelids fluttering. The building vibrated with each slow, penetrating peal of the bell.

"What would Colonel Berkow say," she asked in a hoarse whisper, "if he knew colored people were using his cemetery now?"

Jake allowed the bell to answer with its solemn, relentless tolling.

"Don't you remember what Gloria found out last Christmas," he asked, trying to change the subject, "from the Mormons on the Internet? The name's really Berkowitz. Supposedly they were Polish Jews who immigrated to Tennessee in the early 1800s, then finally settled in the Pinchback district. Berko*witz*, Mama."

"'Partly Hebrew,'" Mrs. Hokum quoted, twisting the signet ring on her finger. "Who in creation would send you a Christmas card saying you're really Jewish?"

"Everyone's Jewish," Ed had commented that Christmas. "Aren't we all descended from Adam's rib?"

"So should we still put up the tree?" Mrs. Hokum looked exasperated, glancing from one son's face to the other as she tried to untangle a string of electric lights. She had just opened Gloria's Christmas card.

"Those of us who aren't descended from monkeys," Jake spit out of the side of his mouth.

"Jacob, stop it." Mrs. Hokum said. "I want peace in this house for the first Christmas without your father. And your brother Edom wouldn't look like an orangutan if he'd just cut all that mess off top his head."

The two brothers had been trading insults of "nerd" and "orangutan" ever since Ed arrived for his visit. Ed was burly, ruddy-faced, and bearded, with a matted shock of graying dreadlocks twisted up into a rainbow-striped Rastafarian cap. Jake had solved his prematurely receding hairline by shaving his head bald. Ed lived in a commune that produced the largest marijuana crop in Mendocino County, although he'd always told his parents he made a living from telemarketing. Jake, who designed graphic software for Adobe, was pale, gaunt, and always dressed in black. Together on the sofa, they looked like a Neanderthal seated next to a Star Trek character.

The only stage missing in their evolutionary diorama was the human.

This was the last time Ed would be invited home for Christmas, Jake had decided. His brother moped about like their father's vengeful ghost, tossing bridles and saddles around the empty stalls then trudging off into the woods to hunt, startling everyone in the new subdivision with rifle blasts. Ed had been livid about his younger brother selling off his father's pine woods to Partridge Estates, and about Jake's plans to convert the now empty barn into his design studio. Jake's cyber startup in Austin had gone bust, and four years ago he'd moved back in with his parents, "temporarily."

"I was planning to come home one day and run the old horse farm like Daddy would have wanted, and now you've taken everything away," Ed said when they were alone in the kitchen, mixing up eggnog.

Jake banged down the bottle of bourbon. "Then why didn't you stay?" There were no more family farms in northern Louisiana. Everyone who hadn't sold to developers had to make it in some other way. "I mean, you could be raising emus and daylilies like the Trotters next door," Jake taunted, "or maybe Christmas trees and Easter bunnies like the Finneys down the way."

The final showdown had occurred ten years earlier. Home again after being kicked out of the third college, Ed had taken LSD, then walked naked into the woods with a gun, a Bible, and a frying pan, screaming that was all he needed from his goddam family to survive.

"Daddy was blind when you had him sign those papers."

"He could see pretty good when his son went back-to-nature, buck-naked in the woods waving Mama's electric skillet. What were you planning to do, run an extension cord to the house?" Jake hissed, trying to calm the hysteria in his voice. "And he could see good enough to find that pot field you planted in the back pasture. And he could see that picture of your 'Sufi bride' you mailed us, which he tore into tiny pieces before Mama could find it. You really thought he'd turn over the farm to you? You broke his hard-shell Baptist heart."

While Ed stood tucking stray dreads into the knit bagful of hair sagging to his shoulders, Jake bolted from the kitchen with a tray of filled glasses.

"Now boys, not everybody in every generation gets along," Mrs. Hokum said, lifting a glass of eggnog. "But having kids helps to iron out everyone's differences. The future belongs to people who have children. Thought by this time I'd have me some darling grandchildren."

Ed looked away, and Jake glared down at him from the aluminum ladder, placing a frilly lace angel on top of the Christmas tree.

The winged statue was a smudge on the horizon, standing out in the coppery fall landscape like a huge rotten tooth. Mrs. Hokum winced when it fell into view, but Jake kept propelling his mother along the curved cemetery path, her stiff leg pointing them toward a meeting with origins.

"Think somebody threw black paint on it? " Mrs. Hokum asked, as they drew nearer. "I mean, because we're 'partly Hebrew?'"

"No, this is the mold of the ages," Jake said as he moved closer, chipping away at the darkened crust with his fingernail. The wistful features of the young woman with the flowing locks faced downward, as if contemplating the sere ground in which she lay buried. She carried a profusion of lilies on her lap, tangled with the finely textured down of feathery wings drooping like an opera cloak from her shoulders. Perched on a block of stone, she was an angel at rest, weighed down by the earth's bounty and her own beauty, unable to soar. Now the dank loam surrounding her was taking her back. "Vengeance is Mine." Jake barely remembered the verses he'd had to memorize. "Sayeth the Lord."

"Think you can save her, sugar?"

"Don't worry. I have those special brushes and marble cleansing powders from the preservation group in New Orleans. See what I can do tomorrow," he said, scrutinizing the statue with a squint. No way is this going to work, he decided.

The white eye sockets stared out from behind scabs of decay so dark that the angel appeared to be wearing minstrel blackface. She was a nurse, a perpetual sitter, keeping watch over the oval bathtubs sunken into the ground in front of her—the grassy graves of all the Berkows—as though they were filled with bathing babies.

"So awful," Mrs. Hokum said. "She was bitten by a brown recluse spider on the morning of her wedding in 1911. Say she was allergic and swole up like a hog. That was long before my time. So she never had children, and I'm an only child. None of my father's brothers had any children, so except for third-cousin Gloria, an old maid schoolteacher, it looks like you and me are the last Berkows left." Mrs. Hokum looked at her son as if they were stranded alone in a lifeboat in the middle of the Atlantic. "Not that Edom doesn't count, but he takes after your daddy. Countrified."

Jake knew what was coming: the apocalyptic importance his mother placed on the end of her family line. "Go forth and multiply," she kept misquoting the Bible, "and ye shall be like the dirt of the earth." Dirt. That's what she'd consider Ed and Judy's four clay-toned kids frolicking naked in the backwoods of Northern California, their nappy heads dusted with marijuana pollen. Edom claimed to have transcended money, Jake thought with a snort, imagining all the dough he must have socked away from wholesale dealing. After all, marijuana was to California what cotton used to be to the South.

"Is there anybody special in your life?" His mother tilted her head, glancing up at him with a flirtatious smile. "You just made thirty-two. Time's awasting."

Jake grabbed the wheelchair handles and carted his mother between the other graves, avoiding the already canned, "somebody special" conversation. The truth was, he didn't believe any more in romance than he did in religion. He had tried various women and even experimented with men. But being part of a two-headed beast just didn't suit him. He counted himself lucky to be free of the delusional convulsions he watched his friends suffer through. Several heartbreaks later, they all wound up alone and childless anyway. Men were extraneous to reproduction, he'd decided. Women gave birth to women who gave birth to women. Where did he fit in? Whenever a woman happened to be ready, the perfect mate was around the next corner. But fewer and fewer women seemed ready these days, at least among those his age in the computer world.

They meandered along chill walkways among the garish funerary monuments of the Gilded Age, bronze statues corroded green, chipped obelisks, the crumbling columns of miniature plantation houses, and iron-lace settees rusting into the ground. Jake couldn't believe what grandiose dreams of permanence these people had once entertained. By contrast, he felt like a wisp of dandelion, a mutant seed bouncing along the ground, the mysteries of where, when, and what he was to become shifting with the seasons. A brilliant abundance of vermilion, ochre, and golden foliage whispered above him as the tires of his mother's wheelchair crunched through dried leaves swept into mounds by the wind.

In the distance Jake spotted what at first seemed like a carnival float moving toward them. He then realized they were hats—wide-brimmed lime, fuchsia, and magenta feathered chapeaux, of the most fanciful confection—perched on the heads of a group of women accompanied by somber-suited men, and followed by a dozen squealing children playing tag around the tombs. This must be the Ticker family returning from their burial. By the time he made out the wedged head of the son leaning on the shoulder of an eggplant-shaped woman, the loud procession was upon them. The woman's face was covered by a black veil studded with teardrop rhinestones.

Suddenly Rebecca Hokum's wheelchair was surrounded by pastel pinafores with matching head bows, and little boys with clip-on ties making monkey faces. They seemed delighted to see the half-stiff corpse of a living white lady being paraded through the cemetery, one who hadn't been buried yet.

"Mister," said a girl with pigtail plaits looking up at Jake, "you sure do look like a hard-boil egg."

"Hey, Humpty-Dumpty," a boy blurted out, covering his mouth. This set off another round of stifled giggles.

"You all having a good old time here in the cemetery?" Mrs. Hokum asked, her birdlike features softening. Her craggy hand reached out to grab the fingers of the pigtailed girl, and didn't let go. The young man with the wedge-shaped haircut drew up beside them.

"I met your brother here at the office," Mrs. Hokum said.

"He our uncle," several children chimed in unison, pulling at his coat tails.

"Sure are a lot of you." Mrs. Hokum's head swiveled around to take them all in with a wide flash of dentures.

"Yes, ma'am. We a family."

"I'm real sorry, son," Mrs. Hokum said, her clouded gray eyes watering. "My mother's buried here. It's a terrible thing to lose a mother. Makes you feel like you got nowhere to go."

"You said it, lady."

"Come on, Mama. We'd better get back to the bed-and-breakfast. I have to clean that angel tomorrow."

"There's our family tomb." Mrs. Hokum pointed out the statue to the rhinestone-veiled woman. "We've come to clean the angel."

"That's my most favorite statue in the cemetery," the woman said in a deep contralto. "Just looking at her give me the unburdening."

Then the Wardell Ticker party was behind them, the ladies adjusting their hats, the children turning around to peek at the old white woman in the wheelchair with her foot pointing through the trees toward the setting sun.

The next morning, when Jake turned from Jackson Street onto Front, he saw plenty more hats outside of the Cook Convention Center. Women were prancing arm-in-arm up and down the street, crowned with elaborately beaded hats, felt ones wrapped with chiffon or gold metallic lace, zebra-striped, leopard-spotted, some frothy, others ferocious, no two alike, all peaked with feathers waving in the breeze. Jake smiled and shook his head, reminded of an aviary of exotic birds preening in tropical sunlight. A big banner announced in red: WELCOME CHURCH OF GOD IN CHRIST. PRAISE THE LORD. WE GOT SOME CREATION GOING ON HERE!

He and his mother were lodged in a Victorian bed-and-breakfast in the Pinch Historic District, where Mrs. Hokum's father grew up. Sitting around in the flouncy parlor of the old mansion, Jake's mother had reminisced about her grandmother presiding over her silver coffee service. The old lady had been such a devout Episcopalian she could afford to tell people, Mrs. Hokum finally recollected, that—way back—her family had been Jewish.

"Now the truth comes out," Jake said.

"She used to joke about Jews and Episcopalians, claiming in her heart she was still one of God's frozen people." This grandmother had grown up in a plantation house, a Daughter of the Confederacy. And her father, Colonel Berkow, had made a fortune in cotton trading, then established the most fashionable dry goods store on Beale Street. "They say the Colonel helped start that country over in Africa for freed slaves. Liberia? But his own son was a slaveholder. Why I bet those two had words. I suspect families didn't get along any better then than they do now."

Mrs. Hokum eventually had talked herself to sleep, reliving a glorious past she'd never known. Her purse was stuffed with Ziploc bags filled with half-eaten sandwiches and packets of cookies so she wouldn't have to waste money on restaurants. She had grown up during the Depression, and her gentleman father, who never held a fulltime job after 1932, had been happy enough to marry her off to a Louisiana horse breeder with a tenth-grade education.

Jake had dropped his mother off for a tour of the Hunt-Phelan plantation home with Gloria, and now was on his way to clean the angel. As he drove under the colonnade of oaks arching over the cemetery, sunlight dappling the car hood made him long to pick up a paintbrush again. After art school, he'd done little else for eight years but fiddle with cursors on a computer screen, submerged in a cartoonish blur of primary colors and beeping boxes that accordioned out. He felt like the boy living in the plastic bubble who could only touch the world through Gore-Tex gloves. The textures of the real world terrified him with their mystical concreteness that couldn't be clicked away.

Yet he was anxious to lay his hands on something—anything—real. And he figured rot was real enough.

The dark angel was waiting for him, gazing at the ground with her wings gathered around her in a gesture of distilled grief. He mixed the powders into a paste, then tried out a patch on the cheek, dabbing on the solution as if he were making up a bride. He covered the face, then the smooth neck above the pleated folds of cloth draping the body. The wings would have to wait until he had mastered the technique.

Jake worked all afternoon, mixing, dabbing, flaking off the dried mixture, and then reapplying a second coat. The last time he'd done any-thing so physical was during his only visit to Ed's, when he'd helped his brother install a sunburst stained-glass window in the group dining room. The commune had been buzzing with activity: Judy baked her own bread and made their clothes, and Ed was always at work composting the vege-table garden. Jake had been so stoned the entire time he didn't remember much from his visit, except carving and sanding fragrant redwood while a tangle of kids and mutts played underfoot to the cacophonous drone of an eternal drum circle. And every event had been an occasion for them to join hands for a Sufi song or some made-up Muslim ritual. He slept in a tree house lit by a kerosene lamp. Not a bad life, he'd decided, if you didn't mind being a grown man still playing Indian fort, watching your life disappear in curlicues of marijuana smoke.

The lazy warmth of the sunny afternoon made Jake drowsy, so waiting for the cleansing solution to dry on the intricate carving of the lily garland, he stretched out in the grass, his head against the statue's stone base. He drifted into a deep sleep, as if the angel had reached over to cover his face with her wings.

In his dream he saw twin escalators side-by-side, one going down, one going up and reaching far into the sky.

The escalator steps were crowded with stout women in church hats, clapping and swaying. Ed and Judy in knitted Rasta caps were playing conga drums, and motley-hued children raced between everybody's legs, singing a cappella. Those going down were waving at those going up, as if seeing them off at the airport on some marvelous trip. At the top of the up-escalator, Jake recognized the sepia features of Colonel Abraham Berkow looking quite pleased with himself, standing in a yarmulke like a department store manager greeting his customers. Rachel was in a wedding gown with a pearl-studded veil, wings fanned out behind her, and people were tossing rice at her.

"Jacob, Jacob, help me get to the next floor. I want to go where they're going."

His mother was calling to him, stuck at the bottom of the up-escalator in her wheelchair. She was wearing a ribboned plantation bonnet, her frozen leg sticking out. He was just about to lift her out of the wheelchair and sling her onto his back to mount the escalator when he was seized by a childhood fear of bare toes getting caught between the meshing teeth of the mechanical staircase. He looked down, and was naked. A series of high-pitched notes—*ding, ding, ding*—rang like a department store intercom as he yawned, neck against the stone, waking to the tolling of the cemetery bell that announced the final burial of the day.

One hand shot to the top of his head, rubbing his baldness. His head was smooth as a baby's bottom. He felt uncovered in the presence of the All Knowing, and shook himself to dispel the awe and shame.

Caw, caw, caw.

All around him in the violet twilight an enormous flock of shiny crows had descended on the cemetery with angry shrieks. They were perched in branches and on the tops of mausoleums, swooping to the ground to peck among shadows at the withered grass for whatever specks of stray life they could unearth. He planted himself in front of the statue, kicking at a few scavengers scuttling toward him, their reptilian heads all bulging eyes and greedy beaks. Their fluttering darkness covered the cemetery as far as he could see, deep into nightfall, far into the future.

Batting at the crows, he took out a hefty flashlight from his canvas tool bag and studied Colonel Berkow's statue. While he slept, as if by magic, the powders had done their work. Everywhere he had touched was now sparkling, as if the lustrous marble were freshly minted flesh. Rachel Berkow seemed to come alive, translucent, shielding virginal eyes from the beams of his light. He pulled on a sweater, tied a red bandana over his head, then buffed the lilies with fine steel wool before beginning on the wings. He was supposed to meet his mother and Gloria at the Peabody Hotel at five o'clock to watch the ducks parade through the lobby and into the elevator. Let them wait.

Losing track of time, he continued scrubbing like a man possessed, arching over the statue as purposefully as prayer, covering her with hands warm as a lover's. All of the gazes that had ever fallen here searching for something lost, all of those eyes hungry as empty plates, bore down upon him. He thought of his mother with her Ziploc bags, of Edom in his stoned exile, of the eggplant-shaped lady with the rhinestone-teared veil and her unburdening. Ever so softly, he hummed an off-key version of "Rock of Ages." Then lifting up a voice long choked inside, he began to sing.

WHY ISN'T EVERYTHING
WHERE IT USED TO BE?

A
t an age when there was little to look forward to except getting into movies cheap, BouBou Glapion got married for the first time. After the modest wedding, she retired at fifty-nine from teaching in parochial schools and moved into her husband's house in River Ridge. For six years she sat in an aluminum lawn chair in the carport, drinking bourbon and crying to herself before the neighbors spoke a word to her. And by the time they did, she'd already begun to forget where she was and how she got there.

Unlike the Victorian shotguns in which she'd grown up in uptown New Orleans, these bungalows were squat brick boxes arranged around circles. This was where World War II veterans and their brides had raised children who then got married—two or three times each, at latest count—expired in boozy car crashes, or otherwise moved on to further glory. Now walkers replaced tricycles, and home oxygen delivery, the Pepsi-Cola man. Shade trees planted in the 1950s had grown tall enough to lend a leafy grace to the stark grid of streets. The dream of gracious suburban living finally had come true, but unfortunately, not until everyone there was widowed, bed-ridden, or in a permanent bad mood.

Never in her younger years had BouBou ever imagined that she would wind up living way out here, even though she was the first person in her family to purchase an automobile and learn to drive. After Sunday dessert, the family would pile into her Studebaker to go visit the "new subdivisions" featured in the *Dixie Roto* magazine. From the parked car, they'd peer out at manicured lawns and split-level ranch houses, studying a future they both longed for and dreaded.

"It's real modren," her nearly blind mother would squeak, trying to get in the swing.

"Naw, MawMaw," a niece would correct. "It's ultra-modren."

BouBou's tipsy father would lumber out of the car and try to take a stroll through the new neighborhood. He'd set out jauntily only to trudge back five minutes later, muttering that not only weren't there any coffee shops, bar rooms, or news vendors, but there weren't even any sidewalks. He didn't understand, never would, and died one afternoon with his checkered vest on, fedora in place, waiting for the Canal streetcar.

These days BouBou couldn't get to sleep at night until she found out who had been shot in New Orleans. She remained glued to the ten o'clock news so she could thank the Blesséd Mother in her prayers for not getting mugged or gang-raped in River Ridge. She secretly thrilled at scenes of the neighborhood she grew up in, people rocking on front galleries or chatting at streetcar stops. For years, as a young woman, she went everywhere on the bus for seven cents. That part of her life had been erased like an old videotape, only to resurface years later on the Channel 4 "Crime Watch." These days, of course, you'd get shot in the head the minute you set foot in the city.

Out here, she thought, were just hard-working white Christians like herself.

The trouble was, people in River Ridge were so bored they often got drunk and took potshots at each other. Three years ago was the Christmas Carol War. The Hendricks and the Bordelons, with houses on opposite sides of the circle, had each mounted garish Christmas displays with outdoor speakers broadcasting carols. And each kept turning up their volume to drown out the other's speaker, until the cacophony from competing versions of "Silent Night" and "Away in a Manger" was getting on everyone's nerves. But people didn't feel it would be Christmasy to complain.

On Christmas Eve Gus Bordelon got drunk on eggnog and shot out the red and green lights of the reindeers leaping in a flashing arch over Bernard Hendrick's carport. Then Hendrick rushed out in a Santa Claus hat with his shotgun and let loose at the life-size plastic nativity scene on the Bordelon lawn, blowing Mary, Jesus, and a couple of shepherds half way down the block.

That's when BouBou had dialed 911. The sheriff cited the husbands for disturbing the peace, and they were sent to bed to sleep it off. Then she, Bessie Bordelon, and Raylene Hendrick wound up sobbing over a half-gallon of Seagram's in her kitchen until dawn.

After that, she was in like Flynn in the neighborhood.

"Where would we be without you?" the butterball Bessie Bordelon gushed as they unloaded Raylene's groceries from BouBou's Pinto. The recently widowed Raylene had come down with acute asthma, and on bad days couldn't move more than a few feet from her oxygen machine. She looked like an extraterrestial in her translucent oxygen mask and metal rollers, gesturing at them through the picture window.

"Hell, I gotta do something. I can't sit inside with that old man all day, the TV blaring and that schnauzer yapping underfoot. I wish I'd never retired, but after Mama . . . went, and I had to put Sissy in the Good Shepherd with Alzheimer's, well it near about killed me." BouBou adjusted her lustrous white pageboy and smoothed her piqué shirtwaist, proud of keeping up her appearance among the baggy shorts and extra-

extra-large T-shirts around her. How could people be seen in public like that?

The life of the neighborhood had begun to emanate from BouBou's house. She crossed the circle twenty times a day as peacemaker, practical nurse, and chauffeur. At dusk, when crickets and tree frogs began to chorus from the swamps, she would sashay from house to house with a go-cup of bourbon in one hand and a filter-tip wand of Merits in the other, cheering up shut-ins with gossip and a raucous laugh.

"That Theresa Comeaux driving me nuts. All she wants me to bring her is a gallon of wine a night and a *TV Guide*. She hasn't cleaned that house in a year, and won't have anything to do with her children. Poor thing. We gonna have to turn the hose on her. That, or put her in a nursing home."

Nursing homes was a disturbing subject on Blue Bird Drive. Everyone in the neighborhood had to visit a relative in one, and privately believed they too would end up there.

"Why the last time I went to visit Sissy," BouBou recounted, "they were walking into walls and colliding with each other like bumper cars. It turns out they all were wearing each other's glasses. So-and-so couldn't find hers on her nightstand, so she put on someone else's, who did the same, and so on. It took days to sort them out."

"Oh, Gawd, one time I visited my poor mama," chimed in Bessie Bordelon, "she was tied into her wheelchair in the hall, and this woman on a walker with Alzerheimer's keeps coming over and saying, 'Daddy, can I come in? Daddy, can I come in?' And so finally I says, 'Sure, sugar, I ain't your daddy, but come on in.' So she starts raising Cain with me like I'm her daddy, wanting to know why I beat up on her mama, and my own mama sitting there with a Whitman Sampler on her lap, taking a bite out of each chocolate then throwing it down on the floor. By the time I got out that place I was bawling."

"Like I used to tell Bernard, may he rest in peace, long as you got your mind, you all right," Raylene said. "But the minute that go, somebody shoot me, quick." Bessie shot her a slit-eyed glance to shut up. For months now they'd been whispering about BouBou's memory. It had all started with little things. But after the weekend spent ransacking BouBou's house, searching for her lost wedding ring that they finally came across wrapped in Kleenex in the vegetable drawer of the refrigerator, they knew it wouldn't be long.

"Don't forget, BouBou, Raylene has her doctor's appointment tomorrow at ten and you promised to take her. So we'll see you around nine-thirty. Remember?"

BouBou went right home to write that down on one of the many lists she kept Scotch-taped around the kitchen. The next morning, she remembered she had to do something, but she forget which list it was on. At quarter to ten Bessie was ringing her doorbell, shaking her head.

After the third call from Jefferson Parish police about a disoriented lady found weeping, pulled over on the side of the highway, Boubou's husband Luke Leggio, a retired mechanic, hid her car at his cousin's across the river. BouBou reported it stolen, and Luke wouldn't let her use his, complaining she stripped the gears on his stick shift. He offered to drive her anywhere she wanted to go, but there was nowhere she wanted to go with him.

She spent a week moping on the aluminum lawn chair in the carport, then set out at a brisk pace one Tuesday morning for the Pak-'N-Save on Jefferson. Waves of heat were shimmering from the tarmac as she made her way along the edge of the highway, past Texaco stations, used car lots, McDonald's, and motels. Until she spotted the parking lot of the convenience store, she had no idea what she was doing stepping in tan Payless tennis shoes along the weedy ridges above highway drainage ditches.

It was as if she suddenly woke from a reverie of shady galleries, frilly skirts, and lemonade to find herself in a glarey Martian landscape of gas fumes and whizzing metallic blurs. *Whooosh*, the sound went straight through her, *whooosh*, drawing her in spirals of vertigo toward a distant vortex. Maybe she had already died and gone to hell.

Wherever she was, she needed to lie down.

Inside the Pak-'N-Save, she floated up and down aisles of shiny packages lurching out to grab her, trying to remember what she wanted. She concentrated on the Muzak version of "Mr. Bojangles" as her mind blinked off and on like a wincing fluorescent tube. In a bright moment she paid for a bottle of Windex and hurried outside, feeling as if she were late—terribly late—for a big test she had to take.

She rummaged inside her taupe handbag for car keys, but found only house keys. She had forgotten the car keys on the kitchen table, and now she would have to take the bus home. Well, Luke could come pick up her car later, so she went back into the Pak-'N-Save to explain this to a puzzled clerk, a stocky young man with a bad complexion who accompanied her across the highway to wait for the Kenner Local bus.

She rode in silence for forty minutes in the wrong direction, following the intestinal curves of the Mississippi, fidgeting with her housekeys and peering out the window, unable to identify a single landmark. All of the gas stations, fast food joints, motels, and billboards swirled together into a whirl of red and yellow lights, like little Sambo's tigers turning into butter. The tigers raced around and around the tree until BouBou could taste butter on the dry toast of her tongue, and realized she was hungry.

At the end of the Kenner line, when she spotted the St. Charles streetcar waiting at the intersection of Carrollton and Claiborne, she smiled to herself and realized why she was hungry: she was supposed to meet her mother on Canal Street for lunch at D.H. Holmes. Why was she carrying a paper bag with Windex in it? Did Mama ask her to buy it?

Never be late for Mama.

Why, that streetcar conductor robbed her, insisting she put a whole dollar and a quarter in the box! She couldn't afford such extravagances on her schoolteacher's salary. She took a window seat, catching her own reflection in the grimy glass. Oh, my, she would have to run by Godchaux's before she met Mama to buy a hat, gloves, and heels. She couldn't be seen like this on Canal Street with her mother. She looked like she'd just come from weeding the garden.

She settled into the swaying of the urban relic, humming under her breath and emitting puffs of air like the little engine that could. As pillared mansions fell into place along St. Charles Avenue, one after the other, an itinerary so familar it felt encoded in her DNA, she knew who she was and where she was going. The farther she rode along the oak-shaded avenue, the further back she was carried, as if the gnarled branches of live oaks were passing her, like tired old nurses, from one pair of rocking arms to another, back to her source.

Her sudden vitality woke up the middle-aged woman in white shoes and stockings dozing on the seat next to her. "Excuse me, miss, we passed by Napoleon yet?" the woman murmured, trying to rouse herself.

"Oh, no," BouBou answered with a burst of confidence. "This is only Joseph Steet. It's about eight stops from here."

"I been on my feet all day by the cosmetics counter at Walgreens, and I can't wait to get home, know what I mean?"

"Oh, yes, indeed. Neither can I."

Miss Glapion's heart leaped into her throat as the clanging streetcar swerved from Carondelet onto Canal Street, a wide elegant avenue bustling with businessmen and well-dressed people carrying shopping bags marked Godchaux's and Kreeger's. This is where she came shopping with her mother and sisters every Saturday, when they would search for

Violet's sheet music at Werlein's and have Sissy's hair done at Maison Blanche and lunch at the coffee shop at the Roosevelt Hotel and then maybe go to a show at the Loew's State Theater.

BouBou stumbled in a daze toward the corner of St. Charles and Canal, still carrying the bottle of Windex. She was looking for Canal Street, the one she had just glimpsed as the streetcar looped back onto St. Charles. Obviously she'd gotten off at the wrong stop. This must be Magazine Street, a shabby thoroughfare of boarded-up storefronts and winos. Mama warned her to be careful on Magazine.

A gristled man with a red knit cap walked in front of her pushing a shopping cart filled with aluminum cans.

"Where's Canal Street?" she barked at him.

"Right here last time I looked, lady," he replied. "Spare any change?"

When BouBou reached to secure her purse, she realized she wasn't carrying it. The taupe handbag was propped next to the conductor's feet as the streetcar rattled around Lee Circle. At that moment, Luke Leggio had gotten up from his doughnut cushion in front of the TV to phone the Jefferson Parish police, and Bessie Bordelon was creeping along in the righthand lane of Jefferson Highway toward the airport, peering down sidestreets and into ditches.

This isn't Canal Street, BouBou thought, as she studied her reflection in the window of a running-shoe store called The Footlocker. And I'm not this old lady. There's been some mistake. I'm here to lunch with my mother and there's death all over the floor and no salt on the table and the rice in my gumbo is burned black. Take it back, I don't want it, take it back.

She trudged up and down Canal Street, past more running-shoe stores, chintzy gift centers selling French Quarter T-shirts, and cut-rate camera shops with "Going Out of Business" banners. Everywhere she walked smelled like piss. The D.H. Holmes clock was gone, the department store boarded up. So was McCrory's dime store. Where Godchaux's had been was a store selling football jerseys and baseball caps. The people were poor, dressed as if they were at the beach. A green and purple bus wheezed down the neutral ground, an island of noxious fumes where the Canal streetcar once passed. The Loew's State Theater, where she saw *Gone with the Wind* twelve times, was a graffiti-covered place called The Palace. "Butthole Surfers—live tonite!" was advertised on its marquee.

That was a picture she didn't want to see.

She wavered in dark doorways of narrow pizza parlors covered with grease, where teenage boys in tank tops and Reeboks looked up from their slices with menacing glances. She wanted to blurt out, *I'm here to meet my mother for lunch but Holmes is boarded up and I've lost my purse and I'm hungry and tired.* Finally she found herself in a McDonald's, where she grabbed a handful of ketchup packets from the self-service counter and stuffed them into the Windex bag. Outside, she tore them open with her teeth and sucked out the contents, ketchup dribbling from her mouth and running down the front of her yellow seersucker dress. She tried to rub out the stains with Windex, creating an enormous orange blotch that looked like a map of South America.

Since there was no D.H. Holmes clock to wait under, she decided to wait for her mother in front of The Dollar Store. She slumped to the sidewalk against the window, huddling with her skirt stretched over her knees. Standing in front of her, a man with a rainbow umbrella hat was screaming into a megaphone about Jesus. At the curb, a young woman in a violet sari stood watch over a card table draped in purple velvet, ecstatically waving sticks of frangipani incense with her eyes closed.

BouBou's eyes were also closed, studying the white crinoline petticoats of the other girls making their first communion march down the aisle of Mater Dolorosa. She was near the end of the procession, and saw the altar moving toward her in a flash of gold and crimson, grandfatherly apostles floating over the church on clouds of frankincense.

BouBou's eyes blinked open into the fulminant gaze of an enormous head, its smile exposing one gold tooth with a champagne glass etched into it, and another with a cross.

"Hey, lady," the head said, "gimme a swig of yours, give you a swig of mine."

The pecan-colored head was of indeterminate age, set without a neck onto a muscular torso perched in the seat of a wheelchair, where the fabric of empty pant legs bunched into a lap just below the navel. A thick arm was holding out a brown paper bag twisted around a bottle.

"Go on, take a swig, the wine'll wake you up. Now gimme your bottle." She handed over her own paper bag, surprised to be carrying it. The head erupted into an uproarious laugher that made the wheels of his chair swivel from side to side.

"Woowee, Windex, now I seen it all! You getting high on this shit, or using it to wipe car windshields? First time I ever see an old white lady hustling that game."

"It's for my mother. To clean the mirror of her vanity."

"Yeah, where your vain mama at?"

"She's coming to meet me at D.H. Holmes."

"She better hurry, honey, cause the place been closed for twenty-five years. Where you stay by?"

"We live at 1232 Upperline Street."

"How you gonna get home? Got any carfare?" he asked with pointed interest.

"I left my purse at Mass."

"Tossed your whole purse in the offering plate? Hey, loony-tune, gimme back my wine," he demanded, tucking the bottle of Windex into the side pouch of the wheelchair. "First, go head, unscrew the top and take a swig."

In one deft maneuver, he spun the wheelchair along side of BouBou, and they began to pass the Thunderbird back and forth.

His name was Breeze, he told her, and he'd been on the streets for twelve years. He knew the ropes, the best places to sleep and how to dodge the cops. She stared at him blankly, mesmerized by the champagne glass and the cross flashing between his fleshy lips. That smile. A much darker color, different clothes, and no fedora, but it was her daddy, that dapper gentleman smelling of bourbon who knew every doorman and sales clerk on Canal Street.

Out of the bulging wheelchair pouch Breeze produced a Hostess cupcake and offered it to her, just as her father would have from the pocket of a rumpled linen jacket. The wine fumes reminded her that it wasn't her mother she was supposed to meet, but him.

"Don't worry, grammaw," Breeze told her. "You sweet. I take care of you." Then ornate street lamps flicked on through the tree tops, and the light inside The Dollar Store dimmed and went out.

On Blue Bird Drive the policeman leaned his potbelly against the squad car's hood, filling out a green form with painstaking slowness under a streetlight. "I forget—how you spell Alzheimer's?" he asked Luke, who threw his hands up in the air.

"Just write demented," Bessie broke in shrilly. "It means the same damn thing. D-E-M-M-E-N—"

"Yeah, yeah, I know. Look, we can send this missing person description to Orleans Parish if you think she got that far. But if we haven't picked her up in a week—"

"She wouldn't set foot in no New Orleans," Bessie protested. "She don't want a bullet in her head. She probably just got lost wandering around River Ridge. These circles are confusing. I hope she isn't stupid enough to walk into the swamp."

"Of course she ain't. She was a schoolteacher, a very educated individual," wheezed Raylene. The neighbors were milling around the circle, even Theresa Comeaux staggering in her plaid bathrobe. Most of them had already taken turns driving in and out of River Ridge's labyrinthine dead ends.

"When they find her," Bessie whispered, nudging Raylene, "it's either bars on the windows or the Good Shepherd for her. I don't think Luke can handle watching her twenty-four hours a day. Ain't it a crying shame?"

The police got several snapshots of BouBou smiling over a birthday cake, and issued Luke a report number. The only lead they found the whole evening was when they stopped by the Pak-'N-Save to buy some Hubig pies and showed the photos to a pimply clerk bleary-eyed from a double shift.

"I could swear that the lady I helped put on the Kenner Local about noon . . . No, sir, the bus was going thataway, toward New Orleans. She goes, like, 'I gotta get home,' and points across the street. Weird how someone from New Orleans would come all this way to buy a bottle of glass cleaner but, hey. . ." he chuckled, downing a swallow of Gatorade.

BouBou pushed Breeze down Tchoupitoulas Street toward the Vision of Zion soup kitchen, both drunk on wine and singing hymns at the top of their lungs. His rich baritone and her off-key contralto bounced off the brick walls of abandoned warehouses and echoed under overpasses.

> . . . to save a wretch like me.
> I once was lost but now I'm found,
> was blind but now I see.

She knew what she was doing. Why was she pushing this legless man in a creaking wheelchair down a deserted street at eight o'clock at night? Because her daddy needed her to.

At the Vision of Zion they feasted on macaroni and cheese, cole slaw, and slices of white bread, then listened to a preacher say we are all children of God, and held hands in a circle. They sang "The Old Rugged Cross" and other hymns, then straggled out of the old storefront. Most of the communicants headed toward the nearby homeless shelter.

"Some rough shit go down at that homeless shelter, grammaw," Breeze told her. "We better off bedding down by that church what got St. Jude over by North Rampart, where I stash my blankets. There a chapel outside filled with candles where the Virgin Mary look after you. They lock the gates up at ten, so we better get a move on."

The lights along the wharf were greenish-violet and cast iridescent patterns on the damp concrete. It was a balmy May night with a breeze blowing in from the river. BouBou was used to seeing the world through a TV screen, a picture window, or a windshield, and walking through the city made her feel like a young woman again. For a change, she felt inside the picture, at home in her own body. She was pushing her little sister Violet in a stroller down St. Charles Avenue, pretending to be the mama. The freedom of being here, a loose-limbed, grown-up girl made her so giddy she almost skipped when she walked. Where had she been all these years? For a second she closed her eyes, trying hard to concentrate on that glarey, horizonless parking lot where she'd sat watching the world like a TV program but couldn't remember, from minute to minute, a single thing she'd seen.

With each step she took, pieces of herself sprang back to life, and they were halfway down Canal to North Rampart before she realized she'd turned the corner, and was almost home.

The iron gates of Our Lady of Guadalupe were still open, and Breeze wheeled himself into an outside grotto filled with candles lit under a statue of the Virgin of Guadalupe. The stone walls were plastered with small plaques that read "Merci, Maurice," or "Gracias, Juana," or "In Loving Memory." He unearthed a bed roll from a cavity between the rocks under the altar, and BouBou hoisted him out of the chair and helped to situate his torso between two blankets on the cement floor.

"In here, you sleep like a babe. Every night there's someone to tuck me in, and every morning the sexton help me back in my chair. She look out for me," Breeze said, pointing at the Virgin. "Tonight she sent me you." The gold champagne glass and cross were glimmering in his wide drunken smile, reflecting the pulsing flames of votive candles. Breeze handed her a third blanket and patted the floor beside him.

"Bedtime, baby." He looked up at her once, then turned away.

Entering the church, BouBou clutched the tattered pink blanket to her breasts as she shuffled down the aisle toward the altar with tears welling in her eyes. St. Jude was decked with wilted red carnations, beckoning her with an incandescent flame shooting from the top of his head. A bronze plaque under the statue read: "Saint of Impossible Cases." She hesitated, then reached down to touch the saint's plaster foot, worn smooth by so many hands.

At six that morning two New Orleans police officers located Mrs. Leggio from River Ridge wrapped in a blanket under the floor-to-ceiling shelves of red and blue novena candles blazing around St. Jude. She had fallen asleep in the alcove behind the statue, directly under a huge Byzantine mosaic in which St. Jude was bearing a golden chalice and Jesus a golden cross. Between them a dove was descending in a shower of gilded tiles.

Her fingers were curled into tight fists, blood oozing from her palms. The intoxicating waxy odor of this oven of faith was translated into a serene paraffin expression on her wrinkled face. They found her lying on her side, bare feet tucked under the hem of a stained seersucker dress, in what the doctor at the Good Shepherd Nursing Home later that day described as a fetal position. Conscious but shaky, she was escorted from the church while the sleepy sexton, who had notified the police, stood wringing his hands at the gate.

Propped up in the back seat of the squad car, her head lay to one side and her mouth hung open. Her final vision of the city of New Orleans was through the limpid police car window. The city disappeared into shadows below her as a golden champagne glass and a cross glinted through the bruise of dawn streaking above the Claiborne Avenue overpass.

It was a miracle, Bessie Bordelon declared that morning, that they found BouBou alive in the French Quarter without a bullet in her head.

KNOCK KNOCK

Before Michael got mixed up with the old sailor, Mr. Malone, he'd wanted to be a streetcar. When he turned ten, he tried to explain this to Miss Francis on the Ding-Dong School TV show for birthday kids. He'd been chosen for the Butch-waxed blond crew cut, blue eyes, and dimpled smile that made him look like the boy eating cereal on the Rice Crispies box. "Such a pretty boy," ladies at church always told him, making his rosy cheeks blush even redder. "What a shame to waste such coloring on a boy," the ladies clucked to his mother, Maxine. Michael had appeared in Schwinn, Ford, and RCA Victor commercials since he was five. That was after his father had left for good, and Maxine began to enter him in modeling contests to make ends meet.

"And what do you want to be when you grow up?" Miss Francis had asked, tilting a lollipop microphone toward Michael.

"A streetcar."

"You mean a streetcar conductor?"

"No." He glared into the camera. "A streetcar."

That summer Michael claimed the streetcars as his own. His post was at the side-window next to the conductor, where he imagined himself clanging the bell and twisting the handles. He would board at Willow Street, and then brace himself for the abrupt turn as the streetcar swung from Carrollton onto St. Charles, changing its course to follow a bend in the Mississippi. St. Charles Avenue seemed like another universe, a broad oak-lined thoroughfare of shadowy mansions far from the weedy shotgun-doubles on Michael's street. He would ride almost until the end of the avenue and get off at the YMCA on Lee Circle, where his mother had enrolled him in the day camp for boys aged nine to sixteen.

Mr. Malone always had a Snickers in his pocket and a knock-knock joke up his sleeve, and was the only one at the Y who could distract Michael from the window that opened onto St. Charles. Michael would stand there for hours tugging at the Venetian blind cord, pretending to ring the bell as he drove his streetcar. Mr. Malone would wait for him in the lobby, reading the newspaper in a leather armchair. For years he'd rented a room upstairs, since he first came to visit his old Navy friend, Coach Harley, who directed the summer program. Mr. Malone had a gray crew cut, a slightly bent, bulbous nose, and a jagged-tooth smile, and was at least fifty or a hundred years old, Michael figured. A retired merchant marine, he had been to every country in the world, and had taken a special interest in the boy. Mr. Malone swore that Michael was the spitting image of Biff, his nephew in California.

"Biff favors my mother's side of the family," Mr. Malone told him. "You and me could be related. Cute little fellow, a real boy."

Michael loved looking like a real boy named Biff in California. Especially since he felt like such a fake boy in New Orleans, Louisiana. California was where TV shows came from, and he hoped one day to make it there to become as real as the people on the black-and-white screen who mesmerized him.

Streetcar conductors began to notice Michael, too. They nicknamed him "Shotgun" because that was where he always rode, a skinny kid with a paper bag containing a clean towel, red YMCA gym shorts, and a sandwich, usually baloney with chow-chow.

"What's your dad do, Shotgun?" the conductors would ask.

"He's away at sea." Once he'd heard his mother tell that to Mrs. Friedman at church.

"So he's a sailor?"

"On a big ship," Michael lied. His father lived in Chicago and called home whenever he was drunk.

The name Shotgun made Michael feel full of "Snap, Crackle, and Pop," even though his world was as gauzy and faraway as a pastel diorama tucked inside a sugar Easter egg. He had stared out of the window so much in fifth grade that one afternoon Miss Umholtz made him count all the cars that passed by. Once he overheard Aunt Jewell, a grammar-school teacher herself, describe him as a "quiet boy." He tried to ape the screaming and jostling of other boys, jumping up and down on cue. Just as in high school, years later, before he stopped pretending, he would cheer and boo with the crowd at the stadium when he didn't know where the ball was, or even which game they were playing.

He was happiest working on his stamp collection, daydreaming of a triangular purple country called Malaysia, or a regal emerald country called Ceylon. For almost a year, he'd spent most of his time in the company of an imaginary Dutch friend named Derrick—Holland had such beautiful stamps. He and Derrick would listen for hours to his *Bozo the Clown Goes Around the World* record on the portable Victrola that looked like a little white valise. In April, Derrick sailed away with Bozo to plant tulips under windmills, just like in the record's picture book. And never came back. Maxine put Bozo in the box with Michael's loopy kindergarten drawings and said, "Time for the real world, kiddo."

So every day she sent Michael to the Y with fourteen cents in his

Daniel Boone wallet for carfare. This was when a ten-year-old could ride public transportation by himself throughout the city of New Orleans. And when children did exactly what grown-ups told them to do.

They had no idea things could be any other way.

Thirty naked Troopers stormed through the showers and scummy footbath, screams ricocheting off the swimming-pool walls in a piercing echo. Coach Harley stuck fingers in his ears and grimaced as if the noise were cracking the enamel on his teeth, then blew his whistle. The boys crouched in orderly rows along the bleachers.

"Look at this, Michael," Stanley Friedman said. He was a fat, freckled kid, the only boy Michael ever talked to—their mothers were friends at church. Somehow, on its own, Stanley's peepee was wagging back and forth like a metronome. Michael studied the swollen knob under Stanley's belly as if it were a gizzard in the poultry shop.

"Hey, you big fruit, knock it off." Jet Musso was looming over them, a Commando, one of the thirteen- to sixteen-year-olds who worked as lifeguards. They strutted around as if they owned the place, their pimply butts sticking out of jockstraps the coach made older boys wear in the pool area. Michael was speechless in the presence of Jet Musso and his Brillcreamed black hair. Jet's fleshy lips, curled into a perpetual sneer, obliterated any trace of Michael's existence.

Days before he met Mr. Malone, Michael had noticed Jet leering at him with eyes green as the panther's at the Audubon Park Zoo. Then one afternoon Jet grabbed Michael by the back of his T-shirt and dragged him across the gym floor. Michael flinched, sure he'd done something wrong, but Jet's touch made his skin tingle, and he went limp in the sweaty Commando's grip.

"This the boy I been telling you about," Jet said, depositing Michael like an offering at Mr. Malone's feet. Now Michael knew he was in trouble. Raised by indulgent women, he suspected men were there to punish you. He could sense Mr. Malone's furrowed brow appraising him, as though the old man could see through to his inner-most secrets, like God. Michael flashed a crooked smile, trying to look harmless and cute.

Mr. Malone's eyes lit up, his ruddy face crinkling. "Knock knock," he said.

"Who's there?" Michael stared down at his Converse hightops.

"You."

"You who?" Michael asked, barely audible.

"Yoohoo!" Mr. Malone boomed. "Hey, no need to shout. I'm right here," he cackled, slapping the boy on the back, then handing him a Snickers. When Jet disappeared, Michael relaxed.

Michael had spotted Mr. Malone and Jet together before, joking and whispering next to the candy machines. Now whenever he and Mr. Malone were alone talking and Jet approached, the words pouring out of Michael's mouth froze in midair like comic-book bubbles. Jet made him feel puny and ridiculous. Why would Mr. Malone want to be friends with him when he had someone like Jet?

"Tuck that midget weenie inside your fat thighs," Jet barked at Stanley, snapping the elastic strap of his badge of authority.

Then the Troopers jumped in the pool, splashing and ducking each other with vindictive savagery. Michael waded alone toward the shallow section, and Jet squatted in front of him. Michael didn't dare look up. All he could see were the curly black hairs sprouting on Jet's wet red toes.

"Hey, little buddy," Jet said hoarsely. "Mr. Malone says he'll meet you by the Ping-Pong table after lunch, okie-dokie?"

Michael bobbed from one foot to the other, flapping his hands with nervous energy, and then felt it starting to happen. Ian Vickers was swimming around him underwater, shimmering like a minnow. He torpedoed to the surface, shrieking at the top of his lungs, "Michael Higgins got a bone-on." Then the fluorescent-lit ceiling seemed to fall on top of Michael amid squeals of laughter.

Michael dreaded the end-of-the-summer award ceremony, and couldn't believe his mother planned to attend. Maxine worked downtown all day as a dentist's receptionist and was too tired at night to do anything except cook dinner, wash her mane of red hair, press clothes, and go to bed after Milton Berle.

"Just kids doing jumping jacks, then the coach hands out some stupid trophies."

"I'll be so proud," Maxine said, testing the iron with her fingertip. Her nails were chewed, with chipped vermilion polish.

"But I'm the biggest spastic in Troopers."

"Have faith in yourself," she said, starting on a shirt collar. "You can do anything you set your mind to. When I was a girl, I wanted a pair of roller-skates so bad I borrowed my friend Emily's, and entered a skating contest in City Park. The first prize was—guess what?"

"A pair of skates?"

"You bet, kiddo. And I'd never been on skates in my life. You should have seen how wobbly my ankles were, like a puppy taking its first steps. I fell down three times, skinned my knees, but golly, I wanted those skates. So I picked myself up—*zoom*—off I rolled. And I won, Michael. Your mother won."

Maxine had also taken apart a refrigerator motor and placed second in a talent show singing "High Hopes" with laryngitis. She had hundreds of stories that illustrated her pep and pluck, and all of them distressed her son, like being too close to a fan rattling at high-speed that any minute might spin out of control.

When the Troopers paraded double-file into the gym, a Sousa march blaring out of scratchy speakers, Maxine was perched high in the bleachers, wearing the shabby, shoulder-padded jacket of the business suit she'd been married in. With her gaunt face framed by a flowered scarf done into a turban, she stood out among the Mamie perms and Ike golf-shirts around her, a figure leftover from a black-and-white movie, a reminder of hard times. Her broad, expectant grin matched the red clutch purse balanced on her knees.

Michael wilted with embarrassment. If only he didn't look at her, he thought, he could get through this.

Trophies gleamed in rows along a table covered with a crisp white tablecloth. The gym swelled with order and optimism, smelling like floor wax and pencil erasers. With other Troopers, Michael drifted through choreographed calisthenics while Coach Harley counted "one, *two*, three, *four*." Michael flailed his arms doing jumping jacks and stiffened pale, froggy legs to complete twenty sit-ups. The eyes of all the parents in the world were burning a hole at the center of his crew cut, studying his shaky limbs and flushed face.

"In third place for Troopers," Coach Harley announced when the awards began, "Billy Blondeau." If I didn't get third, nothing, Michael thought.

"In second place, Ian Vickers," the coach boomed. Ian leaped from the floor and sprinted toward the glittering table.

"And in first place . . . Michael Higgins." Michael wasn't sure he'd heard correctly, and didn't rise until Stanley and Billy started kicking him. Michael floated across the floor to receive the golden statue, a muscular angel with outstretched wings arched over its head, as if it were doing jumping jacks to heaven. His mother sprang to her feet, applauding. Michael blinked, and for a second saw his father beside her, dressed in a streetcar conductor's uniform.

Mr. Malone was approaching the table, where he held up his hand to silence the applause.

"This summer Michael has made the most progress of any Trooper and has shown the strength of Christian character that makes this the greatest country in the world," Mr. Malone declaimed in his broad Boston accent. "To further recognize his achievements, I'd like to present him with this Timex watch."

Then Mr. Malone winked at him, and Sousa started up again.

Michael's first impulse was to see if his father really was there in a streetcar conductor's uniform. Soon his mother was standing over him with enormous shoulders, red lips puckered to devour him with kisses. She was alone.

Michael brushed her off, and she leaned over to embrace Mr. Malone, her eyes moist and glistening.

"Mrs. Higgins, I want to tell you again what a fine young man you're raising," Mr. Malone began. Michael tried on the watch. The chunky stretch band was ten times too large for his pencil-thin wrist. The face was yellowed, the crystal cracked, and it wasn't ticking. Michael tried to wind the stem, but Mr. Malone's Timex was frozen at another moment.

Jet Musso slouched against the gym wall, smoking one of the cigarettes Mr. Malone always bought him. Panther-eyes narrowed, he watched Michael, smoke drifting lazily from his nostrils. He was snickering, as if this were some sick joke only he understood.

"Don't look at me. I feel like a gerbil," Michael sputtered, averting his right cheek so Mr. Malone couldn't see the swollen jaw. Michael had been riding shotgun on the way home from the dentist's office on Barrone Street where his mother worked, and Dr. Roche had just pulled an impacted baby tooth. When Michael spotted Mr. Malone seated by a window in the streetcar, he'd abandoned the conductor and almost leapt into the old sailor's arms.

"Must hurt like the dickens," Mr. Malone said with a slow whistle.

"Where are you heading?" Michael couldn't imagine Mr. Malone's grown-up life.

"Over to see an apartment for rent. You could come visit, and we'd raise a little hell together."

"Neat." Michael's mother and Aunt Jewell never cursed. "Hell" thrilled him. His jaw throbbed and he winced, biting down on the gauze pad. Something was missing.

"Try not to talk." Mr. Malone put his arm around Michael's shoulder, drawing the boy toward him. Michael smiled and closed his eyes, auditioning for the part: everybody thinks I'm sick, and this is my daddy taking me home.

Yes, you can be my daddy.

"Chin up, champ. I'll ring you tomorrow," Mr. Malone said, getting off at Erato Street.

Through the open window, Michael watched the back of the gray crew cut crossing the intersection under a street lamp. He started waving, waving, and suddenly Mr. Malone turned and, with a huge gap-toothed smile, waved back.

Yes, you can. . .

"Later, gator," Mr. Malone shouted to Michael from across the street. A lopsided grin spread across the boy's distorted face. Heads turned, nodding, giving him the odd sensation that he was part of the boisterous world around him.

Yes.

"Jeez, this *puta* in Lima had the loosest twat I ever seen." When Mr. Malone chuckled, his turkey-wattle jiggled.

Michael squirmed, cutting his steak into tiny pieces at the dinette set in Mr. Malone's new apartment in the Dorian Arms, a brick building with fake columns at Erato and St. Charles. He didn't understand most of Mr. Malone's dirty talk, but they never had steak at home, only red beans or brisket soup. So every Wednesday after school he came to spend the afternoon at the Dorian Arms with Mr. Malone, who told him tales about Malaysia, Ceylon, and Holland, every country he ever imagined.

Mr. Malone would prance around the kitchenette, sipping whiskey and grilling steaks. In spite of his bellowing, Michael noticed something old-ladyish about how he fussed with tin foil and dish towels. Everything had to be just-so, like at his aunt's house: which chair he sat in, the rooster salt-and-pepper shakers so far apart, the plastic place mats to the edge of the table.

First they would play Ping-Pong in the spare bedroom with the door closed, and afterward Mr. Malone would fix dinner and they would eat. Then Mr. Malone would start with the stories and jokes: big-tittied ladies in various ports, priests and altar boys, and what fruits on the wharves had wanted to do to him. A queer in San Francisco had told him, "If you got a pickle, I got a nickel." Michael laughed and laughed with a whin-nying gasp, the laughter choked down inside him, trying to get out. It all sounded so funny, although he wasn't sure why.

Michael was most fascinated by the Buddha on the end table near the sofa. Mr. Malone said it was from a country called Formosa. He was a Buddhist.

"Think that sad sack nailed to the planks over the altar is going to bring you peace? Look at him!" Mr. Malone said, stretching the YMCA sweatshirt over his protruding belly. "He wants us to suffer like him, get all bent out of shape by right and wrong. He needs to be goosed. Lighten up, for Christ's sake."

"But Jesus is the Son of God, who so loved the world . . ." Michael protested, reciting from the catechism he was learning.

"Save it for the priests. One thing I learned as a kid, when their mouths are full you can say any damn thing you want. Hey, how about some cherry pie with vanilla ice cream?"

Michael brightened. The old sailor was his best friend, even though he was devastated about Mr. Malone and Jesus.

That evening he didn't ride shotgun, but huddled on the side-seat of the swaying streetcar. The conductor had pulled a ribbed black curtain around himself like bat wings so that he wouldn't be blinded by the glare inside reflecting off his window. Michael contemplated the conductor's oxfords beneath the curtain and thought about the Buddha on Mr. Malone's end table, so ageless and sexless. And with that knowing smile.

"Your T-shirt is in the way," Mr. Malone had said at first.

The next week Michael's blue jeans had to go. After playing Ping-Pong, Mr. Malone had been massaging him on top of the Ping-Pong table. Gives muscle-tone, he promised.

"This is what real athletes do after a game," Mr. Malone said, rubbing his hands together. Unlike most boys, who collected baseball cards and memorized batting averages, Michael couldn't name a single athlete. And he wasn't used to being touched. The pounding and pulling hurt. Other parts tickled. Mr. Malone's calloused hands were rough, but Michael didn't want to complain like a big sissy. He balled his hands into fists and thought of Shotgun, the boy on the Rice Krispies box.

The Ping-Pong table was in the middle of an empty bedroom. As usual, Mr. Malone had closed the door. Michael was lying on a rose towel at the center of the table in white underpants, staring at a stain in the ceiling.

Touch me where?

One of Mr. Malone's hands swept down and grabbed Michael's crotch. Michael shot a glance straight up. Mr. Malone's lower lip was wet and quivering, and his breath smelled like whiskey and peppermints.

Put your mouth where?

A clock was ticking behind the closed door, and a faint roar of traffic filtered in from St. Charles. The ceiling lowered, and the windowless white box dimmed, airless as an engine room. Mr. Malone's hand glided down Michael's smooth stomach.

Make it feel good where?

Michael tensed, eyes watering and toes twitching like in the dentist's chair. Is he going to punish me? Our Father, make this go away.

No, I won't . . .

Michael sat up and reached for his T-shirt, unsure where the words were coming from. "It would be—against God."

"Now I want you to know I've never asked any other boy to do that. You remind me of myself as a kid. You're specially chosen, you know?" Michael saw Jet Musso's lip curl, aiming a cynical stream of smoke at the ceiling.

"Not even Jet?" It just slipped out. Was this what those two did together?

Mr. Malone folded the towel into a perfect square. "I've known Jet since he was your age. We used to be a lot closer, like you and me are now. He said you were the kind of boy who. . . . Why, what did he tell you?"

"He said you were an old fart who bought him lots of stuff," Michael lied, striking back. He kicked on his jeans, then threw open the door.

"I could eat a goddamn horse," Mr. Malone announced to the empty daylight outside.

Touch me where?

The bronze Buddha gleamed on the end table, silent as the Three Monkeys Aunt Jewell had given him: Think No Evil, Hear No Evil, Speak No Evil. Michael was no longer sure that what he thought had happened actually had. He'd made it up in his own twisted mind. While Mr. Malone banged pots in the kitchenette, Michael stared through Venetian blinds slats at the street, thinking about Mr. Malone's red Keds, his nylon gym shorts, his "Go, Tigers!" sweatshirt. Now it seemed like some Halloween costume. He wasn't really a father but some comic-book monster of an overgrown kid.

No, you can't be...

Michael fidgeted on the turquoise section-sofa wrapped around a corner of the room. Outside a streetcar clacked past. He wished he were on it, but felt hungry and knew his mother wasn't expecting him for dinner. Putting on his socks, he could taste disgust on his dry tongue. This was what it felt like to be his father: angry, jumpy, ready to eat and run. He laced up his high tops, and then flipped on the transistor radio lying on the kidney-shaped coffee table. Frankie Avalon filled the room singing "Only the Lonely."

Then steaks hit the pan and started to sizzle.

Bees were buzzing in and out of wisteria blossoms drooping from the vine that grew across the rusty screen of Michael's bedroom window. His desk faced the window, where he squinted with a stubby pencil in hand, filling in the blanks of his sixth-grade science workbook. "(B) Phototropism" matched "(7) Growing toward the light."

Maxine was squealing with girlish laughter next to the squat black phone in the hall, so different from the strict-Mom voice, the tired-Mom voice she used with Michael. The only time she sounded serious on the phone was when his father called. Then she spit out syllables. Afterward her bedroom door slammed and bedsprings sank.

Her radiant face appeared in the doorway, frizzy red hair gathered by a rubber band into a ponytail. "High hopes, I've got high hopes," she was singing in off-key soprano, "high, apple-pie-in-the-sky hopes."

"That guy is a stitch," she said, sitting cross-legged on Michael's bed in a baggy man's dress shirt.

"Dr. Roche?"

"Mr. Malone. And guess what?"

"I've got homework to do." Michael hadn't seen Mr. Malone in months, but knew he still kept in touch with his mother.

"He's going to take you to *Disneyland* after school is out next month," she said, clapping. "He has a sister in Long Beach he's dying to visit, then *you two* can spend a few days in Disneyland. He'll pay for the plane and motel and *everything*, honest Indian. It's like winning a prize on TV. This could be your big chance for the movies."

No, I won't . . .

The lavender scent of wisteria wafted through the window along with the *Father Knows Best* theme from the neighbor's TV. "Starring Robert Young," the announcer said.

No, you can't be . . .

"California!" Maxine reached over to shake Michael's shoulders. "Hollywood. And a room in some swank motel with a swimming pool full of movie stars. Wish I could go."

Touch me where?

Michael's cheeks flushed crimson.

"What do you say?"

Michael stiffened and turned around to face his mother.

Put your mouth where?

"You'd get to fly in an air-o-plane." She stretched out her arms, waving them up and down.

"So why don't *you* go?" he asked.

"He didn't invite *me* along." Maxine's arms fell, and her eyes teared. "Look, honey, I'm sorry you don't have a real daddy. Believe me, nobody's sorrier. But sometimes in this life we don't get what we need from the same people we want it from. So now this perfectly swell man, who's been like a father to you, wants to take you on a trip—"

"Words are all blurry. I think I need glasses." Michael looked up at his mother, and then yanked the silence around himself like a streetcar conductor's curtain.

Mr. Malone and the trip to Disneyland came up every day for a week, then Maxine let it drop. Michael spent that summer lying next to the window abuzz with bees, polishing his new black-framed glasses and reading every book he could lay his hands on. He haunted the neighborhood branch of the library, checking out books from the grown-up section, then sprawling in the tan La-Z Boy his father had left behind, not even closing his book when Maxine came home, plunked down grocery bags, and rattled dishes.

"Such a quiet boy," his mother and Aunt Jewell would comment.

Michael put the golden trophy of the angel reaching toward heaven, the Timex, a plastic sports ring with a genuine ruby Mr. Malone had given him, his YMCA T-shirt and shorts, and the stamp album into a Campbell's soup box.

Then he shoved the box under his bed as far as it would go.

One evening soon after his sixteenth birthday, Michael Higgins sat by a window in the St. Charles streetcar, on his way to a bar called La Casa de los Marinos in the French Quarter to meet Hermine, the girl from English he was in love with. In a faded black turtleneck, he was reading a fat paperback titled *Atlas Shrugged,* scratching the bristly head of hair he had singed the night before with a cigarette lighter and candle.

At Erato Street, the streetcar stopped in front of the Dorian Arms. As far as he knew, Mr. Malone still lived there. After the summer of his eleventh year, he'd lost touch with the old sailor, except for one drunken evening last October with Hermine. Driving past Erato Street, he'd made Hermine stop her Mercury, insisting he wanted her to meet another Buddhist. At the beginning, what had attracted him to Hermine was the bronze Buddha she wore on a leather thong around her neck, and her honey-colored hair and olive corduroys that always smelled of incense. A mutual interest in Nietzsche and Cutty Sark developed later.

"Knock knock," Michael had said as a milky eye appeared through a cracked door.

Mr. Malone blinked. He didn't seem to recognize the scrawny student dressed like Woody Guthrie, but invited them both in.

"This is Hermine, a fellow Buddhist," Michael blurted out, bouncing from one foot to another along the shag carpet. It was important for him to be there with Hermine, although he didn't know why. She'd already met his mother at Dr. Roche's office.

The Buddha was still on the end table, and the door to the Ping-Pong room closed. Two young men lounged on the turquoise sofa watching *77 Sunset Strip* on a color TV. The one in the tight black jeans turned out to be Jet Musso.

While Hermine crouched in front of Mr. Malone's Buddha, Jet cornered Michael in the kitchenette, draping an arm around his shoulder. His shirt was maroon velour, unbuttoned to the waist, exposing a hairy chest. "Turned out different than I figured," he slurred with boozy bravado in Michael's ear.

Michael gave a full-throated laugh at what he saw: Jet the mighty Commando through the wrong end of a telescope. His English Leather cologne and stale whiskey breath smelled of youth gone sour, stuck at a certain hour like the Timex. Jet was still one of Mr. Malone's boys—and always would be—until someday he turned into Mr. Malone.

"After all the grief you put the old man through, I thought you'd be little Miss Priss. You're more like a hobo," Jet said, stroking the wispy hairs on Michael's chin, "but still chicken."

Jet's eyes were hooded and blood-shot, and his raw mouth looked as if he'd been making out with sandpaper.

"Tell you one thing," Jet said, raising his voice, "your girlfriend's got one fine pair of tits on her."

Michael blushed and turned around to survey the living room.

"Everything is just the way it used to be," Michael said. "I remember how—"

"Don't let memory play tricks on you," Mr. Malone cut in, busying himself with ice cubes and cocktail napkins. When he asked Michael for the third time about his mother, Jet's friend disappeared without a word into the Ping-Pong room, clicking the door closed behind him.

That had been Michael's signal to leave.

The streetcar's accordion doors folded shut in front of the Dorian Arms, and then it lurched forward. Michael had spotted Jet Musso only once since, sliding into a silver-haired gentleman's Cadillac in front of a bar on Bourbon Street.

Dog-earing his page, Michael stared past his own sullen reflection in the window pane, into invisible crevices of the darkness outside. The box with the golden trophy and gym clothes and stamp album was still under his bed, bearded with dust balls, and his mother was after him to clean it out. She complained that her child-model and award-winning athlete had become an unkempt stranger who gulped his food, read at the table like a boarder, then slammed closed the door to his room. "Like a complete unknown, like a rolling stone" were the words of a whiny harmonica music seeping at all hours from under his door with the scent of sandalwood incense. Michael had no idea who the things belonged to in that box his mother kept harping on.

They were somebody else's.

Michael sank back into *Atlas Shrugged*, lulled into a trance. Approaching the lights at Lee Circle, the streetcar conductor wrapped himself behind his night drape. Michael glanced up from his book as the streetcar swung past the YMCA then veered right onto Carondolet Street, the second place it changed course to follow a sudden bend in the Mississippi. Again, it was as if the river had said *no* to the land but continued flowing, in a different direction. The conductor, a silhouette as mysterious as fate behind his curtain, clanged the bell as the streetcar rattled through a corridor of office buildings, bringing Michael toward the Greek and Latino sailor bars that lined the dark, narrow streets of the port.

II
THE ISLE OF DENIAL

LA VIE EN ROSE
CONSTRUCTION CO.

"New Orleans a city built on top a swamp," the airport shuttle driver recited as the Garden of Memories loomed to the right. "Bodies are sealed above ground in them little white houses. You can't put 'em in the ground account of the water table."

The haggard man winced behind dark glasses as the driver's spiel worked its magic with the rowdy conventioneers in the van, who began to sing off-key choruses of "When the Saints Go Marching In." Every time he flew in or out of New Orleans, this information was there to greet him like a gargoyle at the gate. He had just bid goodbye to a friend dying of breast cancer, and now he was coming home to his ailing mother. This gargoyle and he were old friends, but he hoped this once to be spared acknowledging it.

The pirate Dominican taxi had been by at five that morning to pick him up for LaGuardia, and still flush with Cuba Libres and goodbyes, he had maintained an animated discussion with the driver about—what else?—how the hell could anyone live in New York? He had been gone the whole month of August, hadn't slept in two nights, and all he wanted was to sip a glass of wine in his courtyard and crawl asleep between the sheets.

Over the past three years he gradually had been moving back to New

Orleans, and in his suitcases was the last load of rugs, papers, and photographs. This time he had even taken the silverware. He was hanging up his freelance photography business in New York, capitulating to origins. He had won every battle, but had lost the war for independence from this place. And as the shuttle turned onto a narrow street of wrought-iron balconies spilling over with begonias, he was relieved to admit it.

With his last burst of strength, he trundled the bulging suitcases from the van and threw them against a green gate, behind which was a serene rose-colored courtyard. He identified with this aspect of Mediterranean architecture, nondescript on the outside, like this shabby fence, but with a luxuriant interior landscape hidden behind walls. He couldn't wait to slam the gate shut onto the world, with its incurable diseases, honking horns, and aggrieved parties.

Unlocking the wooden gate, he was met by the glare of eight men in purple T-shirts, black pants, and gold baseball caps. Slouching on patio chairs in the shade of the live oak that dominated the courtyard, they were sitting around a battered blue water cooler set on his grandmother's oak table, leisurely chipping mortar from bricks heaped in piles at their feet. In the shock of intrusion, he and the men just stared at each other, as once, while washing dishes at his sink on West 14th Street, he had locked eyes with a cat burglar passing along the fire escape. His own resentment wilted in the waves of misgiving he felt coming at him. Lowering his eyes, he wheeled his suitcases one by one across wobbly bridges scattered over dank trenches of corroded pipes. The purple T-shirts read, in flowery script, LA VIE EN ROSE CONSTRUCTION CO.

"How's it going?" a portly man growled. "You Mr. Weems in apartment B, right?"

"Yes I am, and I'm real tired. You all doing a little work out here?" Mr. Weems ventured, defying the obvious.

"All these pipes in the courtyard gotta come up. They a gas leak here, big time. We been at it for a month, be at it for another one to come. Just got the toe-mice out your kitchen. Had to tear down a coupla walls."

Hoisting the largest suitcase over the apartment threshold, the wheels popped off. He bent down to scoop them up with pale, shaking hands while the eight men studied him. Then he walked inside, choking on the fine white dust that covered everything. All the family antiques he had so carefully restored were stacked in one corner under a shroud of cement chips. His table lamp squatted on the floor with the shade ripped off, an outdoor spotlight beaming into his eyes.

He kicked the door closed and sat down on a suitcase to survey the damage as, on the other side of the green storm shutter, an electric saw blade cut into a length of pipe.

Derwood Weems didn't even begin to unpack his suitcases for three days. Most of that time he spent in bed in chili pepper boxer shorts eating fudge-ripple ice cream with ear plugs in.

Halfheartedly he studied the "for rent" classifieds in *The Times-Picayune*, but in the end, didn't make a single call. He hauled the construction debris out of his bedroom, swabbed the floor three times, then closed off the rest of the apartment. He kept the jalousie shutters shut and the bedroom air conditioner running, sealing himself inside like an eggplant forgotten at the bottom of the refrigerator. He cancelled his photographic shoots and didn't return calls.

Beep. "Hello, Woody honey, Mama. Guess you decided to stay longer in New York, because I been ringing you forever. Your number up there's been disconnected, so I don't know where in the world you are. Everything's fine here. That new medicine is working real good, and I don't have so much fluid. Now you ring me soon as you get in, hear?" *Beep.*

He let the message erase.

Like people enduring a siege, his neighbors only emerged at dusk to scamper to the corner store or dry cleaners, then bolted themselves inside, away from clanging pipes, jackhammers, and crashing loads of bricks. On the second evening home, when Derwood at last stumbled outside after the workers had packed up, he ran into his neighbor, Irene Guidry. Fingering the leaves of her shriveled bougainvillea, she reminded him of a photo he printed last spring of a Bosnian woman who had endured the shelling in Sarajevo by hiding for two years in a crawl space.

"Guess the dust smothered these," she was murmuring to herself. "I see you're back, Derwood. Bet you wish you weren't."

"Irene, when are they going to turn the water and gas back on? How long is this going to last? I'm definitely moving."

"That's all I thought of . . . for the first month," she snorted. "That's when I asked the workers about their progress and tried to reason with Eustice."

Eustice LaRose, their landlady's light-skinned handyman, had been in and out of the courtyard flashing his gold tooth and dusting off his chinos ever since Derwood moved in. He was the kind of fast-talking man his father had taught him to avoid at the racetrack.

"The day after you left," Irene began with a deep breath, already exhausted by the litany of disasters she was about to recount, "Eustice found what he calls 'toe-mice' in your kitchen wall, and proceeded to call the termite man. The termite man drilled into the courtyard to bury bug poison and proceeded to hit a gas pipe. The gas man came and proceeded to impound the meter, and Eustice sweet-talked Conchita into replacing all the service pipes in the courtyard and the woodwork in our kitchens, though most of this doesn't need to be done. He started his own company and will be a millionaire by Christmas."

"By Christmas?"

"You know Eustice. Every night he probably runs home to study the *Time-Life* books on plumbing and carpentry so he can tell his crew what to do the next day. Now I just accept it as Allah's will, and hide upstairs all day while they tear out my kitchen floor, looking for Formosan termites. I haven't had a bath in ten days. Yesterday at Mass they offered me litera- ture on the parish homeless shelter."

"Isn't this an awful mess? Hi, Woody, welcome home, sugar."

They were joined by their landlady Conchita, tiptoeing in stiletto heels along the plywood over the trenches with her blind Lhasa apso waddling behind. "Over here, hon. Come on, Choo-Choo."

Conchita Claret Charbonnet, from Hammond, was accustomed to tour the courtyard at dusk every evening with a highball in hand, surveying her kingdom. She was a sixtyish former Strawberry Queen whose hair got bigger and bigger as it turned blacker and blacker. Conchita had been a sec- retary who retired to marry her boss and lover, Monsieur Charbonnet. The elderly Parisian dressed up every day in a loop bow tie and double-breasted brown suit, as if he were about to promenade along the Champs Elysées, although he never moved from his glass of Johnny Walker Red in front of the blaring TV. Nobody knew how old he was, but if it was any indication, he claimed Edith Piaf as an early conquest. "After she make sex with me," he told Derwood last Mardi Gras, "her voice it really improve."

An engineer, Monsieur Charbonnet had been invited by Governor Huey P. Long to teach Louisiana how to drill for oil. During that era he bought this Creole cottage, built in the 1820s, and fixed up the slave quarters behind it into apartments. His first wife, an artist, had made the complex beautiful, and it appeared in several Vieux Carré patio books. Conchita had made it interesting for herself, filling it with the handsom- est young men she could lay her hands on, including Eustice LaRose.

"That fat plumber, the minister, thought I was flirting with him," she confided hoarsely to Derwood and Irene. "He said, 'I do believe you flirt- ing with me, Miss Conchita. You and me should step out some time. I like white women.' The nerve. I told him, 'Look, Reverend, I'm a married lady, and besides, I don't date nigras.'" She furrowed her clown-white brow to whisper in mock horror, "You think I want to get Ebola?"

Sniffing among the rubble, the Lhasa apso almost slid into a ditch. Conchita screamed, "Choo-Choo, remember you've had your bath!" Derwood yanked the yelping animal by its collar back onto the bricks as Monsieur Charbonnet appeared through the shutters, grasping a cane in each hand.

"Stop this sheeet!"

"Sweetheart, Choo-Choo almost fell in a ditch. His cataracts won't let him see where he's going to make peepee."

"I bet he can still smell pussy," Monsieur Charbonnet remarked. "I am so tired of this sheeet. All day long, *boom boom boom*. If they are not finish by Friday, I fire them all." And swiveling his toothpick body around on two canes, he faced Conchita. "And you, too!"

Derwood led the dog by its collar across the courtyard to the Charbonnet's door. Irene scurried into her kitchen, and Derwood let the gate slam behind him as he burst onto Burgundy Street, where the gay bars were hosting a weekend celebration called Southern Decadence.

The devil sure was flexing the biceps in his left arm tonight, Derwood thought, stepping out of the gate into a group of balding men in black leather chaps and bare butts with hardware dangling from every crevice and joint of their bodies. They were carrying go-cups of beer toward a corner bar called The Rough House, where a crowd of identical creatures milled under a canopy of white and baby-blue helium balloons. Derwood decided he might as well stroll in that direction toward the A & P.

Once, while fixing the kitchen sink drain, Eustice LaRose had told Derwood his vision about homosexuals. Eustice was not only an ordained Pentecostal minister, but also considered himself a prophet. "When homosexuals die," he explained, loosening a socket with a wrench and looking straight at Derwood, "they go straight into the left arm of the devil down in hell." Then he tightened the socket with a grimace.

"Now a while back, I had me a woman who was mighty fine in bed," Eustice continued, cleaning the drain trap, "best I ever did have. But I gave her up to please the Lord, and to marry a woman who'd be a good mother to my children." Derwood thought about what unhappy people plumbers always were, mucking around in other people's waste all day. And he suspected, trying to make sense of this conversation, that the woman who was so mighty fine in bed probably wasn't a woman at all.

Derwood's trip to the A & P on Royal Street was waylaid into an all-night drunk on dollar-fifty well drinks at a bar called Your Little Red Wagon on North Rampart. That night the club featured an ancient drag queen who looked like a tax auditor and sang "We're in the Money" in pig Latin in front of a gold lamé backdrop tacked across the storefront window. You can lead a whore to water but you can't make her drown, Derwood chuckled to himself as he fell into the hairy arms of a bald man with no eyebrows named Earl. Earl's keys jangled when he walked, and his slow smile exposed rotten front teeth. "Duke, Duke, Duke," he kept singing, "Duke of Earl," a song that Derwood hadn't heard since high school.

"I'd love to invite you home for a drink, Earl," Derwood protested, coming to his senses, "but they're tearing the damn courtyard apart to put in new plumbing and didn't even have the decency to turn my water back on before they split this evening. I won't have water all weekend."

"For true? Who's doing the job?" the Duke of Earl asked, with a sudden professional interest.

"Some outfit Eustice LaRose put together called La Vie en Rose."

"That Vie en Rose don't know shit. I'm a plumber, hear, and it ain't nothing to turn someone's water back on if the pipes is laid right while you working on them. Lemme go by my daddy's on Dauphine," he said, shooting Derwood a sweetly rotten smile as he massaged his thigh, "and get my wrench, know what I mean, Woody? Gimme your address on this napkin."

My God, what have I gone and done? Of all things, a plumber! Derwood's head was spinning as he lay stretched out on his crummy sheets, hoping the doorbell wouldn't ring. But it did. He stumbled barefoot in his shorts across the plywood bridges toward the courtyard gate, ready to make any excuse. When he opened it, there stood an enormous woman with a cascade of curly red locks in a kelly-green dress, hand on hip.

"Woody, where y'at? It's me. So whatcha think, cher? Pretty foxy?" the figure gushed, doing a runway twirl and voguing in through the gate.

"Man, look at this mess. Them guys don't know they ass from a hole in the ground," Earl mumbled in disgust, swaggering bowlegged in beige half-heel pumps that went tap-tap-tapping across the plywood bridges. Yanking a wrench out of a beaded handbag, he hiked the slip up to his crotch and squatted like a bull frog to inspect the water main.

"Piece of cake," Earl said.

Leaning over too far, his thin soles slipped on the mucky plywood, and he skidded feetfirst into a sinkhole under the pipes, up to his knees in fetid water. With a sucking sound, he step-kicked one meaty calf over the pipes to strike a vampish pose with one bare foot resting demurely on his knee.

"I'll get you out. Here, grab my hand."

"Whoa, not so fast. Where my shoe at? Don't rip them twenty-dollar panty hose, hear?"

As Derwood and Earl grappled over the ditch, Conchita's pale yellow kimono appeared framed in the French door of the Charbonnet's apartment. "Woody, is that you, honey? Who's that lady in the ditch? She with you?"

Conchita padded out in velour slippers to get a better look.

"It's the plumber, Conchita. Everything's all right," Derwood boomed in a business-like baritone. "We're just trying to turn my water on."

"Turn *who* on? At this hour of the morning? Hey, she's a redhead. She's a red-headed plumber! I never seen such a red-headed plumber before." Conchita thought this a hilarious observation, and insisted on helping hoist Earl out of the ditch, her mascara-smudged eyes widening as she grabbed hold of his thick, tattooed forearm. "How would you and the plumber like to come in for a teensy-weensy nightcap?" she slurred. "My husband's gone beddy-bye."

Heavy-lidded, she gave the mud-splattered Duchess of Earl a slow up-and-down. "You sure you a plumber?"

Earl was furious. He'd lost a new Dillard's pump in the sinkhole and wanted to go straight home to change his dress. The offer of a shower tempted Derwood, but when he considered the Duchess's other charms, he declined. They exchanged phone numbers, and for the next few days—during which Derwood was on the phone to New York every minute of the day and night telling everybody he was moving back—Earl didn't call.

"Mama, I've tried everything to come home, but it isn't working out. . . No, I don't want to own a house here anymore. . . Because my expectations have changed. I expect things to work, and for things to work people have got to. It takes more than a pound of crawfish, a couple of beers, and a carnival parade to make me happy these days. I guess New York has changed me. . . Thanks, but you don't need to remind me this is where I'm from—it's a great place to be *from*. And a great place to come *back to*, once in a while. In the meantime. . . Permanently? Inside that tomb with you. That's where I'll end up permanently. Then I'll settle down for a century or two. But right now, to find another apartment and move again, I might as well move to Paris for all the trouble. I don't know. Something tells me I may never get out of here.

How you feeling? . . . Well, why did he change the medication if the other one was working so well? Try it for awhile, I guess. . . Yeah, I'll be out to see you this weekend. First thing I'll do is check out your hot water. . . I love you, too."

Derwood always knew New Orleans would be his undoing, he thought as he hung up. It had taken him twenty years to get out, and another twenty to get back, transformed from a blond catalog model into a mature photographer. Unlike most New Yorkers, who thought they could take the slow, sensual Crescent City by storm, Derwood understood the value of lifelong contacts. No, here he wouldn't edit and print for the World News Service, but at least he could shoot the right weddings and Mardi Gras courts. And this would leave him time for his own projects, like the photo essay on New Orleans cemeteries. The creative possibilities here seemed endless.

And so did the destructive.

At night he could feel the city sinking back into the swamp it rose from, a miasma of hereditary alcoholism, violence, and dementia. He could sense hideous tumors blooming like bayou orchids inside the lethargic bodies that sleepwalked the streets. Swatting at mosquitoes on his balcony, he stared down into the Venice of trenches in the moon-lit courtyard below, examining for signs and portents the brackish entrails that lay two feet beneath the surface of a city that so charmed visitors. Just below the pipes floated a soggy bed of cypress logs placed by French settlers and their slaves on top of a snake-infested swamp.

I know where I'm from, he thought.

Mosquitoes already had begun to breed in the stagnant ditches, and Formosan termites were devouring the city alive. The termites could only be stopped here and there, a bathroom or kitchen at a time, by endless restorations like this one. Sixty percent of the primordial live oaks shading the city were already being hollowed out from below by these insects brought over from Taiwan aboard World War II freighters. This species only swarmed during three or four evenings in May, ferocious to fuck each other and then nest before their double wings fell off at 10 p.m. like a Darwinian Last Call.

The wrought-iron courtyard furniture had been abandoned to the August rains, and in a matter of weeks was as barnacled with rust as the heaps of corroded pipes that lay next to it. The spongy night drove Derwood back into the air conditioning, where he slipped into a deep sleep. He dreamed of a dark reservoir filled with naked swimmers. They were clamoring for him to *jump in, jump in,* but he knew the tank was bottomless, stretching into the bowels of the earth. He hesitated at the edge of the water that wound deeper and deeper down into nowhere, and woke with a start at the first low rumblings of thunder.

It was about to storm.

For two nights Derwood Weems was held prisoner in his slave quarter. All lines to the outside world were cut—electricity, gas, water, and telephone. He survived on sardine sandwiches and brushed his teeth with Dr. Pepper. The hurricane had passed yesterday, but still the shutters were locked tightly from the outside. Through the louvers, he could see the courtyard was nothing but flooded moats with pipes sticking out at jagged angles.

All of his neigbors had escaped days ago, when the workers from La Vie En Rose Construction Co. got into a violent argument with Eustice. After they had done the most backbreaking part of the job, digging ditches and pulling up old pipes, Eustice wanted to lower their wages, or he threatened to fire them and bring in even cheaper workers. That was their side. Eustice, on the other hand, admitted these guys were just preachers and homeless men he'd recruited at the Vision of Zion soup kitchen on Perdido Street. Now that he had to connect new pipes, he needed trained plumbers and electricians, and these other men could continue working as assistants. Derwood didn't know whom to believe.

For several mornings leading up to the blow out, Derwood was woken up by the stentorian voice of a minister gesturing in the shade under the live oak, preaching about Joshua. "Now Jericho was an old city, and Jericho was an evil city, eaten up by weevils and sin. And Joshua had him a trumpet and stood outside them gates, blowing to let a little *light* in, blowing to let a little *justice* in, blowing to let a little bro-ther-ly *love* in. . . ."

"And the wall come tumbling down," was the uproarious response of the men, listening with shovels and pipes in hand.

This was not a good sign.

Work came to a standstill, and within a few days, Eustice fired the crew. But without a week's severance, they refused to allow new workers in. They camped out in the courtyard overnight, so Derwood heard more about corrupt Jericho, Joshua, and his golden horn. He let them keep beer in his refrigerator and call home from his phone, and only stopped short of offering them space on the floor.

That evening Conchita waltzed in from Arnaud's in a lilac mother-of-the-bride's dress and marched around and around the courtyard with a tumbler of scotch in her hand. "Go home and go to bed, you naughty boys," she screeched, "before I call the cops."

At three in the morning Eustice brought over the sheriff to evict them for trespassing. Conchita told him that the takeover had driven off all her tenants, which was almost true, although Derwood didn't know how much longer he could have taken it. So early the next morning, when hurricane Diane unexpectedly veered west from Pensacola and headed toward southeastern Louisiana, Eustice came by to test the storm shutters. He double-latched all door and window shutters from the outside while Derwood was upstairs sleeping off the battle of Jericho.

By the time Derwood got up and stumbled to a balcony door, the hurricane was already starting to hit. He noticed a broken wire flapping in the wind outside. When he tried to call Conchita, his line was dead. The last time he saw her, from between the louvers, she was trying to fold Monsieur Charbonnet's palsied limbs into the Buick in the driveway. A suitcase had blown open, and undergarments were twirling furiously around the courtyard. Conchita was screaming "Choo-Choo, Choo-choo," trying to find the Lhasa apso. Later Derwood heard the car start up, and after ramming every shutter in the apartment with a solid brass coat stand, he curled up in bed to listen to stinging sheets of rain whip across the house, bombarding the roof with tiny green acorns.

The bloated Lhasa apso with a rhinestone barette was floating belly-up in a trench, next to a beige pump. A mandarin silk pajama top, an alarming red, dangled from the top branch of the fig tree.

The waters had receded, coating everything with a primal gray slime.

Derwood kicked through the acorns and branches that matted the slick courtyard, his blue eyes blinded by morning glare. He'd lept up to embrace the flashing grin of his jailer and liberator when Eustice arrived to unfasten the storm shutters the second morning after Diane hit. Like a trapped animal, Derwood had almost destroyed the apartment trying to gnaw his way out. In one particular hole, over the stove, he had burrowed with a butcher knife as far as the original brick wall of the slave quarter.

Eustice apologized for his terrible mistake, but otherwise was all business.

"Yes sirree, it's a new day for me," he kept repeating, as he tossed tools into canvas sacks. "Lucky the Charbonnets asked me to come by to look for they pooch," he said, glancing at the dead dog floating in a trench, "or you could've been locked in there till kingdom come. They staying out by her sister's house across the lake till Thanksgiving. Mr. Charbonnet ailing and Miss Conchita ain't about to drag him back to this holeful of toe-mice."

"When will the work start up again?" Derwood wanted to know, calculating how long it would take to haul his things out.

"Not for a long time now. I'm bailing out of this town and following the storm down the coast. La Vie en Rose got a brand new bag, and we gonna be cleaning up after the hurricane. We're talking exclusive home reconstruction and insurance megabucks, get me? You should see Biloxi. It a mess. By the way, babe, got a plumber gonna work with us name of Earl who says if I see Woody over by Miss Conchita, be sure to tell him 'way to go!'"

A flock of sparrows, driven off by the construction project, had returned to the live oak, now split to one side. Morning birdsong joined the high whine of an air conditioner in allegro accompaniment to the Creole Queen's calliope on the levee, belting out "Do You Know What It Means to Miss New Orleans?" The worse part of his incarceration was Derwood had run out of cigarettes, so he and Eustice sat smoking on the rusted patio chairs under the tree, Derwood plotting how to revive his career in New York, Eustice flush with plans to make a killing on the devastated Gulf Coast.

Suddenly the sparrows surged all at once from the tree top into a black funnel of wings shrieking to a nearby roof. The sound almost tore the top of Derwood's head off. The two men jerked backward, gazing up into the quivering branches, but before Derwood knew what was happening, the quivering became a massive sway.

And then a splintering.

The tree trunk split open like papier-mâché, tumbling down on top of the two natives smoking together after the storm. Derwood could feel the warmth of Eustice's limbs entwined with his own, but couldn't lift either his arms or legs as a salty syrup that tasted like blood seeped into his mouth. He thrashed his head in the struggle to free himself, finally surrendering his panic to a familiar comfort that closed over his head like dark water.

A group of early-morning revelers with sausage balloons tied around their heads stopped to marvel. The top of a huge live oak had just come crashing to Burgundy Street through a green wooden fence, exposing the radiant pink flesh of a French Quarter courtyard. "Whoa, did you see that?" they asked each other, as a parked car smacked by a gnarled limb let out its supersonic wail. Then, checking their map, they ambled toward the Mississippi, looking for the blackjack tables and another cold one.

OPEN MIKE

There must be hundreds of kids who have wound up dead in the French Quarter. Eva Pierce was just one of them. Everywhere you walk in the neighborhood you see fliers about them Scotch-taped to lamp posts: *Information Wanted* or *$5,000 Reward*. And below is a blurry snapshot of some scruffy young person. After Eva's body was discovered, bundled inside a blue Tommy Hilfiger comforter floating in Bayou St. John, the girl's mother moved down here from Idaho or Iowa or Ohio—however you pronounce it—and blanketed the Quarter with those signs. She even printed her daughter's last poem on the flier, but no dice. The fifteen hours between when Eva was last seen and when her body was found in the bayou remained a blank.

That's when the mother rang me. I'm listed in the Yellow Pages as *Need to Know, Inc: Off-Duty Homicide Detective—Missing Persons—Surveillance.*

Mrs. Pierce met me under the bingo board at Fiorella's restaurant at the French Market. It wasn't my suggestion. I hadn't been to the market since I was a kid, when my daddy used to take me on Saturday mornings to squabble with his wop relatives while we loaded up at a discount on their fruits and vegetables. On my daddy's side I'm related to everyone who ever sold a pastry, an eggplant, or a bottle of dago red in the Quarter, and on my mother's side, to everyone who ever ran the numbers, pimped girls, or took a kickback. I peeked inside the rotting old market but sure didn't see any Italians or tomatoes. Now it was just Chinese selling knockoff sunglasses to tourists.

Mrs. Pierce was short and round as a cannoli, with a stiff gray bouffant and a complexion like powdered sugar. With those cat's-eye bifocals, she looked like someone who might be playing bingo at Fiorella's. But when she opened her mouth . . . *Twilight Zone*. Mrs. Pierce said it wasn't drugs or sex that did her daughter in but—get this—poetry.

"And the police aren't doing anything," she said with a flat Midwestern whine that made me want to go suck a lemon.

"Look, lady, I'm a cop—Lieutenant Vincent Panarello, Sixth District—and the police have more trouble than they can handle in New Orleans. They don't pay us much . . . I got a wife and three kids in Terrytown, so that's why I moonlight as a detective."

"My daughter loved moonlight."

"I bet."

"She read her own original poetry every Tuesday night at that rodent-infested bar on Esplanade Avenue called the Dragon's Den." She was twisting the wrapper from her straw into a noose.

"Yeah, that used to be Ruby Red's in my day. A college joint, the floor all covered with sawdust and peanut shells." I didn't tell her how drunk I used to get there in high school with a fake I.D. While I was going to night school at Tulane, Ruby Red's was where I met my first wife Janice, may she rest in peace.

"Well, the place has gone beatniky." Mrs. Pierce leaned forward, her eyes watering. "And do you know what I think, Lieutenant Panarello?"

"Shoot."

"I think one of those poets murdered my daughter. One of those characters who read at the open mike. And that's where I want you to start. To listen for clues when the poets read. Eventually one of them will give himself away."

"Listening to the perms will cost you extra." And so will the French Quarter, but I'd already averaged that in when I quoted her my fee.

"I'll meet you there Tuesday at 9 p.m. It's above that Thai restaurant. Just go through the alley—"

"I know how to get up there." I could have climbed those worn wooden steps next to the crumbling brick wall in my sleep. That's where I first kissed Janice. Funny, but she also wrote poems she read to me on the sagging wrought-iron balcony. The life I really wanted was the one I planned with her. The life I settled for is the one I got.

Mrs. Pierce handed me a picture of her daughter, a list of her friends, and a check. I eyed the amount. Local bank.

"What your daughter do for a living?" I pushed back my chair, antsy to blow Fiorella's. I could already smell the fried-chicken grease on my clothes.

"Why, she was a poet and interpretive dancer."

"Interpretive dancer. Gotcha."

I studied the photo. Eva was about twenty-four, pretty, with skin as pale and powdery as a moth's wing. But she was dressed in a ratty red sweater over a pink print dress over black sweat pants. Her dyed black hair was hanging in two stringy hanks of pigtail like a cocker spaniel's ears. Who would want to kill her, I wondered, except the fashion police?

When I got down to the station I pulled the report. Eva was last seen at Molly's bar on Decatur Street at 4 a.m on a Tuesday, where she told her roommate, Pogo Lamont, that she was going home to feed their one-eyed dog named Welfare. They lived on Ursulines at Bourbon, upper slave quarter, uptown side. She never made it home. After an anonymous 911 tip, her body was hoisted out of the bayou at 7 p.m. the next evening. One clean shot through the temple, real professional. No forced sexual entry. Her purse was lying open on the grassy bank, surrounded by a gaggle of ducks trying to get at the bag of stale popcorn inside. A cell phone and twenty-five dollars were tucked in the bag, so the motive wasn't robbery. Also inside the purse were a red lipstick, a flea collar, a black notebook filled with poems, two 10-mg. Valiums, an Ohio picture I.D., a plastic straw that tested positive for cocaine residue, and a worn-out restraining order against Brack Self, a bartender and "performance artist" who turned out to have been locked up the whole time in Tampa for beating on his present girlfriend. That, and an Egyptian scarab, a petrified dung beetle supposed to be a symbol of immortality.

Which didn't seem to have worked for Eva Pierce, poet and stripper.

I made it to the Dragon's Den on a sticky Tuesday evening, with a woolly sky trapping humidity inside the city like a soggy blanket. It had been trying to rain for two weeks. The air was always just about to clear but never did, as if old Mother Nature were working on her orgasm. I carried an umbrella, expecting a downpour. The place was right next to the river and hadn't seen a drop of paint since I last walked in the door thirty years ago, with all my hair and a young man's cocky swagger. A whistle was moaning as a freight train clacked along the nearby tracks, and the huge live oak out front shrouded the crumbling façade in a tangle of shadows. An old rickshaw was parked outside, where an elfin creature with orange hair sat scribbling in a notebook. He shot me a look through thick black plastic glasses, and then went back to writing.

Guess I'd found the poets.

I slapped a black beret on my head as I headed through the clammy alley, the bricks so decrepit that ferns were sprouting from the walls. I needed to blend in with the artsy crowd here, so I wore a blousy purple shirt and tight black pants, and carried a paperback by some poet called Oscar Wilde that I'd had to read at night school. A wizened old Chinese guy was squatting over a tub of vegetables in the patio, and the air smelled like spices. Something was sizzling in the kitchen. I felt like I was in Hong Kong looking for my Shanghai Lil.

Except for the Far East decor, the bar upstairs hadn't changed that much. A small stage and dance floor had been added at the center, and the tables were low, surrounded by pillows on the floor. Is that where poets eat, I wondered, on the floor?

"I'll have something light and refreshing, with a twist of lime," I lisped to the two-ton oriental gal behind the bar, waving my pinky. A biker type in a leather cowboy hat was observing me from across the bar.

"You a cop?" he yelled.

"Why no," I said, batting my eyelashes, holding up the lavender book so he could read the cover. "I've come for the poultry."

"Hey, Miss Ping," he shouted to the bartender. "Give Lieutenant Girlfriend here a wine spritzer on my tab."

Just as I lurched forward to knock this asshole's block off, in walked Mrs. Pierce with that orange-haired garden gnome from out front.

"Here you go, Lieutenant Girlfriend," Miss Ping said, setting down the drink.

"Lieutenant," Mrs. Pierce said, "this was Eva's roommate, Pogo Lamont."

"Lieutenant Girlfriend," Pogo cackled, extending his hand.

"Come on, son, I want to talk to you on the balcony," I said, grabbing him by the shoulder.

"Unhand me this instant!" the little creep cried out.

"Watch out," grunted the joker in the leather cowboy hat, "Lieutenant Girlfriend's already hitting on the chicken." Miss Ping barked a throaty laugh.

The kid followed me onto the balcony, which was pitching precariously away from the building. I steadied myself as if stepping into a boat, not trusting the rusted iron-lace railing to keep all 250 pounds of me from rolling off.

"Okay, you know why I'm here," I said, plunking down my drink on a wobbly table. "Who's this Brack Self character that Eva took out a peace bond against?"

"Oh, that snarling beast," Pogo said, curling up like a cat into a chair. "A former beau who used his fists to make a point. Black and blue weren't Eva's most becoming colors."

"She liked it rough, huh?"

"Oooh, Lieutenant Girlfriend," Pogo squealed.

"Say, you little—" Play it cool, I thought. This was just a job.

"She met him here at the open mike when the poetry series first started. That first night he got so wasted he just unzipped, whipped it out, and pissed sitting right at a table. While I was performing, I might add. Now that, honey, is what I call literary criticism. Eva mopped it up, and never stopped. And ended up mothering him."

"How long they together?"

"Until the third occasion she summoned the police."

He couldn't have killed her from a jail cell in Tampa. Maybe he had friends.

"How long you been coming here?"

"Since I was a boy. When Mother couldn't find a babysitter, she'd haul me here when it was Ruby Red's—"

"I used to come here then, too. Who was your mom?"

"Lily."

"Lily Lamont?" She was the fancy-pants, Uptown debutante who used to cause scenes whenever I was here with Janice. In those days the port was right across the train tracks from the Quarter, and Lily Lamont was usually being held upright between a couple of Greek or Latino sailors. Once I swung open the door to the can to find her on her knees giving one of them a blow job while a rat looked on from the urinal. That was when I stopped bringing Janice to this dump.

"Did you know Mother?" Pogo squirmed in his seat.

"Only by sight." So this was the stunted offspring of one of those Ruby Red nights. If Janice were still here, we'd have children his age.

"Your mother still alive?" I asked.

"If you care to call it that. She's secluded inside her Xanadu on Pirate's Alley."

I softened to the little creep. He told me that as a kid, his mother would often show up at their apartment on Dumaine with a strange man, and they'd lock themselves inside her room for three days with a case of bourbon. Now Pogo lived on a trust fund from the Lamonts, which paid the rent on the apartment. He was finishing a book of poems dedicated to his mother titled *The Monster Cave*.

"Where did Eva strip?"

"At Les Girls on Iberville. She gave it up soon after she moved in with me. You see, I paid for everything. Because Eva was my teacher and muse."

"She ever bring any guys home from there?"

"Not guys. Other strippers sometimes."

"So she swung both ways?"

"Oooh, Lieutenant Girlfriend." Pogo nudged my leg with his foot. "Do you?"

I heard some ranting and raving from inside the bar, and edged my way in to listen. The place was packed, with a permanent cloud of cigarette smoke hovering in the spot light. First up was Millicent Tripplet, an obese woman with ruby lipstick, who recited a poem about how oppressed she felt when she was being fucked by a certain guy, and how depressed she felt when she wasn't. That got a howl of appreciation. Then a rapper named

Pawnshop took the stage, coked out of his gourd, to blow the trumpet and rap about how all the bitches and ho's weren't down with his skinny black ass in the baggy jumpsuit. His rhymes were catchy but the rhythm was a snooze. Then came a comic from the racetrack who sounded like my Uncle Dominic; next up was some nerd in a plaid sports coat who read a sonnet about peat moss and death; and then some anorexic lady dressed in lilac who choked up in the middle and had to sit down. I couldn't figure out what her poem was about. I think her pooch died.

One thing I clocked: the better the poet, the shorter the spiel. The worst ones droned on forever. I gave Mrs. Pierce an empty shrug, as if to say, *No clues here, lady.* Then she took the stage, hands folded, looking like a Methodist Sunday school teacher. She held up the flier and announced that she would read the last poem her daughter ever wrote:

> *I've always known you*
> *though we haven't met.*
> *I know how your name tastes*
> *though I've never said it.*
> *You linger on the last step*
> *of stairs I never descend,*
> *I stand with my address book*
> *on a landing to which you never*
> *climb, and every day we stop*
> *just short of each other.*
>
> *I invoke you to appear,*
> *to kiss childhood back*
> *into my skeptical mouth,*
> *rain into this parched air.*
> *I invoke you at the sudden angle*
> *of smoke, secrets, and zippers,*

at the hour when ear lobes,
skin along inner thighs,
a smooth chest is tenderest,
love unfolding like a hammock
to fit whatever is nearest.
I invoke your breath's fur
on my neck, your curve of lips,
the blue seaweed of your hair where
we'll weave a nest of lost mornings.

The words sent a chill down my spine. It was as if Eva had been waiting for her murderer. Had a date with death. All I could see was Janice, her face bent over a glowing red candle holder, her straight blond hair swaying as she read poems to me. I had to rush out onto the balcony where I could sit alone and be twenty again, if only for a moment, and remember what a love so fragile felt like.

Finally it was raining, coming down in torrents, the oak branches and curlicues of iron lace dripping fat, dirty tears. "Drip drop, drip drop." That's how the Irma Thomas song began, the one we were always listening to in those days. "It's raining so hard, brings back memories." An ambulance raced past, its flashing red lights hellish on the slick street. And I had to endure it all over again, her body dragged from the driver's seat of our crumpled red Chevy. She had been coming home with a birthday surprise for me, and the McKenzie cake box was soaked with her blood. I never thought I'd be sitting again with Janice on the balcony at Ruby Red's, listening to the rain.

I began to haunt the Quarter for the first time in years, trying to get a handle on Eva's world. Mostly she hung out in what they used to call Little Sicily, around the French Market and lower Decatur Street, where my daddy grew up. Like all the Sicilians in this town, his family had lived over their corner grocery store, Angelo's Superette at Decatur and Governor Nicholls. My only relative left in the neighborhood was Aunt Olivia, a butch little old maid who used to run a laundromat with her mama on Dauphine Street. She owned half the Quarter, and my Uncle Dominic, who hadn't worn anything but pajamas for the past twenty years, owned the other half. When I was young, everyone was always going *Oh, jeez, you got family in the Quarter, you should visit them.* But like my mama always said, "Me, I don't go by them dagos none. They just as soon stick a knife in your back."

The neighborhood was a different place now, and I couldn't understand what anyone down here did to make a living. You hardly saw any grocery stores or dry cleaners or fruit vendors or florists or printing offices or notions stores. Mostly the shops were Pakistani joints selling Mardi Gras masks made in China. Even the criminals were candy-assed, just a bunch of two-bit drug dealers and purse snatchers, nothing like the outfit my mama's family used to run. In those days, if a girl didn't cough up to her pimp, she got a Saturday-night makeover with acid splashed in her face. The girls used to roll the sailors right and left, slipping mickeys in their drinks or switch blades between their ribs. Now I walked around at night unarmed with a couple hundred bucks in my pocket. The streets were filled with gutter punks, their mangy mutts, and older kids playing dress up. These kids thought they were being *bad bad bad.* They'd snort their little powders and do their little humpety-hump on somebody's futon. Then they'd ride their bikes and eat their vegetables, just like their mamas told them. They even recycled.

I figured with all these Pollyannas floating around, older predators were bound to be lurking in the shadows, dying to take a bite out of this innocent flesh. So the first place I hit was where Eva used to strip, Les Girls de Paree on Iberville between Royal and Chartres. This block of seedy dives was the real thing, the way the whole Quarter used to look when I was coming up. The Vieux Carré Commission must have preserved it as a historical diorama. A hulking bozo with a mullet haircut held the doors open onto the pulsing red lights of a dark pit belting out bump-and-grind. Inside, Les Girls smelled like dirty drawers in a hamper. Or to put it less delicately, like ass.

Some skanky brunette with zits on her behind was rubbing her crotch on an aluminum pole and jiggling her store-bought titties. You'd have to be pretty desperate to throw a boner for a rancid slice of luncheon meat like that. Only two old guys were sitting in the shadows, and I couldn't figure out how this joint sucked in any bucks. Finally Mullet Head waltzed over to ask what I wanted.

"I want to talk about Eva Pierce."

"Miss Ivonne," he called out, eyeballing me up and down. "Copper here."

This over-the-hill fluffball with champagne hair clopped over to my table. I couldn't take my eyes off her lips. "What can I do for you, officer?"

"Eva Pierce" is all I said. Her lips were pink and puffed out like Vienna Sausages. They must have kept a vat of collagen under the bar.

"I've been waiting for this little bereavement call," she said, sliding into a chair. "I'm still broke up about Eva. She didn't belong here, and I was glad to see her leave. All she ever did was write poetry and sip 7-Up. But she sure attracted the chicken hawks."

"Anyone in particular?"

"I don't rat out my customers."

"Eva liked it rough, and swung both ways, right?"

"Where you hear that, babe?" She yanked a Vantage from inside her bra and lipped it.

"Her roommate Pogo."

"Me and his momma used to have the best damn time," she shrieked, pounding the table. "But don't ever cross that woman. No, siree."

"You know Lily Lamont?"

She slit her eyes at me. "You sure get around for a cop."

"Some people pay me to."

"Look, officer," she said, shooting a stream of smoke toward the ceiling through those lips, "Eva went home with a couple of the girls here, but they just wanted somebody's shoulder to cry on. Eva was a mommy, not a dyke. She took care of stray animals and people. Like that Brack creature and poor Pogo. She was like Dorothy in the goddamn *Wizard of Oz*. All she ever talked about was that farm in Ohio."

"So who'd want to kill her?"

"You got me," she said. "Maybe the wicked witch with her flying monkeys. Or the blue guy."

"The blue guy?"

Miss Yvonne stifled a laugh. "Buffed up psycho used to come in here, hair and beard dyed cobalt blue. He wore a cat of nine tails around his neck. Sure took a liking to Eva, but I run him off."

I was walking back down Chartres Street, thinking about Janice, when I heard a dog leash rattling behind me.

"Oh, Lieutenant Girlfriend." It was Pogo walking this dust mop named Welfare, now squatting at the curb. I hadn't seen Pogo since last Tuesday at the Dragon's Den. I was becoming a regular at the open mike, and starting to get a kick out of it. It was like a cross between a gong show and the observation room on Acutely Disturbed at DePaul's.

"Been meaning to ask you," I said. "Eva go to the movies a lot?"

"Never," he said, picking up a dog turd between two fingers with a plastic baggie. "She preferred to star in her own epic drama."

"So why was she carrying popcorn the night she died?"

He stopped. "Popcorn? I never thought about that. Maybe she swung by the Cloister after she said goodnight at Molly's. Sometimes the bartender there hands out bags of popcorn. Just before dawn."

I smiled. The Cloister. A few doors down Decatur from Molly's.

Pogo put the plastic baggie in his pocket. Who would've ever thought that one day the Quarter would be filled with rich people walking around with dog turds in their pockets? The dagos moved to Kenner just in time.

"Ever see Eva around a man with a blue beard. Blue hair and beard. And a whip?"

"Oh, him."

"She date him?"

"He followed her to the open mike from Les Girls. She wouldn't have anything to do with him. Now we have to listen to his poetry."

"His perms any good?"

Pogo pulled out the baggie of dog mess and waved it in my face. "See you at the open mike, Lieutenant Girlfriend."

If the garage rock band at the Cloister banged out one more song, I thought my skull would pop. I nursed several Seven and Sevens while I jotted down random thoughts in my notebook, hoping Swamp Gas would finally run out of steam. The crowd was twenty-somethings dressed in black with all the hardware in Home Depot dangling off their mugs. I wondered if they got snared in each other's rings and things when they got down to business and had to use a wire cutter to separate themselves. Nobody seemed to be having a particularly good time. Janice and I'd had more fun eating thirty-five-cent plates of red beans and rice at Buster Holmes. A steady stream of couples was going in and out of the bathrooms in back, but not for any lovey-dovey. They were wiping their noses and clenching their jaws when they walked out. That explained the coke residue on the straw in Eva's purse.

Finally I was getting somewhere.

Swamp Gas petered out at about five in the morning. I was getting ready to leave when I spotted this geezer with a snowy white pompadour hobbling around in his bathrobe and slippers. When he turned around, I had to laugh.

"Hey, Uncle Dominic, it's me, Vinnie. Chetta's boy." I hadn't seen the old guy since my daddy's funeral.

"Vinnie, let me get a look at you." He cuffed my head and patted my cheeks. "Not a day goes by I don't think of my sweet little sister. How she making?"

"Same old same old." Mama was still fuming about how Uncle Dominic had gypped her on the inheritance. *He stuck a knife in my back*, she growled whenever his name came up.

"Remind her she still owes me three hundred bucks for property taxes the year she sold out."

"What you doing here at this hour," I asked, swiveling my hips, "getting down with the girlies?" His robe was covered with lint balls.

"Just checking on my investment. Got six, seven other buildings to see this morning. You?" he asked, swiveling his own hips. "Thought you was married. You just like your papa."

"Here on a murder case. Know this young lady?" I flipped out the picture of Eva, and he fished glasses out of his robe pocket. "Killed the night of March 28."

"Let me think," he said, staring at the snapshot. "Yeah, yeah, I seen her here that morning. Last time I come in to check on my investment. Around this time. I axed her what she was writing down in her little book, and she says 'a perm.' Looked like a bunny with them funny pigtails."

"She leave alone?"

"Yeah, yeah. No, wait—" He slapped his forehead. "Madonna, how could I forget? She left with that *pazzo* what got the blue beard."

Blue Beard.

Bingo.

Then somebody handed me popcorn still warm in the bag.

The next morning I radioed Blue Beard's description in to the Eighth District station in the Quarter, and rang Pogo, Miss Ivonne, Miss Ping, and Uncle Dominic to ask them to contact me the minute they spotted him. Uncle Dominic told me he wanted a cut of the reward, and lost interest fast when I told him there wasn't any. But both he and Miss Ivonne promised to make a few phone calls to help locate Blue Beard. Mrs. Pierce sputtered "God bless you" when I reported that I was zeroing in on the killer.

Where the hell could he be? It wasn't like a man with blue hair could hide just anywhere, even in the French Quarter.

That afternoon I got a staticky message on my cell phone.

Lily Lamont.

A husky, spaced-out voice said she needed to talk with me in person. That evening. She left an address that at first she couldn't remember right.

My heels echoed on the flagstones in deserted Pirate's Alley like the approaching footsteps in those radio plays my daddy used to listen to. A mist had rolled in from the river, wrapping St. Louis Cathedral in fog, and I squinted to make out the address under the halo of a streetlamp. I pictured Lily Lamont blowzy and toothless now, passed out on a filthy mattress cradling an empty bourbon bottle.

Nothing could have prepared me for what I found.

After I was buzzed in, I mounted a curved mahogany staircase that swept me up into a cavernous Creole ballroom under a spidery bronze chandelier. In a zebra upholstered throne, there sat a mummified lady with white hair pulled back tight from her porcelain face, buttering a slice of raisin-bread toast.

"I'm famished," Lily Lamont said, taking a bite. "Would you care for some toast and tea? That's all I ever, *ever* eat."

I shook my head. Perched in the zebra chair next to hers was a bulky goon with a body like a boxer's gone to seed. He was caressing the top of his shiny bald head, several shades paler than his face.

"I don't believe we've ever formally met, Lieutenant Panarello," she said. Her bones, thin as chopsticks, were swallowed by a red silk kimono fastened by a dragon brooch.

"Not face-to-face." What was I supposed to say, tell this lady I saw her on her knees in a men's room thirty years ago?

"And this is my associate, Lucas," she said, gesturing to Baldie.

I nodded, taking a seat in an elaborately carved bishop's chair under an alabaster lamp of entwined snakes.

"Nice place," I said. The floor-to-ceiling windows were draped with damask swags. Outside, shadows from the extended arms of a spot-lit Jesus loomed over the cathedral garden.

"I bought this house last year from your uncle, Dominic Zuppardo." Her sharp little teeth gnawed on the toast like a rat's. "At a pretty penny. Actually, I paid him twice as much as the sale price we registered. That helped with my property assessment and his capital gains taxes. Smart man."

Bet Uncle Dominic is kissing her butt now, I thought. So that was who tipped her off to my investigation.

"Met your friend Miss Ivonne," I said, since we were having a family reunion. "Place where Eva Pierce used to strip."

"How is Ivonne?" Lily asked with a tight smile. "I set her up with that club. I've never been in it, of course." Her frail shoulders shuddered.

Ditto, I thought. Miss Ivonne probably called her, too.

"Look, I won't beat around the bush," Lily Lamont said, brushing

{ 113 }

toast crumbs from her finger tips. "I want you to call off your investigation into Eva Pierce's death. The killer is probably in Timbuktu by now. Questioning all of these people is silly."

"But I know who did it. A guy with blue hair and beard."

"Have you ever seen him?" Her enormous hazel eyes studied me slyly over the gold rim of an ornate tea cup.

"No, but he used to come to the open mike at the Dragon's Den all the time to read his lousy perms."

Baldie winced. Then a shit-eating grin spread across his face. Why the hell would he care about Blue Beard's poems?

Unless he wrote them.

"Do you have children, lieutenant?" Lily's voice was filling with church choirs.

"Three. A boy at De la Salle, a girl at Mount Carmel, and another girl starting out at Loyola University next year." That was why I moonlighted, to pay all those tuitions. The older girl worked at a pizza parlor after school to save up for Loyola. Her dad, you see, was a New Orleans cop.

"And wouldn't you do anything to help your children?"

"Anything short of—"

"Eva Pierce was a horrible influence on my son." Lily swayed like a cobra as she mouthed the words in a slow, woozy monotone. "She turned him against me. You should read the venomous words about me she inspired him to pen. She was just using him."

"Maybe he liked being used," I said, locking eyes with Pogo's mother. "Maybe it's all he's ever known."

"Here, this is for you." Her long indigo fingernail flicked an ivory envelope across the coffee table toward me. "It's a check for $25,000. Eva's mother hired you to investigate. I'm hiring you to stop the investigation." She arched a penciled eyebrow. "Simple."

I stood up. "Can I used the john?"

"Lucas will show you the way."

I studied the rolls of skin on the back of Baldie's head as I followed him down a long corridor, trying to picture him with blue hair and beard. The smartest thugs know the best disguise is something attention-getting but dispensable. And who would testify against Lily and this hit man? My uncle? Miss Ivonne? Trust-fund Pogo? The whole Quarter owed Lily Lamont a favor.

In the bathroom I tore open the envelope with an Egyptian scarab embossed on the flap: 25,000 smackers, made out to cash. I folded the check into my wallet. It was five times what Mrs. Pierce was paying me. I splashed water on my face and took a long look in the mirror. The jowly, unshaven mug of my daddy stared back at me, the face of three generations of Italian shopkeepers who worked like hell and never managed to get ahead. *What, you crazy or something*, they screamed at me. *You want your daughter to graduate from college? Take the damn dough and run, Vinnie.*

I picked up the plush blue bath towel folded next to the mirror. Underneath was a syringe, a packet of white powder, and a silver iced-tea spoon.

I rang Mrs. Pierce as soon as I'd escaped the junkie fog in Pirate's Alley.

"Look, lady," I told her, "the investigation is off. Your daughter just got mixed up with the wrong crowd, that's all. Blue Beard is probably unidentifiable by now. He could be anywhere. I can't, in good conscience, waste any more of your money." All true.

Mrs. Pierce started sobbing and then hung up. She'd been right. It wasn't sex or drugs that got her daughter killed, but poetry. Me, I was never so glad to drive home to Terrytown, to the wife and life that I've got.

. . .

I didn't make it back to the Dragon's Den until one sweltering August night later that year. The air smelled like river sludge, and the façade was shimmering in the heat like a mirage made of shadows and memories. The old Chinese guy was still hanging over his tub of vegetables in the patio. He shot me a thumbs up as I mounted the stairs, mopping my face with a handkerchief.

Every step was an effort.

"Look what the cat drug in," Miss Ping said, setting me up with my Seven and Seven.

"Where's that sign-up sheet for the open mike?" I asked her. She pushed a clipboard toward me. With a shaky hand I scrawled *Vinnie P.*, third name on the list. I couldn't believe what I was about to do. It seemed like jerking off in public. So I sat on the balcony to calm myself down and go over what I'd written.

"Hey honey, what you doing in the den with the TV off?" my wife had asked me. "You sick?"

"Writing a report." I swatted her away.

What I'd been writing for two weeks wasn't exactly a report but some buried feelings—poems, I guess you'd call them. I couldn't sleep or concentrate, and had even thought of going to Saturday confession, but then nixed that dumb-cluck idea. I couldn't tell the Father who would marry my kids and christen my grand babies that I, a cop, was the accessory to a murder. Those poets that I'd listen to during the open mike, something like this was eating them up, too. Their girlfriends left them or their parents never loved them or they felt lonely and empty—I don't know—they just needed to spill their guts and be heard. By anyone. Just *heard*. They didn't tell it straight but in a symbolic way, you know, twisting it up enough so that it wouldn't be only their story but everybody's. So that's what I'd been writing: what happened to me investigating Eva

Pierce's murder. And with Janice. Where it all went wrong and how I wound up feeling the way I did, as old, corrupt, and dirty as this French Quarter.

I had to get it off my chest.

Pogo stuck his face onto the balcony, eyes popping out at the sight of me.

"She's a vile bitch," he hissed, biting his lip. Then he waved me inside.

Only about ten of the usual suspects were sprawled around the room. The first two poets went on forever. I was so wound up I couldn't concentrate on a word they said.

Finally the clown with the leather cowboy hat held up the clipboard.

"And here, ladies and gentlemen," he announced, "is a rising star in the Quarter poetry scene. A man of the law who will grace us with his debut reading. He came to bust us, and now he's one of us. Put your hands together to welcome Lieutenant Girlfriend."

Everyone clapped like crazy as I stepped onto the stage feeling like a horse's ass. Pogo was jumping up and down, waving his arms like a cheerleader. I shuffled through the pages to get them in order. My voice caught as I started to speak.

Miss Ping plinked an ice cube into a glass. The air conditioner coughed.

Then a huge gray rat scurried across the room, stopped in the middle of the floor to take in the audience, and disappeared under the stage I was standing on.

Everyone jumped to their feet.

"Okay, you assholes, sit down," I said, adjusting the mike. "That rat has to wait its turn just like all us other poets. This is called 'Janice and Eva Swap Lipsticks in the Changing Room to Hell.' I bet you lunkheads aren't going to get it, but here goes."

ALL SPIDERS, NO FLIES

Tomorrow I've got to bail my boyfriend out of jail. As if I'm made of money, which is what everybody thinks. But he's better than some of the people who have crashed here. Like that one-armed carpenter who begged me to go on jobs with him to hold the damn nails. Finally, I said look, honey, and gave him four hundred dollars to lease a fruit stand in a truck parked in front of St. Louis Cemetery. First week someone ripped off all four tires. Now it just sits there propped up on cinder blocks with ratty cardboard signs advertising strawberries from the country.

And everytime he gets a hard-on he takes the day off.

They call me a "remittance man." Means my family pays me to stay away. That's how come I'm back in New Orleans, where years ago I finally finished at Tulane with a thesis called "Madonna: A Woman of Gender," which I won't go into now. If I hadn't gone to Tulane, I wouldn't know who I am. I mean, socially. Even if I do live with a penniless old alcoholic and am in love with a dreamy hustler named Ernest Royal Breaux, who's in for assault.

Like everyone I meet these days, I had a miserable childhood. My mama was a drunk, my daddy chased women, and my grandfather was the governor of the state of Louisiana.

I'm not telling you which one he was—I'm too ashamed—but I will say PawPaw escaped over the state line with a paper bag over his head after my grandmother Mimi tried to have him committed. Then he gave a press conference from a motel in his drawers, eating grits without his teeth in. They broadcast that over the whole world, and I just about died. Especially about the teeth, which PawPaw forgot on the back of a commode in the capitol washroom, he was in such a hurry to get the hell out of Louisiana.

When they brought him back, Mimi was like, "You go play bourrée with him, boy, and keep him quiet." This was back around when Mama and Daddy were getting their divorce, so I was staying in the mansion a lot. PawPaw and I had played bourrée together while he decided on some important legislation, emptying a bottle of bourbon in the process. One thing I can say, he cheated at bourrée.

That's only part of my miserable childhood. Fact is I'm a flaming faggot.

"We don't care if you a hoMOsexual, Bib," my big sister always goes, "but why you have to turn out a flaming faggot."

Then I go, "We don't care if you a WOman, but why you have to turn out a fat sow with a kid hanging off each of your six tits. Or those supposed to be your knees and elbows?" That gets her every time. She really does need to reduce.

Daddy caught me the first time. I'd managed to hogtie myself in the stable, bare-assed except for Mama's bra, and was rolling around in horse shit. He beat the tar out of me because he said I was aroused. What really got him: so was his favorite thoroughbred. That was the beginning of shrinks and military schools.

They said they wanted to make a man out of me but really just wanted me out of sight, like PawPaw when he wound up with the paper bag over his head.

"Puh-lease," I pleaded, flipping bug-eyed through a military school yearbook, "don't send me away to be locked up with all these muscle-bound boys in uniforms." But they wouldn't listen to reason. So by the time I was kicked out of the last one, Culver Military Academy in Indiana, for starting the midnight action in the wheelchair-access bath-room, everyone was calling me Longjohn. Cadets are a bunch of size queens, if you want to know the truth. My first name is John, though everyone calls me Bib.

And I'm not telling you what my last name is.

I've been back in the French Quarter ever since I broke up with my second husband, a dentist named Bernard I lived with in Daytona Beach. Why a dentist? I ask myself in moments of introspection. But after the plastic surgery, I feel comfortable with doctors. They can see me for who I really am, beyond all the glamour.

Only with all the Percodan and coke we were doing, Bernie and I started working each other's nerves. After smashing every piece of glass in his condo one night, I took off with a guard who had just been fired for running a security golf cart into the lagoon looking for a bottle of vodka he'd stashed behind a philodendrum.

Too Too is a sixty-two-year-old alkie I used to pal around with while Bernie was off doing root canals. Too Too listens to opera and is into butt plugs, one of the sweetest men I've ever known. I drink a lot, too, if you want to know the truth, so I took him hostage and caught the Amtrack to Baton Rouge. We got there just in time for my thirty-fifth birthday. After two nights at Mama's, she made a few brisk calls that set me up with an apartment in the Quarter and a check every month. She had discovered one of Too Too's playthings wedged into her La-Z-Boy.

"I'm getting too old for so much commotion," Mama says. She

dried out a long time ago.

"Rehab is for quitters," I tell her. She just shakes her head, says stay in touch.

One thing, as the daughter-in-law of a former governor, Mama has flawless taste. The apartment she got me on Dauphine is a restored shotgun with crown moldings, bronze fixtures, hardwood floors, and glass chandeliers. I really didn't mean to trash the place. Things have just gotten out of hand.

The day I moved in I met Crystal, a forty-year-old crack whore who strips at Les Girls de Paree. She had just been evicted and was circling the Quarter with a U-Haul filled with all her stuff. Her fourth husband, a teenager who works as a clown on Jackson Square, bought me a half-gallon of vodka and convinced me to let them keep everything here for just one night. I didn't have much to move in except for a boom box, my Madonna poster, and Too Too, who had managed to lose his suitcase on the Greyhound.

Our welcome to the neighborhood wasn't exactly cordial. The director of the Vieux Carré Commission, who lives across the street, said he didn't particularly object to Crystal's five-foot cage on the gallery with the squirrel inside who thought it was a human being. Or to her mangy white cockatoo in another cage. What got him was her leatherette couch we couldn't fit through the door. Said it was tacky and had to go, and suggested cane rockers or a swing or a loveseat in white rattan. All my new friends were on the floor next to the dishwasher getting high. I didn't want to ruin my first evening fussing with that old queen.

Now you know how the Quarter is on a July night.

At dusk everybody comes scampering out like roaches hiding from the scorching light. Then the neighborhood is one big cocktail party. Music blares out of open bar doors. Hunky guys in tank tops and cutoffs lean against car hoods sucking on ice cubes, rattling go-cups at you as you pass. People scream to each other from balcony to balcony, hang out on their stoops, draining beers and mopping their brows and shooting the shit with everyone who walks by.

It's too hot to touch. And too hot not to.

So I slipped on bathing trunks and some Mardi Gras beads Crystal gave me, found a garden hose, and wet my curly self down every half hour. Dauphine Street was the only place I ever wanted to be, stoned on the steps with a Screwdriver and my boom box, carrying on with everyone in the street. I kept turning up the Stones, singing "Wild, wild horses couldn't drag me away."

That first night I was drunk as a monkey, rolled up in one of Crystal's old sheets in front of the floor-to-ceiling window that opens onto the gallery, when somebody crawled inside on all fours. I said to myself, "Bib, honey, prepare to expire." But then the intruder curled up beside me like a lost lamb—or should I say ram? He was sporting a monster down there, and it wasn't until the first rays crept in through the jalousies that I realized he didn't have any top front teeth and smelled like a free box. But by then I didn't care. It was a new morning, and he was mine.

Said he grew up in Crowley and his name is Ernest Royal Breaux—I do believe that's the only true thing he's ever told me—and he's a veterinarian at the Audubon Park Zoo. He's twentyish with wavy chestnut hair and soft green eyes, tanned and built like he's been doing hard labor, not another gym bunny hanging out in the free-weight room like those Muscle Marys in Daytona.

"So what's a veterinarian from the zoo doing crawling into my cage in the middle of the night?" I wanted to know.

"Last week three assholes mugged me at the ATM," he explained with a coonass accent. "Niggers punch my teeth down my throat, take all the money out my account, then leave me broke and bleeding in Pirate's Alley."

"So you crawl in anybody's window you please like a dog in heat?" I don't fall in love before breakfast. That's my policy.

While I was in the shower, I heard Royal in the kitchen informing Crystal and her clown, who was putting on his makeup, that he's a golf pro who will be judging an open competition at Elmwood Country Club. I was some mad. Then, tossing everything out my suitcase trying to find something to wear, I hear the golf pro tell Too Too—get this—he's the director of the Vieux Carré Commission.

I maxed Madonna on the boom box, sashayed onto the gallery, and threw myself onto the leatherette couch. Everybody was already high and talking to that stupid squirrel like it was a human being.

"Let's get something straight, Royal," I hissed, lighting a Kool and tossing the burnt match in his direction. "The director of the Vieux Carré Commision lives right across the street, and yesterday him and me had a little tête-à-tête. And I know you're not him or a golf pro or a fucking veterinarian at the goddam zoo. You can't con a con man. Who are you really?"

Now whenever you ask anyone in the Quarter who they really are, pull up a chair, loosen your girdle, and get ready for a real pack of lies. Ernest Royal Breaux said before he won the "New Meat Night" contest at The Rough House and became a hustler, he was a member of a white militia on his sister's survivalist ranch in Alabama.

"If PawPaw could see me now, he'd be so proud," I said, casting my eyes heavenward.

Like all hustlers, he said he has a girlfriend he adores who serves him champagne barefoot, but he just can't stay off the pipe. And in his sick mind, he becomes his tricks. Takes on their identities. Ever since that time he ripped off a trick's wallet and impersonated him across the country on a drug-crazed credit-card spree.

"Last night I tricked across the street," he said, pointing at the door of the director of the Vieux Carré Commission. "That guy has a security camera that's not a prop, like most around here. Lays in bed jerking off watching his front steps on video, and when he sees someone setting there he likes, he comes out and yanks him in. He's into spanking, so we have to tell him how bad we been while he spanks our butts. So he throws me out at five in the morning and tells me I can probably crash on that tacky sofa cross the way. Then I see you sleeping in there like an angel and come in to keep you company. Tricking's lonely."

That afternoon we hung out on the gallery and organized Crystal's stuff into a sidewalk sale. And met more neighbors, like Earl, the bald drag queen who lives in the slave quarter out back with his eighty-two-year-old father. Royal stayed around until evening, when he took his shirt off, stuffed it in his back pocket, and went to stand on the corner. And around dawn, he crawled back in through the window to curl up with me, and in the morning handed me a twenty and a bunch of change.

That was how I got started with Ernest Royal Breaux. Believe me, walking on the street with him is like being with Mae West. Everybody's like in awe until they check out the teeth. At least he pays his own way.

Too Too, on the other hand, doesn't have a dime to his name and plans to retire on Social Security in Mexico next year. He only has one shirt and a pair of pleated gray slacks, so he started spending the day dressed in nothing but a beach towel. He's the one who cooks, so he slept on the floor by the stove. Until Earl showed up one day with a cot after the ambulance left. That girl was a mess.

"Dad just died," Earl said, all puffy-eyed. "Can y'all use his bed? I can't stand to look at it no more."

"You mean that's where he died?" Too Too wanted to know. He opened it up to inspect the mattress for stains. "Hey, you want a drink?"

So they had a good bawl, and now Too Too lolls around on the Bed of Death all day like a beached whale, listening to opera, wrapped in a towel that says *Surf's Up!* When the black football players drop by to see him, he closes the kitchen door. But it still drives Royal crazy. Last week he threw a hissy-fit.

"Take your tricks out to the alley," he screamed. "Decent people have to eat in here."

But then Royal started scoring rocks off Too Too's tricks, and on New Year's, some defensive end from LSU even brought over a bottle of Dom Perignon. And that's made an uneasy peace between the watermelon queen and the white survivalist.

In the meantime, I've kicked everybody else out, the one-armed carpenter, Crystal and her clown, and the eighteen-year-olds who would hang out all day rolling joints and grabbing my remote. I can't take it anymore. I started feeling like the Mother Teresa of hustlers and con artists, running a soup kitchen in the quarter of lost men.

Wherever I go, they find me, and like PawPaw, I never learned to say no until it's too late. They fall in love with me because I listen to their stories about who they were, or who they think they are. No one else bothers. Just fuck 'em, pay 'em, and throw 'em out. Their raps are all lies, I guess. Although sometimes they're telling the truth, sprawled on my scuzzy mattress and staring up at the chandelier. They go on about their grandmas and their dogs, stuff like that. And know I don't want anything from them except maybe a hit off their joints. I can't help it. I like damaged people because I'm one of them.

Like that blues song goes, don't roll those bloodshot eyes at me.

Earl, the only neighbor I get along with, has moved out.

After his dad died, he went on a bender and emptied all the drag out the armoires and chiffarobes into the middle of his bedroom floor. He threw the scarves, skirts, wigs, and padded bras into Seagram boxes, along with makeup, tweezers, and everything else he called his "woman's stuff." Then he took the day off from his plumbing job, stacked the boxes in the back of his pickup, drove them to the Goodwill, shoved them across the counter and announced, "I quit."

I see Earl in the bars, and his eyebrows have grown back in. He took his dad's death real hard.

So except for Royal and Too Too, no one's left to hang out with this January. It's damp and cold, and I feel like a lizard at the bottom of a well. Tonight I stopped by Your Little Red Wagon to say hello to Miss Mamou behind the bar and find Royal. Just a bunch of hustlers playing video-poker or nursing beers in the corner—waiting for a ride to their mama's wake, it looked like. It was all spiders, no flies.

Except for an old black gentleman who comes in every night—a choir director or voice teacher, something like that—who was trying to have a birthday party. Half-eaten paper plates of gooey cake were all over the bar, and he was wrapping the leftovers up in the McKenzie box, tying it again and again and looking at each of the guys like, *now what?* He kept twisting the red string around the box like he couldn't believe nobody loved him on his birthday because he was old.

I mean he couldn't keep his hands off his cake.

So I went over and hugged him and told him happy birthday and how handsome he was. One day I'll be wrapping up my cake in a bar like this, after the party has been over for twenty-five years but nobody's told me. So while this guy is revving up the story of his life, Miss Mamou comes over to tell me Royal has been popped.

"Dude's a beeper queen," Royal cackled. I'm his one call, and the phone was ringing when I walked in.

"A new one on me." I never believe a word he says, but I listen. "What happened this time?"

"I tie him up in his bed, just like he says, set his beeper to *vibrate*, slip it in a condom and shove it up his ass. Then I shut the door, go into the kitchen, crack open a cold one, dial his number, and hit redial every few minutes."

"Ever do a three-way with Call Waiting?" I asked.

"Hey, no shit. He works for the phone company, so he's got all kind of gadgets and beaucoup bucks. But tries to pass me a twenty when we settled on fifty. So I punch out his lights, and he gets the cops to pick me up. Says the jab to his kisser wasn't 'consensual.'"

"Look, this is the last time I bail Ernest Royal Breaux out of jail. Try to stay out of trouble till I see the bail bondsman in the morning."

So I just got off the phone to Baton Rouge. And tomorrow I have to hightail it over to Merrill Lynch on Poydras, then take the bus to Parish Prison on Tulane and North Broad. I told Mama I need some dental work. God forbid I tell her the truth. Not that she'd recognize it if I did. Or anyone in this town, for that matter. Everytime I start what Too Too calls that "governor's grandson shit," he walks out of the room. I don't care if he or anyone else believes me. It only costs a drink or a joint for someone to believe you. Or at least listen to you.

And I haven't run out of people yet.

THE BOUNCING LADY

M inette Ferrier never had gotten the attention she deserved.
But she knew how to fix things. So one September afternoon, a month before the Overture to the Cultural Season
began, she arranged a blond wig, a bottle of Jack Daniels, and a pearl-
handled revolver in a magic triangle on her rosewood dining table. Then
she put her unpublished novel at the center.

"How do I get the right person to read my book?" she'd asked Eula.

Eula had rustled her violet robes and turned up the Queen of Cups.
"It'll have something to do with being blond and getting drunk. But
be careful," she added, furrowing her brow as she turned up the Five of
Swords. "I see danger."

That was why Minette put the pistol on the table. Drunk blondes
needed all the protection they could get, she figured, especially in the
French Quarter.

Everything else Minette ever wanted eventually had come her way.
After finishing at LSU, she signed a waiting list for an apartment in the
upper Pontabla building on Jackson Square. While she waited, she settled
for dingy efficiencies here and there in the Quarter. Every morning she
would set out in Bermuda shorts, with a big bag and a book she never

read, *The Lonely Crowd*. And every afternoon she would wind up in front of the Pontabla, staring up at the wrought-iron balconies overflowing with bougainvillea and cape jasmine.

One day, she'd promised herself, I'm going to live there.

Five years later her name came up and now here she was, a grande dame with burgundy velvet drapes and her grandmother's sterling coffee service, which she kept covered with a plastic dry-cleaning bag so it wouldn't tarnish.

Or take Louis Duiplaisir, her boyfriend, who for the longest time didn't know she existed. But Minette had her sights set on him. Lou was a security guard at One Shell Square, where she worked as a decorator, filling beige office suites with overpriced antiques from Royal Street. When he was laid off, Minette found him a job right outside her bedroom window as the bodyguard for her friend Eula Austin, the crippled Tarot reader.

Everybody in New Orleans knew that Jackson Square had turned into a Moroccan souk of veiled and plumed Tarot readers squabbling over prominent spots. One day Eula was bonked on the head by a Honduran fortune-teller who claimed Eula had stolen her corner. So Minette talked Eula into hiring Lou as her bodyguard. Lou had a job, Eula made out like a bandit, and on one of his potty trips to her apartment, Minette and Lou had tumbled together into her French Provincial bed.

Minette Ferrier knew how to fix things.

It was almost as if she had discovered a smudged magic lantern on one of her junking expeditions to Magazine Street, and taken it home to polish. Now she was working on her third wish: if only someone would publish her novel. She'd been writing it ever since Elwood, the Happy Line tour guide she once dated, told her that in the 1920s Sherwood Anderson had lived in her third-floor Pontabla apartment. According to Elwood, who did a lot of coke, this was where Anita Loos brought tall glasses of moonshine every morning to a weird little man from Mississippi who vowed he couldn't get up in the morning without a drink. Elwood never shut up, not even in bed, and once told Minette during sex about Faulkner's war wound, and how the writer needed great quantities of alcohol to ease the pain because he had a metal plate in his head.

Minette dumped the cokehead, but for three years after wrote like a soul possessed, with visions of Anderson and Faulkner hovering over her laptop. Minette tried literary contests, she tried conferences, and she tried sleeping with agents, but had no luck in finding a publisher. She told everyone that her book was "an opera of passion and intrigue," just like the life she led.

"All you ever do these days is type, type, type," Lou complained, zipping up on the chaise lounge after one of Minette's spontaneous showerings of affection. He was still a handsome man. The diet was working, although the hair transplant wasn't.

"It's because of the metal plate in my head," Minette piped up from the bathroom in her little girl's voice. "Listen, I hear Eula screaming. She's probably being attacked again by that fat Honduran. You better run down quick quick."

The continual circus in the square was shattering her peace of mind, and Lou was beginning to get on her nerves. Just the way he stood around watching her do things, like wash her hands or fry an egg, as if demanding *what next?* Whatever was next didn't include him.

Why was it, she wondered, that every time she had great sex, she wound up cooking somebody breakfast for the next ten years?

If Minette were possessed, it wasn't by Anderson or Faulkner but by the ghost of Anita Loos. She lifted the wavy blond wig from its box and studied herself in the beveled mirror over the marble mantle. It looked ridiculous on her five-foot-three frame, accentuating her dark eyebrows and olive complexion. She fluffed out the wig, put an index finger to her cheek, rolled her shoulders, and mimicked Marilyn Monroe's sultry singsong:

The Bouncing Lady

After you get what you waaant
You don't waaant it.
If I gave you the moooon
You'd get tired of it soooon.

Then she threw herself on the chaise lounge to practice what she'd learned at the psychic fair: Positive Visualization. She's in Manhattan, a blonde in a tailored hounds'- tooth suit, stepping out of a taxi on Madison Avenue. After a packed signing at Barnes & Noble, she's on her way to pick up a check at the agent's office, fumbling in her wallet for a twenty. Copies of her novel are spilling out of a leather shoulder bag, horns honking, the driver gunning the motor. Let them wait, she tells herself, gathering like lost children the dust-jacket photos of herself staring up seductively from the curb. She kisses each photo on the forehead as she places the books back in her bag.

"Water," Eula intoned with her tortoise eyelids half-closed and jowls quivering. "Success will come through water." Then she turned over the Three of Cups. "Women dancing in a circle. Success will come through women."

Water, Minette mused. She thought of the stinking Mississippi and polluted Lake Ponchartrain. Women. She thought of flappers and flippers and goggles and gals in bikinis sunning around hotel pools. Then she flashed on the pool at the New Orleans Athletic Club, a crumbling turn-of-the-century gym on North Rampart. Elwood had told her that Tennessee Williams used to swim naked there and be massaged by a one-armed man.

That was how she came to join "the bouncing ladies," which was how male lap swimmers in the steam room referred to the aquasize class. They were older women who stood in a circle, doing jumpy and kicky things with their legs while keeping their coiffures dry and in place. So for an hour, twice a week, they gossiped and bounced, gossiped and bounced.

Minette soon sorted out who was who and zeroed in on Yetta Blitz, a
top-heavy woman with peach lipstick and a black chignon.

"Why don't you and Fox come for dinner on Thursday the 15th,"
Minnete asked Yetta one evening, bouncing on one foot. "Louis and I
will be having a few other writers over."

"A terrible date. That dreadful awards dinner at the Monteleone Hotel
for the Overture begins at eight, and Fox has to be there. He's served on
the board since Bienville landed. This year our guest writer is, you know,
what's his name? He's a hundred years old and costs a fortune. Oh you
know, *Appointment at Appomattox, The Boll-Weevil Chronicles....*"

Minette's eyes widened. "Beauregard Mandible? I thought he was
dead."

"Rotate, *dip*, rotate, *dip*," the boyish instructor called out. The
women swiveled to the left, curtseyed, and then swiveled to the right,
waving their polished nails under water like sea anemone.

"Then drop by at seven for cocktails," Minette said, swiveling to the
left. "I want to show y'all the room where Faulkner slept it off."

The bouncing ladies lived in the Quarter or worked downtown and went
to cocktail parties in each others' courtyards. So invitations were cordially
received. That was how Minette got Yetta and Fox Blitz—of the drugstore
Blitzs—to her apartment on the night of the Overture to the Cultural
Season's awards gala, where Beauregard Mandible was going to speak.

Water, Minette thought, water everywhere. But danger, be careful:
not a drop to drink. She perched on the locker-room bench, drying off
like a cat licking herself clean with a scratchy pink tongue. By the time
she'd slipped into her skirt, she knew exactly how she was going to get
her novel published.

"Fox will get a bang out of meeting you," Yetta shouted over the whir
of a blow-dryer aimed at her head.

...

Then came the crash. For ten days before the gala, Minette could barely move from a kitchen chair to the chaise lounge and back into bed. She closed the burgundy drapes and lived on soft-boiled eggs and daytime television. Between crying jags, she would call Lou to tell him how she wanted to disappear into a crack in the sidewalk.

"So you and everyone else who thinks they're so smart," she said, "can step on me and break your poor mamas' backs."

She avoided the balcony, afraid she might throw herself off onto the Tarot readers' card tables and portrait painters' easels. Everything she'd turned into was a lie. She vowed to become a legal secretary, join a church, and move into an apartment complex in Metairie.

The day of the gala, she started on the Jack Daniels at noon and then vacuumed the apartment twice. At three she began trying on every outfit in her closet, searching for a look both genteel and sluttish enough to seduce an octogenarian man of letters. Then she collapsed into a heap of clothes on her bedroom floor and took to reading her novel out loud, making corrections in purple with a drugstore ballpoint while she knocked back a few more on the rocks.

When the doorbell rang she glanced in the mirror to straighten her wig. In her sensible heels and "Indispensable Black Travel Dress" from *Vanity Fair,* she thought she looked like a fifth-grade teacher from Indiana out for a night on Bourbon Street.

"Look at you. A blonde!" Yetta shrieked as she waltzed in, followed by a myopic scarecrow in a cutaway tuxedo clutching a stained manila envelope. "Fox, this is my friend from the gym, Minette . . . Monroe, Marilyn's sister. Minette, my Fox," she said, giving his shoulder a squeeze.

"How are you this evening, Miss Monroe?" Fox asked with a deep bow and twitching eyebrows.

"Hell-bent, honey. The darker my mood gets, the lighter my hair." Minette pointed them to the open steamer trunk she'd converted into a bar. "Dig in."

"Wow, what a view," they enthused, catching sight of General Jackson spot-lit beyond the drapes, charging. They drifted like sleepwalkers onto the balcony, drawn by a melancholic tugboat siren moaning on the hazy river at twilight.

"Minette, before I forget," Yetta said, as they raised glasses toward the luminous façade of the cathedral, "you probably have a hot date for this evening, but my friend Lily Lamont couldn't make it, so we have an extra invitation to this shindig. And since you're such a big fan of Beauregard Mandible, we thought you might want to come along. It's just around the corner."

Minette responded with a slow smile. She knew how to fix things.

While Fox Blitz practiced delivering his speech from the balcony like Jackson addressing his troops, Minette yanked Yetta into her bedroom, saying she just had to change. Then she dug through piles of clothes on the floor, looking for the ivory charmeuse. Five outfits later, they emerged, Minette in a rose décolleté cocktail dress with her wig on crooked, gripping a bottle of Jack Daniels by the neck.

"I want to eat the night raw as an oyster. Why are you just standing there?" she demanded, turning to Fox. "Adore me!"

"But we do," he stammered, collecting his papers, "particularly your ghosts and this gorgeous view."

"*I am* the view," she said with a gesture that took in the square, the bend in the river, and the whole state of Louisiana. Yetta and Fox exchanged glances as Minette stumbled toward a closet to retrieve a black velvet jacket and a bulging vinyl portfolio. On one last unsteady sweep between the mounds of clothes in her bedroom, Minette resisted the urge to lock herself inside and never come out again. What would she say when she met that old man? Trembling, she tucked the pearl-handled revolver into her satin opera bag.

"Danger," Eula had warned. "I see danger."

Once out of the front door, their voices echoed in the cavernous stairwell. The bald pate of a turnip-shaped gentleman was approaching from below. He was trudging up one step at a time, pulling himself along the curved mahogany banister with a folded *Times-Picayune* under his arm and a Styrofoam carton of takeout in one hand.

"Oh, Mr. Abadie," called Minette. He glanced up reluctantly at the descending clop of her backless heels. "There's something important I've been meaning to tell you."

As they passed him, she glared into the sagging face half-averted into the shadows of the landing. "Live, Mr. Abadie. Live. LIVE!"

"How's that?" he asked, cupping a hand around his ear.

Pumping her fist in the air like Mick Jagger, she raced down the stairs past the startled neighbor shouting, "LIVE, Mr. Abadie. LIVE!"

Yetta and Fox trailed behind, sobered by what they'd gotten themselves into. They looked relieved when the Baroness Pontabla's massive cypress door slammed behind them, and they stepped once again into the importance of their evening.

Yetta and Fox managed to lose Minette the minute they reached the buffet line in La Louisiane room at the Monteleone. Later Yetta told reporters that she overhead everything at the adjoining table, where Minette placed herself next to the Dean of Arts and Sciences at the University of New Orleans and his wife.

"I'm Minette Ferrier, Yetta Blitz's close friend," she said, plopping down her portfolio and highball and extending a hand around the table, "and I only associate with rich and famous people."

"I'm Grandich Kropp from UNO, and I generally associate with people much richer and more famous than I," the dean replied, turning perplexed to his wife as she raised a forkful of beef Wellington to her mouth.

Minette lunged across the table. "Why are you *eating*?" she demanded of the woman, who stared back with sad green eyes.

"It's delish," she responded, placing three fingers delicately over a full mouth. "Aren't you going to get a plate?"

"I only feed once every six months. I live on air and poetry," Minette announced with an air of religious ecstasy. The food nauseated her. She was too wired to take a bite.

"Are you on that new Santa Teresa diet?" Dean Kropp drawled as the faces at the round table rotated like a field of sunflowers toward a goateed young man with a paisley bow tie and cummerbund, who was describing his new poetry workshop in the ruins of Tikal called "Mind-Trips: Safaris in Personal Creativity."

"What about jaguars and creepy-crawlies?" asked the dean.

"Everything will be taken care of. We'll be occupying the Club Med compound near the air strip."

"And as for the exiled Zapatista revolutionaries who will be conduct-ing the workshops," inquired the Women's Studies chair, "how will they approach gender issues with the women students?"

"Relax. They're all Jesuits. A real bunch of queens."

"So it'll be a gendered experience in the jungle?" asked the Women's Studies chair.

"*I'm a queen,* the queen of the jungle," Minette burst in, tired of the small talk. "I grew up in Lafourche Parish," she ad-libbed frantically, "and for a living I shoot alligators and sell their meat and hides. That's how come I can afford to live in the lap of luxury and be a famous writer. Shooting, skinning, and filleting isn't the hardest part, it's cleaning the bones to sell to gift shops. Finally I found the perfect solution...."

She paused, basking in the attention, everyone's silverware poised in midair.

"I lug the smelly carcasses onto the levee, smear them with honey, and then cover them with shovelfuls of dirt from fire-ant hills. Fire ants eat those bones clean as a whistle in no time," Minette announced, pounding the table like a Sicilian.

Everyone at the table put down their knives and forks in unison. The dean's wife began to play with the clasp on her charm bracelet, and in the distance a fork tinkled against a wine glass. There at the podium stood Fox Blitz, Adam's apple bobbing. Beside him an elderly man with a ruddy complexion and shock of white hair was dozing off.

Minette emptied her glass in one gulp and clapped wildly at all the wrong places through Fox's introduction. When the ovation had died down and the keynote speaker was shuffling through his papers trying to wake up, Minette leaned across the table to pluck a red carnation from the centerpiece. Scooping up her belongings, she climbed the steps to the podium with a look of schoolgirlish devotion, holding the flower high above her by its stem. Her face glistened with a sheen of sweat. Now or never, she thought. Live! Live!

The audience broke into warm applause as she curtseyed, flashing a generous view of her plunging neckline, and fixed the carnation into Mr. Mandible's boutonniere. With watery eyes, Yetta Blitz sat transfixed by this spontaneous ceremony.

"Maybe we were wrong about her," she whispered, tugging at Fox's sleeve. "This is like McDonogh Day," referring to that holiday when the city's school children used to line up to place bouquets at the statue of their benefactor.

"Mr. Mandible," Minette cooed sideways into the microphone, "I've always been a admirer of your great literature, and dreamed on some occasion I might have the honor to meet you."

Then she plunked her portfolio down on top of his typescript, pulled the pearl-handled revolver out of her opera bag, and pointed it at his head.

"So sit down and shut up for a change," she commanded, glowering at the audience, "and no one will get hurt."

As the old man staggered back into his chair next to the podium, the hush in La Louisiane Room was thick as upholstery. Flames flickered in silver candelabras on linen tablecloths, diamonds gleamed from earlobes as women turned to catch their husbands' eyes, and servers in vermilion jackets stood at attention behind carving stations and dessert carts.

Waving the gun over Beauregard Mandible's snowy locks with one hand and slipping her manuscript from the portfolio with the other, Minette hissed one last order into the microphone. "I want the waiters to turn around slowly—ever so slowly—close and lock the doors, and not let anyone in or out until I've finished."

"Thanks very much," she said, her voice catching in her throat. She shifted her weight from one foot to the other. The heels were killing her. Aiming the revolver at Mr. Mandible's temple, she announced that she was going to read from recent work, beginning with a 350 page novel-in-progress. She cleared her throat, buried her nose in a glass of water, and then emerged like a mermaid carved on a ship prow, cresting a wave to leap headfirst into the spotlight.

Minette didn't last long.

Halfway into the second chapter, she announced that she had to visit the little girl's room and handed the revolver to Beauregard Mandible, pale as a marble bust. A vein was pulsing at his temple during an attack of what turned out to be angina pectoris.

"Mr. Mandible, sir, please keep an eye on those sneaky bastards out there," she instructed, "and shoot anyone who tries to get away."

Hotel security found her locked in a stall in the men's room, slumped shoeless on the tile floor making corrections on chapter three with an eyebrow pencil.

"Now you gentlemen be careful, I have a metal plate in my head," she warned, taking the arms of the two officers who escorted her barefoot down Royal Street to the Eighth District station. One of the cops carried her heels dangling by the straps.

The next morning the story made the front page of *The Times-Picayune* under the headline WOULD-BE WRITER HIJACKS ARTS GALA. A flustered Yetta Blitz was interviewed about how she'd met Minette Ferrier at "the bouncing ladies," a term she later denied using. In a color photograph Minette was featured mugging for reporters at the police station, clutching the manuscript to her breast with one hand while holding an imaginary gun to her head with the other. Elwood Toups of Happy Line Tours, "a close personal friend," was quoted in part as saying that "Minette is a pillar of the Quarter community but, like us all, has her ups and downs." Stan Abadie, a Pontabla resident, described Ms. Ferrier as "a great neighbor, if a touch nervine. But that little gal really taught me to live."

Before he died, Beauregard Mandible went on to have one last minor success with *Bang*, a novel set in New Orleans, but never again appeared in public. And Minette never did publish her novel or return to the bouncing ladies, although her name came up often. Somebody heard she'd spent time in a mental hospital in Shreveport and was doing well on lithium. Then she resurfaced on cable TV. One of the women spotted her selling gold tennis bracelets on the shopping channel, and then another swore she saw her in a rerun of *The Mating Game*. Several slipped and got their hair wet when it was reported one evening that Minette Ferrier had married a TV evangelist. Every Sunday morning there she was, escorting sinners down the aisle during the *Hour of Decision*. Dressed like a casino hostess, her eyes twinkled through a raccoon mask of makeup as she delivered her slogan: "Let the Lord fix it."

"What's left but Jesus after you bomb out in this town?" asked Yetta, swiveling to the left, then to the right.

THE VAMPIRE-TOUR DIARY

July 16:

I t's against the law now, godammit. And still those vampire people are disturbing my peace, the peace I worked so hard to earn in a town I never liked, among people I never liked, neither the living nor—if the sad truth be known—the dead.

For thirty-five years I slaved and scrimped as a funeral director at the Still Waters Mortuary in Minneapolis, Minnesota, slugging uphill day after day through the snowdrifts of a lifetime of winters to finally arrive at this wrought-iron balcony in the Vieux Carré, brimming with magenta double-hibiscuses, lakeview jasime, cascading purple verbena, and pink impatiens. And every evening here on the rue Chartres, while I stand with a goblet of Merlot in hand, Bach pouring through the floor-to-ceiling windows onto my gallery, while I stand here trying to forget the smell of formaldehyde and the texture of coffin satin, what do I see?

I see the upturned faces of hundreds of those vampire-tour people crowding the street below, fanning themselves silly with cardboard fans in the shape of skulls.

Your Honor, my name is Merlin Withers. My attorney has advised me to keep this diary, may it please the court, both to record the frequency and numbers of the groups, and to document the mental anguish they've inflicted upon me.

From six in the evening until ten at night, seven days a week, one group follows the next, popping flashbulbs and whirring video cameras, enthralled by the stentorian voice of some tour guide draped in black, done up in a top hat and white face paint, flinging his arms to punctuate the morbid monologues. I know all their spiels by heart. Word for word. Most of those vampire people's gazes have swiveled like heliotropes toward the house next door, a moldering Creole museum by day, once the site of the Café des Éxilés, where corrupt Caribbean colonials plotted and schemed and drank themselves into a tropical stupor.

But always a few in the crowd are staring up at me, as if this pale, thin Midwesterner perched on his balcony possessed the secret of immortality, as if because of my intimate proximity to what the guides claim occurred next door, I were Nosferatu himself rather than a retired funeral director with loose upper dentures and strands of tinted hair combed over his bald spot.

From what I hear, that house was once the scene of unimaginable horrors among the undead. French casket girls did, in fact, board upstairs, hoping to find suitable mates among the Creoles at the café below. Only according to the guides, their so-called caskets weren't filled with embroidered linens for their trousseaux but with families of royal vampires who paid their maids to stow them away to the New World after they lost their castles during the French Revolution. These vampires supposedly fed on the babies birthed by nuns at the Ursuline convent down the block, who delivered their bastard infants to-go, nestled among the baguettes in bread baskets, as if they were pizzas.

Poppycock.

These are stories concocted by dropped-out slackers high on crack cocaine who are making a bundle, the only people in this impoverished little Haiti of a city pulling in a damn dime. They, and those sharkish real estate agents, who have turned every termite-eaten slave quarter and rat-infested Creole town house into a luxury condo for goldenagers who want to add a dash of romance to their final years.

Like the story of Nosferatu, mine begins with a real estate transaction. How was I to know what I was getting into when I purchased this apartment? And for a small fortune, I might add. Todd, the buffed young go-getter from Hot Tin Roof Realty who sold it to me, brought me here on a sepulchral Tuesday morning. The only discernable activity on Chartres Street was that obese museum guard next-door, sucking his teeth and passing gas. Todd even flirted with me, and silly old Lutheran queen that I am, I took it seriously. But the paperwork went through in a snap, even after the slap. "No skin off my butt what makes you hot, Pops," Todd told me with a smug gym-bunny smile. "Sign here."

And pointing at the museum next door, he had the gall to suggest how quiet the apartment should be, since all my neighbors would be ghosts.

A far cry.

Lean over the balcony to ask those vampire guides to please lower their voices, and they snarl, baring nicotine-stained choppers at you. Request that they please move their Disneyland gangs aside so that I might enter my carriage way, burdened as I often am with groceries in one hand, mail and a newspaper in the other, and their shrill, crack-addled laughter rings off the slate rooftops of the cottages across the street. Their black-clad lackeys stand to one side, tattoed arms folded over muscled chests, packing thirty-eight snubs, I've heard tell, and waiting for any trouble.

Your Honor, you must understand, we don't have vampire tours in Minneapolis, Minnesota.

July 17:

I'm having trouble sleeping. Last night I was up again until dawn, kept awake by scratching sounds, as if some small, clawed creatures were scurrying around inside the walls. I may have rats.

On the evening in question, July 15 of this year, I dined alone on the balcony, as is my custom, after repotting two flats of wilting impatiens I'd purchased that afternoon. Then suddenly below appear a sea of faces from two different tours, jostling for space. One group must have had a hundred people, the other forty. And they are standing twenty feet apart, both guides engaged in a shouting match to be heard over the other.

"FAMILIES OF BLOODSUCKING ARISTOCRATS STOWED AWAY IN HOPE CHESTS . . ." one screeches, making clawing gestures with his filthy fingernails.

"BASKETS OF BREAD FRESH FROM THE CONVENT OVENS, AND BUNDLED INSIDE . . ." the other booms, rocking his bony arms with a pathetic cradling motion.

All this before dessert.

Meanwhile, half of the vampire people are glaring at me, as if the wine in my unfinished glass of Merlot were babies' blood. In my day I've buried many a baby, let me tell you. I started my career from the ground up, working as an embalmer, and I know all about the smell and feel of blood. Your Honor, this is too much. Besides, they are breaking the new law, which as you know limits each group to twenty-eight tourists, and stipulates they cannot use bullhorns, block sidewalks, or station themselves less than fifty feet from any other group. So I pick up my wireless to call the cops.

"You are in violation of the law, and I've summoned the authorities," I call down to the guide bellowing under my balcony. My voice is trembling, but I'm exhilerated by my own boldness. "And would you please ask your group to step across the street, because I am about to water my wilting impatiens."

I wait a minute or two, then pull out my hose and begin to spray. A few of the tourists squawk, but I continue in a fury, as if hosing down the embalming room at the Still Waters, washing every last trace of blood and viscera out of the tile corners. I hit the baskets of Boston ferns, then the hibiscus, then the poor impatiens.

About an hour later, long after both vampire groups have disappeared, a squad car finally pulls up under my balcony. No fewer than three policemen step out. Although still in gardening togs, I race downstairs to greet them, pleased my complaints will finally be attended to.

But oh no, they haven't come to register my complaints, but to issue me a summons for assault on forty people with a garden hose. The guide had each of the people in his group take out their cell phones to call in a complaint that they'd been splattered during the vampire tour.

I am speechless.

"You ruining the image of New Orleans," a cop tells me, his face so flushed with booze it looks like a baked ham. "People pay good money to come down here."

"Sir, I'm a retired professional from out of town—"

"We don't care who you is," another cop replies in that thick Brooklyn accent the people down here speak with. "Could've been my momma and daddy on that tour getting all sopping wet. Last night another bozo emptied a cat box on top them vampire people."

"I certainly have the right to water the flowers on my balcony. And look here, those tour guides were breaking the new laws—"

"Mr. Withers, those laws ain't on the books yet," the third policemen cuts in, shoving in my face a summons to appear in court.

And that, Your Honor, is what took place on the night of July 15. And when I return to my balcony to calm myself down with blood-pressure medication and a cocktail—it's a double, several doubles, if I remember correctly—I have the distinct impression the water still dripping from the leaves of my plants and down onto the street below is blood. My own blood. And that as it collects into puddles at the base of the posts that support my gallery, roving packs of skeletal rats are lapping it up.

And that this defines my relationship to the city of New Orleans.

July 18:

Last night I was up until dawn again, then slept the day away. This is becoming a pattern. I dreamed of a coffin in the room with me, one that contains the remains of my dead self. I am trying to explain to my neighbors when the body is to be discovered and what will happen to his possessions. Yet I am still myself and in my same body, and seem to have other plans. I wake up charged with energy.

Tonight I'm watching my blood pressure, hiding behind closed shutters from the circus in the street. Peeking outside, I count eight different groups with approximately sixty tourists each. Have you ever wondered, Your Honor, what sends these hordes out on vampire tours?

In my profession I've comforted countless bereaved people, and have learned that many have lost their religion. Nowadays they get their images of the beyond from kitsch calendar art. Take unicorns and angels. For centuries they were subjects of esoteric fascination to scholars, theologians, and mystic hermits in caves. Only recently have they begun to appear on coffee mugs, stationery, address labels, costume jewelery, and pocket agendas, reflecting a craving for some benevolent form of eternal life. Vampires have gone the way of unicorn pins and angel mugs, but suggest darker, more disturbing thoughts about the hereafter. At one time, seekers set out on pilgrimages, entered monasteries, fasted, or prayed to gain some glimpse of immortality. Now they buy a pair of angel earrings, or pay fifteen dollars a pop for a vampire tour.

So every night, hundreds stand slack-jawed in front of my balcony, gazing up as if at the façade of Chartres Cathedral, as if the building next door contained some secret that, could they but capture it, would make them special mythical creatures, too, instead of mortal, workaday slobs.

It seems these vampire-chasers are all fat morning people watching their cholesterol, obsessed by slim nocturnal creatures gorging on bloody flesh. Maybe these fans just hate to get up in the morning, and worship those who don't. But these people aren't actually interested in achieving immortality. What they want is an immortality T-shirt.

Merchandise is the only myth left. I journeyed to the realm of the undead, and all I got was this lousy baseball cap.

July 20:

I do have rats, although I've yet to spot them. I don't understand where the infestation is coming from, but the entire apartment reeks of leaf mold and wet animal fur. A white cobwebby fungus hangs in the air, sticking to my clothes and furniture. This morning I dream that a huge rat corners me, bares its bloody fangs, and warns me to get out of town while I can. A slow night in the crypt. The heat and humidity make me feel swathed in rolls of damp cotton. This evening's body count: 285 vampire people in front of my house.

"Vampires?" barks my Aunt Ora from her bed in a nursing home across the river. "You got vampires? That's rich. Wish that was my only problem."

"I said I have rats. The vampire tours—"

"Vampires, rats." She shakes her head. "Never thought I'd live to be this old."

Then Aunt Ora fills me in on the latest details about her broken hip, osteoporosis, and macular degeneration. The body in decay is terrible to witness. And nursing homes. Will that be my fate? Aunt Ora claims that last week her roommate was boiled to death in the bathtub by an orderly who let the water get too hot. When they found the roommate, my aunt swears, her hands were gripping the tub rim, long red fingernails clacking against the porcelain sides like a lobster in a pot.

Aunt Ora is my mother's only surviving sister, always considered something of a floozy by Minneapolis standards. They say I take after her. She's one of the reasons I decided to retire to my mother's hometown, although she's my last relative in the city. On my frequent visits, we gossip about the Quarter, her old neighboorhood. For years she was a cashier at an oyster bar on Iberville Street. When I was a kid she'd be perched high on a throne behind the cash register, ruby-lipped and chignoned, waving a filter-tip Chesterfield and smelling like bourbon and oyster shells. She used to let me spear paid tickets on the spike next to the cash drawer.

"The Tarot readers on Jackson Square are suing the painters," I tell her, "the street musicians are fighting with the clowns and fire-eaters, and politicians bribed by tourism are squabbling with politicians bought by real estate. The place is a mess."

"Didn't used to be that way," she says, sniffling. "The mob and the cops used to run it together, real peaceful-like. Left us alone, except when a pimp killed one of his girls. But the city's done run off cotton, shipping, and oil. All it's got left is that falling-down old French Quarter. That's why everybody in town trying to squeeze it hard for every last penny they can get. Merl, hand me that box of Kleenex, would you, hon?"

And you know something, Your Honor, Aunt Ora is right.

Occasionally in the evening, on my way to the A & P, I stroll past the cathedral, where the vampire tours recruit their victims among the candle-lit tables of Tarot readers. Six different companies are vying for the business, and each has some gamine young goth in tattered veils handing out leaflets, or some Hell's Angel-type dressed as a ghoul sporting a sandwich board dripping with red letters. They obviously hate each other, and often the guides are screaming about who saw whom first, or who has dibs on which suckers. It has all the subtlety of a slave auction, and this goes on just as six o'clock Mass in the cathedral is letting out.

On my mother's visits home, she and Aunt Ora would sometimes take me into the scented hush of St. Louis Cathedral. I was seduced by the stained glass and candles and statues. That's probably why I went into the funeral business, because I wanted everything always to remain as eternal and soothing as inside that church.

Now I can't bear to step inside. Even crosses gives me the creeps.

July 25:

I've set out traps and hired an exterminator, but can't seem to kill the rats. I'm convinced they're immortal.

This evening I miss the vampire tours to discuss strategies for survival with a neighborhood residents' group, Peeved Property Owners on Parade. First on our agenda is termites; second, vampires. And third, another round of Bloody Marys, with Barbra Streisand cranked up loud.

Most of the members of PPOOP are my age or older, retired from various parts of the country. Many of the other gentlemen let their hair down (only two are actually wearing wigs), and I realize that many of us are "friends of Dorothy," as we used to say during my youth in Minneapolis. That certainly sounds a lot better than "queer." What are we supposed to call ourselves now? BLT. No, wait, that's a sandwich. It's GLBT, which stands for Gay, Lesbian, Bisexual, and Transsexual. My dear, so many choices. I'll take the bacon sandwich.

The other old PPOOPs are horrified when I report how the police issued me a summons for assault on forty vampire people.

"You pulled out your *what* to sprinkle those tourists?" asks Stan Abadie, a sweet man from the Pontabla building with a hearing aid.

"He said his garden hose, Gladys," shouts his partner Timothy, the director of the Vieux Carré Commission, sending a jet of mentholated smoke toward the crown medallion over the chandelier.

"What I did for a while," offers an odd little vegetarian of inde-terminate sex named Tootie, "was to direct my speakers to the street, and every time the vampire tours came by, blast that song that goes 'I went on down to the Audubon Zoo, and they all axed for you.' That really stopped those vampire people in their tracks. They make me feel like an animal in a zoo. But then neighbors started to complain about *my* noise."

"We can't make noise to drown out noise," I insist. "But any direct action we take will get us arrested."

"Not if we all act at once," growls portly Jason, a retired Spanish professor from Purdue. The room is heating up.

"What do you mean?"

"Okay, Merl, if on a given night," Jason says, "we all stand on our balconies or lean out our windows and squirt them as the vampire people congregate below, it will overload the system. Like Ghandi, or Martin Luther King."

"Look, the only way to get anything done in this town is to throw a *fab*ulous party," chimes in Timothy, lighting another Salem. "What if on the same night we all have vampire-watering soirees on our balconies, and invite oodles of friends."

"They'll arrest the person holding the hose." I know of what I speak.

"What if we're all masked?" suggests Timothy.

"Then they'll ask who did it," I reply.

"Not if each vampire-waterer steps forward to answer, 'Officer, I did,'" Jason says. "It's a ploy from a Lope de Vega play, but if it worked in the *Siglo de Oro*, why shouldn't it work in the French Quarter. That's why I moved here. This place is just like sixteenth-century Spain, only with go-cups and gay bars."

"And what will we mask as?"

"That's easy," says Stan Abadie. "Vampires."

Giddy with our plan, we repair to the Sunday afternoon singalong at Tinkles, the corner piano bar. When the bartender asks which of us gentlemen ordered the double Bloody Mary, all fifteen of us answer in unison, "Officer, I did."

July 28:

Tonight I hear from Reynold, one of the old PPOOPs. He calls to tell me he's dropping out of our vampire-watering protest, set for August 5. I finally worm the truth out of him. He's sleeping with a vampire-tour guide, a man half his age.

"They have to make a living, too," he says. "Besides, he's kind of cute."

These queens. How could anybody betray our cause for a piece of ass? Especially a sleazy piece of vampire-tour ass.

The costume we decide on is basic black, plus those translucent plastic masks worn by the riders on old-line krewe carnival floats. They are horrifyingly expressionless, like the mug of a serial killer. You can buy them by the gross from Mardi Gras wholesalers. Timothy offers to run up a couple of hundred black acrylic capes on his Singer so that we can't be identified by body type.

When we try on our outfits, it kills the party. We can't speak, drink, or smoke with the masks on. But we do look identical, like a roomful of horny cadavers.

Somebody grabs my crotch, and for the life of me I can't tell who it is.

Your Honor, does it appear we're acting "with malice?" My peace of mind has been shattered by these vampire people. I'm up all night, eat little, and am tormented by the squealing of rats and incandescent memories of my early years as an embalmer, when I'd ride home on the bus every night picking dried blood from under my fingernails. I've lost ten, maybe fifteen pounds, and my libido, once comfortably mummified, is rearing its ugly head again with a vengeance. All night I'm on the prowl, making the rounds of pick-up bars, from the smokey alcoves of Your Little Red Wagon to the dim back room of The Rough House, places I'd never set foot in before. The younger and tenderer they are when I get my claws on them, the better. I'm beset by unspeakable fantasies, and my blood pressure, which I monitor twice a day, is through the roof.

Tonight: seven groups. Body count: 463 people. During the final tour, which passes at 9:50 p.m., the guide uses a bullhorn as he describes the blood of used babies seeping from the baskets stacked at the café door and trickling throught the cobblestones into the open sewers.

I see red, and scamper from my apartment to The Rough House, beside myself. I must have company, and of a particular kind. I hunt all night, and find no one. I return home parched, famished, and settle for a glass of Merlot and a bacon sandwich.

August 5:

What happened this evening is a drunken blur, Your Honor. You might find a more accurate account in the ambulance report.

About 6:00 p.m. thirty black-clad friends stomp up the stairs to my apartment already in a state of high hilarity over what they call "Halloween in August." Once the martinis start to flow and capes are put on, the guests become hard to control. Several people have brought water pistols, soon filled with Grey Goose that they squirt into each other's mouths. Over cries of "squirt me one, girlfriend" and "hit me up, Dracula baby," I explain the scenario.

"At this moment, throughout the Vieux Carré," I announce, "lined up in windows and on balconies such as this one, groups of citizens costumed as vampires will attempt to take back their streets from the vampire tours."

This is greeted by cheers and stomping. I catch a stream of vodka in my left eye.

"When a tour group comes by, put on your masks, wrap the capes around your bodies, and one of you—nobody will know who it is—grab the hose and wet them down real good. When the police come by—now listen up, this is important—and ask who did it, we are each to respond, 'Officer, I did.'"

"Officer, I did," the whole balcony chants, flapping their capes and squirting each other with vodka.

Police sirens shriek in the distance, edging closer. And around the corner shuffles a two-by-two column of vampire people, already looking a bit soggy. The cardboard skulls are drooping off the sticks of their fans. They cringe, facing yet another balcony filled with lunar masks glowing against a backdrop of figures in black. We must be quite a sight.

One tourist holds up his arms in a cross. And hisses.

As somebody next to me reaches for the hose, another tour group marches in from the opposite direction and stations itself several feet from the first. The guides glare at each other, puffing out their chests like fighting cocks. They are just about to begin their shouting match when down the block, under the languid fronds of a weeping willow, a heavyset man with bleached-blond hair clutches his chest and doubles over to the sidewalk, moaning.

The only movement on the street is the mosquito buzzing in my ear.

Then the woman accompanying the man on the sidewalk jerks out a cell phone, and in a snap, a blaring fire engine has pulled under the balcony, its pulsing red lights reflecting off our blank plastic masks. Men with *FIRE* stenciled on the backs of their shirts yank a yellow stretcher from under the ladder, then an ambulance wails in behind them. The man is lifted from the sidewalk and strapped into a gurney, Haiwaiian shirt unbuttoned. His gelatinous belly is spot lit like an enormous pale pudding under a streetlamp bent at a tipsy angle.

The vampire tour guides back off. Trafficking nightly in tales of blood and gore, they are turned to stone by the sight of a fat man having a heart attack. Both groups disappear around the corner as a squad car swerves up behind the ambulance. As a policemen emerges, the masked crowd on the balcony shouts in chorus, "Officer, I did, officer, I did."

"Not now, you fools," I mutter between clenched teeth.

The policeman looks up, stunned, and is about to say something to us when he swats us away like insects and approaches the gurney, his brow furrowed. Transfixed by the man's heaving stomach, my guests take off their masks, put down their vodka pistols, and begin to murmur. The vampire-watering party is over.

After everyone has wandered back down into the street and I'm folding shiny black capes and cleaning up the last of half-finished cock-tails, the telephone rings.

"Merl Withers?"

It's the nursing home across the river. Aunt Ora has just died.

August 6:

An eerie silence reigns on Chartres Street.

I pick up *The Times-Picayune* on my way to make the arrangements for Aunt Ora's funeral. Even though our party was disrupted, the protest was a smash in other parts of the neighborhood. An article headlined "LOCAL VAMPIRES ARMED WITH HOSES ATTACK TOUR GROUPS" reports that "due to a massive altercation with French Quarter residents, the vampire tours have been temporarily suspended." With the story appears a photo of several drenched tourists.

"It was a mess," one of them is quoted as saying, "but I've never had such a hoot in my life. I can't wait to come back to New Orleans."

August 7:

I wake in a panic. While I was asleep, a rat must have bitten me on the neck. There's no other explanation for the small, precise teeth marks. I call the exterminator, who laughs and says, "Face it, mister, your rats are imaginary." But I've observed them scurrying along the electrical cables between the museum and this building, long queues of them like hoary refugees from history. Where they hide I have no idea, but I hear them, and feel their icy presence. It's too late to see a doctor today, so I bandage the wound before falling into a feverish state.

In my delirium I have the sensation that I'm alone in my coffin, hands folded over my chest. Suddenly I feel someone touch me. I jump up from the sofa screaming, "Who are you?"

No one is there. Nobody I can see.

I've been alone for centuries, as desiccated as a tuberous root dug from a cleft between two rocks. Sheer white curtains are billowing between the living room and balcony, and in my black bathrobe I step through them into the violet haze of late evening. A demented wind is blowing; bolts of lightning split the sky. The plants are dried sticks, the ferns, baskets of spiny bristles, and white rats are swarming over the balcony floor. The puffy faces of hundreds of vampire people are staring up from the street, not at the museum but, with excruciating longing, toward me.

Their tour guides are nuns carrying baskets, offering me their charges, beaming.

"Master," the crowd moans, "master, usher us into endless night."

I take out my cosmetics case and with great care make up each of their faces. Then I tenderly tuck each body into a casket lined with quilted satin. My hunger is satiated, and the service just about to begin.

III

DISSOLUTION PROPERTIES

LUCILLE LEBLANC'S
LAST STAND

One December, Celestine lay down in the middle of the parlor and stayed there for three weeks. "I don't know whether to call a priest or a crash truck," Lucille complained to my grandmother on the phone. "How I'm gonna move her without a hook and ladder? I can't have y'all over for Christmas with that woman moaning between the Motorola and the piano."

"Jack, go over there and see what you can do," my grandmother urged me. But trying to do anything about the LeBlancs was like trying to do something about the Civil War. It was over, and I was just getting started.

Celestine was a massive, gold-toothed woman who shook the floorboards when she walked. Lucille was wiry and smart-mouthed, with mottled skin two shades of white and one of brown. She was better off than her sister Mignonne, who used a walker and was so deaf she couldn't hear the telephone ring. But standing up made Lucille so dizzy she couldn't wait to sit back down. All three were over seventy-five years old and, as Lucille liked to say, had one good pair of legs, ears, and eyes between them.

For twenty-five years Celestine had worked for the LeBlanc family in their dilapidated West Indian plantation house on Bayou Road. She'd kept order and cooked grillades among the squawking eccentricities of six Creole brothers and sisters, none of whom had ever married or held a job. Celestine's voice thundered from the kitchen to the front gallery, commanding everyone in its path. On Sundays while we ate in the dining room, she'd perch on a high stool in front of her stove, engaged in an ongoing conversation through the door with everyone at the table, telling us what to eat and how much, and serving up side dishes of advice and gossip. Any difference of opinion at the table awaited her final word, which came booming in with the next course. Lucille would change the subject rather than give in to Celestine.

Yet Celestine was as terrified as the LeBlancs of the deteriorating neighborhood beyond the picket fence on Bayou Road, and ventured out even less than they did. She was afraid, she said, some young fellow with a loud radio and a big stick would knock her down at the bus stop. Except for the walk to morning Mass at St. Rose de Lima, during those final years only Lucille ever left the house, putting on her hat and pearls to "go to town" (as she still called Canal Street) to visit with the lawyer and banker or to fight another battle with the "big monkey-monks" at City Hall.

First the Department of Public Health condemned the chicken and duck coops the LeBlancs had always kept in the yard, forcing them to eat store-bought meat. Then the city sealed the well and cistern, obliging them to wash down store-bought meat with tap water from the Mississippi River. "Them health people trying to make us sick for sure," Lucille ranted to anyone who would listen. The last straw was when the city condemned the fireplaces. Then they had to huddle all winter in the cavernous rooms around electric space heaters connected by dangling extension cords to the crystal chandeliers.

None of the old downtown families still kept chickens or drank rainwater from a cistern, my grandmother told me, although she remembered doing so as a girl when they lived next-door to the LeBlancs. My grandmother had gone to convent school with the LeBlanc sisters, but compared to Lucille and Mignonne, she was a Thoroughly Modern Mémère. She smoked Salems, drove a car, and probably owned the first MixMaster and electric rotisserie oven in the state of Louisiana. "Times have changed" was her motto. Long before he became president, she liked that handsome actor on the General Electric TV show who said every week, "Progress is our most important product."

Around the time the city condemned the fireplaces, the remaining LeBlancs went into mourning and never emerged. They continued eating a long, leisurely dinner at one o'clock in the afternoon and then napping, as though the buzzing nine-to-five world of rush hours and freeways didn't exist. Meanwhile, the house fell apart around them, jerry-rigged in that style of managed decay endemic to the tropics. Burst pipes were wrapped with rags and duct tape, swatches of mismatched linoleum covered termite holes in the floors, and broken shutters were wired closed. The garden grew wild, and when I got older, after Sunday dinner I'd change into an old pair of jeans and do what I could to weed and trim. They often threatened to sell the house and move to the country, where their cousins had a sugar plantation, but the plantation eventually was bought by an oil company, one thing led to another, and they never did.

First Euphèmie, the youngest LeBlanc, became convinced that her sisters were trying to poison her. During our Sunday visits, she would suddenly appear at the creaky pocket doors between the dining room and parlor, her oval eyes lowered to the floor like a novitiate, hands wrapped around her elbows at the small of her back. Her downy gray hair was cropped short as a boy's, and she must have weighed no more than seventy-five pounds. She spoke in a loud whining voice, making sounds like a deaf girl mouthing her first words.

Once, when I was about fourteen, she came in, curtsied, and kissed me shyly on the cheek. "Why did Miss Euphie do that?" I asked Lucille, blushing.

"She thinks you that good-looking boy Èmile used to call on her from Bayou St. John. But Papa ran him off, and then he went over there and got himself killed by the Kaiser. Euphie Marie, she never got over that boy, I hope to tell you."

The next time Euphèmie made one of her appearances between the pocket doors, I gallantly kissed her hand, playing my part as the ghost of a Creole suitor. Euphèmie ran shrieking from the room, and we could hear Celestine tussling with her in the kitchen. When she finally got her quieted and tied to the bed, I asked Celestine what happened.

"She thinks you the trash man. Come back here screaming something about how the trash man done licked her hand, and make me wash it five or four time to get the smell off."

Lucille refused to have her sister put away, as her cousins thought she should, and always said she couldn't sell the house as long as Euphèmie was alive. Where else could she find a place big enough so that neighbors couldn't hear her scream?

After Euphèmie starved herself to death, Sylver, the older brother, started up. He took to his bed, refusing to move until he died. He would sit propped up, wild-eyed and unshaven, and demand Dixie beer and Lucky Strikes. To catch the ashes, Celestine held a silver tray under the cigarette drooping from his mouth, terrified he would set the bed on fire. He called and called on the merciful Lord Jesus to take him, until one Sunday I heard Celestine march in to tell him—in no uncertain terms—he should be ashamed for calling on the Lord to do something He had no mind to do at the moment.

That was the night Sylver died.

. . .

Those visits to the nineteenth century lasted all afternoon, especially the formal gatherings after Christmas dinner, when my grandmother, mother, sister, and I would come to exchange presents with the dwindling circle of LeBlancs. Their two cousins, the mean-mouthed Lanoux sisters from North Miro Street, would always be there, along with a daughter Adrienne, and her boy my age, Jerome. The parlor smelled like the inside of an old leather suitcase, and I sat up straight for hours with red foil wrapping from a new pair of cuff links balanced on my lap. My grandfather had knotted my tie so tight I could barely swallow the cherry bounce in a cordial glass.

Everyone spoke at once, to no one in particular, in French, in English, and in both. To American ears, they always sounded as if they were arguing, even when they were agreeing. This was a conversational style known as *cancan*, as boisterous as the dance but not as naughty. Nodding in the direction of the cancan, I would run my hands against the nap of the prickly horsehair chair I was sitting on.

"*Margot, dites-moi encore l'âge de ce garçon, oh la, il est grand.*" Then Lucille would turn to me. "I say, Ti-Jacques, you want a Barq's or Big Shot? Maybe you not big enough for cherry bounce. *Ma cousine le fait en la campagne pour la famille toutes les fêtes de Noël mais* maybe it too strong for you."

I was in a cage filled with giant lady parakeets dressed in flowered rayon dresses with clunky black shoes and long wisps of white hair held in ornate barrettes. They were chirping and shrieking and filling the cage with feathers, beating their wings and hopping from perch to perch. Balanced on the edges of their chairs, they'd dip their beaks rapidly into tiny glasses in their hands. Outside, I could hear pine cones dropping onto the rockers on the front gallery and sense the sun motionless at the center of the pewter sky.

Inside the crystal ball from the whatnot cabinet, it was always snowing when I wanted it to be.

The whatnot cabinet was also lined with cut glass bowls reflected in beveled mirrors. The high ceiling was the color of pages from an old book, the paint peeling back in long strips. The parlor reminded me of an antique shop on Royal Street, overflowing with china urns, candelabra lamps, still lifes of blowzy dahlias in gold frames, chairs with caning the color of tobacco-stained teeth, and an obstacle course of back tables and end tables. Overhead hung a huge ceiling fan like an ornamental propeller that didn't move. The piano seat did move, and my sister spun around and around on it in her yellow pinafore with starched petticoats underneath, her new Mary Janes almost touching the floor. A small Christmas tree glimmered on top of the piano, and the plaster Magi and camel crossed the piano lid—nailed shut—in search of their blinking silver star.

The Christmas after the city condemned the LeBlancs' fireplaces, their cousin Goozy Dordain ordered for them from the Montgomery Ward catalogue a cardboard fireplace with a revolving spotlight behind a sheet of red cellophane. Not to hurt his feelings, Lucille set it up every year, and we sat in chilly parlor shadows with red light wavering across our faces as we sipped cherry bounce, rearranged space heaters, and silently watched snow falling in New York on the new Motorola TV.

"It's real pretty," everyone agreed. And we left early.

Lucille had the Montgomery Ward fireplace box in the front hall, ready to set it up, when Celestine lay down in the middle of the parlor. For years each brother or sister had lined up to be the next to die, until only Lucille, Mignonne, and Celestine were left. Out of the blue, Celestine decided it was her turn.

Like the white ladies she worked for, Celestine had never married. "Who would have her?" was the way Lucille always answered the question, out of earshot. Celestine was from the country in Assumption Parish, and was given to odd beliefs. She kept an assortment of small animals in and around the house, which she claimed were her spirits. Looking for sugar inside the screened cupboard in the pantry one day, I was bitten by a box turtle hiding among the canisters. Rubbing my hand with alcohol, Celestine said the turtle was curing her.

I was in my first year of college by this time, had long hair, and went to civil rights demonstrations. And so, smarting from my turtle bite and guilt about segregation, I sat face to face with Celestine at the kitchen table—I'd never done that before—and we talked about reincarnation. We both believed in it.

"Nothing die," Celestine told me. "It all go on from one thing to the next. These animals I brung here are my people from the country. They can suck the misery out me and put it back in the ground. One day I be them, or they be me or Miss Lucille or your Mémère. They our people, too."

My sit-in in the kitchen with Celestine discussing hippie ideas didn't go over too big with the LeBlancs or my family. They made Celestine put the turtle in a hole under the house and get rid of the lizards, field mice, and garden snakes she kept tucked away in every nook and cranny of the kitchen. And the next time I visited, Lucille exploded. "I hope you don't mind if I tell you to your face that you'd look a lot better without all that hair hanging off your head." As she lurched to the sideboard for her barber shears, I excused myself to jump on the bus.

Whatever Celestine was trying to cure with the box turtle was awfully real, because the house smelled so foul that all but their most faithful friends and family stopped visiting. I first noticed the stench when my grandmother explained in a stage whisper, "Celestine has soiled herself." We exited the kitchen onto the back gallery. But an odor of stale urine began to seep into the woodwork, linen, and marquisette curtains. The smell was aggravated by a Creole fear of drafts, so the shutters were kept tightly shut. Lucille and Mignonne didn't notice it; they lived with it. But the first blast on entering the house on a summer afternoon was . . . well, I asked myself how could people live like this?

After the smell came the trash. I was amazed at the number of shopping bags my grandmother kept carrying out of the house and stuffing into her car after visiting the LeBlancs. One afternoon I lugged three, she, two, and they weighed a ton. At first I didn't ask, thinking they were old clothes for the Sisters' Home for the Incurables or a lifetime supply of fig preserves and cherry bounce. Finally I couldn't resist.

"Don't tell anyone, Jack, but Celestine won't let Lucille or Mignonne throw out anything. She's got it into her head that the garbage is invaluable. Newspapers, milk cartons, tin cans, it's all piling up in the house to the point where Lucille has to sleep on the couch in the parlor because her room's filled with stacks and stacks of trash."

I reached around to the back seat to peer into a shopping bag. It was filled with Holsom bread wrappers and French Market Coffee & Chicory cans.

"And so we decided each visit I would, you know, make like I was just coming from Maison Blanche with shopping, and get rid of the trash that way. Sad thing is, we didn't know Celestine banks her money between the old newspapers until six one-dollar bills slipped out. Now we have to thumb through the papers first and put her money under the Bible she keeps on the mantle in her room. That's where she saves the money for her funeral."

The garbage smuggling went on for several months, until the day Celestine made her pallet in the parlor and lay down to die.

Lucille called us every day with the latest report. "She likes to sleep on the floor . . . like you"—Lucille paused for emphasis, exposing once more our hippie conspiracy—"but usually sleeps in the back hall next to the kitchen. Lord knows it'd take me till next Easter to clean out that room of hers. For ten years I been begging her to see a doctor, but she say she don't have no use for doctors. And every time I mention an ambulance, she commences to holler. You hear, there she goes again. I got to go. I'm waiting on that woman like she was the Queen of Sheba. Tell your Mémère I'll ring her later. Pray for me."

Seated on the gossip-bench next to the square black telephone, Lucille went down the list, asking each of her relatives what to do. Her cousin Tante Sis from North Miro Street suggested that Lucille "launder Celestine's step-ins." Lucille performed this chore every night in the bathtub, diapering her with a fresh pair of drawers every morning. Celestine moaned and cussed and called on her Maker as Lucille struggled to change her, but a least the smell wasn't as suffocating during our last visit with Celestine.

She lay sprawled under a pile of patched blankets, even though it was an unusually warm December day. The acrid piss smell lingered, in spite of laundered step-ins. Rays of strong sunlight, strained through closed shutters, cast a zebra-pattern across the room, catching motes of dust falling in slow currents from the overhead fan. The air had an exhausted gray tinge. We stood over Celestine as though over an impromtu grave.

At first the deathbed seemed like a mound of rags with a big green rock balanced on top, heaving up and down. When I looked closer, only Celestine's ashen-blue face was exposed, pocked with beads of sweat, eyes rolled back in her head. The turtle rested on her formidable stomach, tail and legs withdrawn inside its parched shell, its head protruding with yellow carmine eyes staring defiantly at us. It seemed to be guarding her, and I remembered it bit.

I thought I heard it hiss. I didn't get too close.

Lucille ushered us out onto the gallery, and Mignonne clanked after us on her walker. "She says it draws the misery from her, that turtle.

Says her soul going to go in it when she pass, and then I should put it back under the house," Lucille said. "I got enough on my hands without fooling with no dirty cowan. I tell her I'm gonna make a soup out of that cowan, and she holler some more."

Mignonne, rocking herself into a trance in her worn rattan rocker, stared down the long shaded walkway that led to the gate, as if imagining her own last exit from Bayou Road. Shaking her wilted head, she cut in at regular intervals with "Lucille's right!" and "We done all we could."

"Have you tried to make other arrangements, called a nursing home or something?" my grandmother asked, trying to bring the conversation back to earth. "I hear the Good Shepherd has wonderful care, for white and colored both."

Lucille swept the suggestion aside as if it came from another planet. "Every day I get down on my knees and ask the Blessèd Mother what to do. And yesterday I got an answer loud and clear: *call her family*. So finally I talk to some woman in Assumption Parish who claims Celestine as her great-aunt. She says, 'You got Tante Celestine?' and I say, 'If she your kin, come get her. That woman suffering bad. Us, we got one foot each in the grave, my sister and me.'"

Three days before Christmas, I'd just finished my final exams when Lucille called to tell us Celestine had died, and that her niece had taken the body to Assumption Parish. On the morning of Christmas Eve, my grandmother drove Lucille and Mignonne in her turquoise Plymouth to the country for the funeral. I heard that at one point Lucille hung her head out of the window, carsick in her new rose hat. Before she left, she asked me to do something with that turtle. I coaxed it into a shoe box and carried it back to its hole under the house, where I had my own funeral rite for Celestine with votive candles and a mayonnaise jar of holy water I took from Mignonne's prie-dieu.

While I was scurrying under the brick pillars that raised the house above the flood-line, a crack of thunder announced one of those flash Louisiana storms that unexpectedly sets the moment in parentheses from the rest of the day. So I spent a while under the cypress floorboards, lighting votive candles and singing a Choctaw poem I'd ripped out of my literature textbook, hypnotized by the torrential downpour. The damp loam smell reminded me that Bayou Road had first been a muddy Indian portage between the Mississippi and Bayou St. John, bricked over into a street at the turn of the century. I imagined a procession of Houmas with bark pirogues hoisted over their heads treading toward the bayou, shook a few more drops of holy water from Mignonne's jar into the turtle's hole, and buried them there, too.

Lucille had often told me her mother's story of how a rich voodoo named Jean Bayou had buried gold under the house. And to my boyish fascination, she'd promised that before she ever sold the place, she and I would rent one of those metal detectors and crawl under the house to search for it. Studying the recession in the ground where the intractable turtle lay, I figured that must be where the gold was. So I sprinkled the rest of the holy water there and buried Jean Bayou along with his gold for the turtle to guard, and Celestine with her misery, and—although I didn't know it at the moment—the past, both my own and one from long before I was born.

Lucille and I never did rent a metal detector to dig for Jean Bayou's gold. The day of the thunderstorm was my last visit to Bayou Road. We didn't celebrate Christmas there the next day, and within a month Lucille and Mignonne, abandoned in what suddenly felt like a drafty ruin, put the house up for sale. They moved into a cinderblock room their cousin Goozy constructed behind his tract bungalow in Destrehan, connected to the main house by a corrugated tin breezeway. With a suppressed shudder my grandmother discouraged me from visiting, reporting that

Mignonne wasn't responding and Lucille was becoming disoriented, packing her suitcase to walk back to Bayou Road to pass the dust mop, or something like that. I was in college; I couldn't relate.

Both Lucille and Mignonne died in the cinderblock room within a year after leaving Bayou Road, and my grandmother said it was for the best. I now live in another city of another state, where free-range chickens, bilingualism, drinking rainwater, recycling trash, and dying at home are the cutting edge. I have to shake my head and laugh out loud, imagining what Lucille would think. She always had something memorable to say as she stubbornly dragged the last century by a mule harness halfway into this one.

Just before my grandmother died she mailed me a clipping from *The Times-Picayune* about how some dot-com baron from San Francisco had turned the house into a bed-and-breakfast where TV stars stayed when they visited New Orleans. "Times have changed!" she scrawled under a color picture of Mary Tyler Moore sitting on the front gallery. There were photos of beige wall-to-wall carpeting around a sunken whirlpool bath in Mignonne's room, and of a swimming pool where the chicken coop used to be. I could drive into any suburb and see the same thing, so I threw the article away.

After Mémère passed away, we had the piano the LeBlancs gave her shipped up here. The fragile upright was delivered during a snow flurry, a week before Christmas, and my wife wanted to pry up the rusty spikes right away, have it tuned, and play carols on it. But I shook my head, insisting we keep it nailed shut. If only to humor me, she gave in after I told her what that Yankee soldier did the night Lincoln was shot.

The story went that the LeBlancs' grandmother had been playing it that evening, when New Orleans was an occupied city. When a Union soldier came by to warn her to stop playing because the city was in mourning, she kept right on because she didn't understand a word of English. He came around a second time, and she showed him to the door, smiling, and resumed playing. The third time he returned with a hammer and nailed the lid shut. Not a note has been played on the piano since the night Lincoln was shot, and the dank silence and defeat should stay buried in there like a ghost sonata.

For whatever it's worth, that's all I have left of home.

Every Christmas we have a small to-do here. Friends come over for something to drink, and I usually wind up seated on the revolving stool at the mute piano, telling this story about the last December on Bayou Road. And for my little boy I line up the Magi and camel along the piano lid, still searching for their star.

THE TOWER

"**L**ooks like the Summer of Love is finally over," Narda mumbles, flipping through the endless pages of a Thirty Day Notice to Terminate Tenancy. It's addressed to Ms. Penny Davenport from Grumbel & Goodfellow, Attorneys at Law. Narda collapses onto the futon sofa in the Bay window, yanks open the Tibetan-flag curtain, and stares out. The firehose nozzle of Coit Tower is spot lit above, still presiding over her life. Only tonight she sees it as a Tarot card. A zigzag of lightning is striking the tower, flames shooting out, and she is tumbling from the top window wearing a diaphanous kimono and a tiara.

She averts her gaze and, out of habit, checks the ceiling for falling elephants. Above the molding, a black-and-white frieze of elephants circles the Victorian room. She printed the woodblock elephants when she moved in, twenty-five years ago. Every year she gets up on a ladder to staple gun loose elephants back into place. Friends have died. Neighbors have been evicted. San Francisco has changed, but the yellowing procession of paper elephants remains, swaying trunk-to-tail around and around the room.

Narda slides off chunky ivory bracelets, untangles herself from a flamenco shawl, and unzips snakeskin boots. What else is in the mail?

Maybe a million dollars from a secret admirer so she can rent another one-bedroom in North Beach? No, just the Friday paycheck from the temp agency, a "Thinking of a Special Friend" card from her mother, and a singles' club brochure from MillenniumHeart.com.

"You naughty boy," Narda coos to Catscan, one of the feral cats she's rescued. "You're sitting on Grumbel & Goodfellow. But these papers are for Penny Davenport. Do you know who she is?" she asks in high-pitched baby talk, scratching Catscan's ears. "I don't. Penny died and went to Wal-Mart. She's her mother's special friend in Pasadena. I'm Narda, Narda Onyx, and nobody can throw us out."

Three whiskered noses emerge from under furniture, drawn toward her voice. "Come here, Katmandu," she calls to a regal tiger tom perching on the arm of a velvet chair. She courted him with Kibbles for a week, luring him from under an abandoned car. Catamaran is skidding along a kilim, searching for the other end of a strand of red yarn.

"I have something to tell all of you. This computer mouse named Rhoda Reuters wants to move her awful gray machines in here. She wants to scan us into a CD-Rom called 'La Bohème.' Catastrophe!" Narda claps her hands at the black Siamese leaping onto the bookcase, rocking a Chinese urn already glued back together. "Down, Catastrophe, down!"

Narda raises the curved window. At the corner the new neighbor in the stucco condo is out with his push broom and blue dustbin, sweeping the sidewalk for the third time today. He even sweeps the asphalt street and under parked cars. With his white buzz-cut and squared shoulders, she imagines him a retired colonel with a loaded arsenal, some dot-commer's daddy who wants to live near the kids. She has kept her distance.

She misses the Vecchios and Impastatos, the Lees and Hongs, who used to own the neighborhood. They hung laundry and dried their fish on the picket-fenced rooftops, and she watched their children sprouting up next to the cash registers in their corner stores. Now these same kids are selling their childhood homes for millions to Silicon Valley techno-brats, who think it so chic to live around bohemians like Narda that they kick them out and move in. North Beach is now nothing but plate-glass bistros and cafés she calls "Crayola joints." Whenever she walks in, the patrons form such a wall of milk-fed postpubesence that she feels like handing out crayons and tablet paper. Narda rounds her shoulders and shrinks into herself just thinking about them.

They make her feel old and poor.

Twenty years ago, the painted floors and collaged Frigidaire and Rube Goldberg stove pipes of her rent-controlled apartment were what North Beach looked like. But now, even to her friends, Narda's apartment is a museum, festooned with Guatemalan huipiles and Tibetan tankhas and Bhutanese ceremonial headdresses. Dressing is a matter of pulling down a costume from the wall, slipping it on, and gathering her accessories from heaping African baskets as she hurries toward the door, always late.

Narda's mother likes to tell her that she's stuck in hourly office jobs because she doesn't dress for success. "Always a temp, never a bride," she chides, as if there were any other kind of work in the city. "And you'll never catch a husband at that dog pound," meaning the SPCA shelter where Narda volunteers on weekends, bathing and de-fleaing strays she can't bring home.

But Mrs. Davenport is still talking to Penny, who ran away from the second semester of accounting at Pasadena Community College in the spring of 1967. Narda Onyx was born that summer, belly dancing in Golden Gate Park with the Rainbow Gypsies on a tab of Orange Sunshine. Still sacred is that moment in the Rhododendrum Dell. Dwarfed like Alice by huge prehistoric ferns, she vowed never to come down.

True to her visions, she has come to haunt the neighborhood, vestige of another era, emerging from the fog at the top of the hill like a wild parrot, a blur of tropical color and eccentric plumage. Charging down the slope, she seems to be rushing home, several decades late, from the ongoing costume ball the city once was. These days she is surrounded by nylon gym togs and taupe pantsuits, and she certainly isn't going to give up Narda Onyx to look like *that*. Artist friends—those few who are left—have created books and paintings and performances. She has created herself.

The French Empire phone bleats, but Narda doesn't have the strength to pick it up.

"Free Tibet!" Her voice message clicks on. "Free Leonard Peltier! Talk to me."

"And free fried chicken, too," a twangy baritone booms from the machine. "That's what I'd like to hear. Honey, when you going to change that message? I've got comps to the ballet on Friday, so put on something fabulous. . . ."

Narda grabs the receiver. "Cyrus, I'm being evicted." There is a silence, much like years ago when friends first began to confide in each other the results of their blood work.

Cyrus King finally speaks: "And now you."

"I just got the papers. The new owner, a lawyer named Rhoda Reuters, is doing an owner move-in. She's part of some real estate outfit called Dissolution Properties."

"How fitting," he says. "She'll stay just a few months, jack up the rent from three hundred to three grand, and then dissolve all our raggedy-assed properties, one by one. You'll never find anything else you can afford in this town. It's over, baby doll."

"I know."

"Next stop, Redwood City."

"Don't be cruel."

"You, of all people. This is like the death of Mick Jagger."

The henna tint takes three hours to dry, and Narda's hair is twisted into muddy red peaks when the doorbell rings. She's been chopping scallions for a stir-fry, so she races to the door clutching a meat cleaver, fumbling to fasten the frogs on her Chinese dragon robe. She peers out. It isn't Cyrus but some plaid undergrad with a bottle of Evian in one hand, a cell phone in the other, and a confused look on her face, as if she can't decide whether to hydrate or network.

Must be Greenpeace, Narda decides, opening the door.

"Hi, I'm Rhoda Reuters. You're Penny Davenport, aren't you?" the woman asks, slipping the phone into her canvas shoulder bag and stepping backward as she extends a limp hand.

"Not recently," Narda answers, aghast, clutching the dragon robe closed around her neck. The cleaver shoots toward Rhoda in an involuntary handshake as the robe flies open, exposing tiger-stripe tattooed breasts and black lace panties. "I mean not in this lifetime," she stammers, juggling the cleaver as she struggles to close the robe.

"Ms. Davenport," Rhoda whines, averting her eyes, "it's inappropriate to wave that weapon at me." A tic twitches above a lip with a Herpes sore.

"Weapon?" Narda asks with a mysterious smile. "I've been chopping up things."

"I can see." Rhoda is staring wide-eyed at the termite mound of peaked hair. Red streaks have dribbled and dried across Narda's brow and temples. From inside, a bamboo wind chime rattles like bones.

"We heard Mrs. Wong sold the building," Narda blurts out, glancing down. Above the white rubber marshmallows of Rhoda's running shoes, flea collars are buckled around both ankles. Damn, Narda thinks, she's heard about the cats.

"I feel total solidarity with where you're coming from," Rhoda says, trying to peek over Narda's shoulder into the apartment. "You must really love the place. But really, I'm sleeping on my office floor in Palo Alto, and am virtually homeless—"

"Homeless? The in-house attorney for Whoopee dot-com. I've heard you own three other buildings in the neighborhood. With all those people sleeping on the street, aren't you ashamed—"

"I'm trying to be fair," Rhoda says, her face hardening inside the expensive haircut. "You have thirty days, plus a thousand dollars for moving expenses."

"You're not evicting me from these rooms, but from this city, from my past. I could never be me anywhere else."

"Look, I'm prepared to increase the moving stipend to three thousand," Rhoda says, taking a suck on the pacifier of her water bottle, "if you vacate the unit by the first—"

"The quote-unquote unit is my home. Twenty thou. Or see you in court." Narda hopes to stall the eviction with a tenants' lawyer.

"Just where do you get your sense of entitlement?" Rhoda zeroes in, playing to the jury. "Or don't you think I have the right to live in property I've purchased?"

"The moon's not for sale. Not yet. Money's not everything. You should've thought of this before you bought a rent-controlled building in a historic district."

"You're the one who's history."

"Tough titty," Narda screams, slamming the door.

On the flat rooftop outside of the kitchen window, pigeons are goose-stepping through the drizzle like barrel-chested guards. Wrapped in gray gauze, the Golden Gate Bridge is a faint outline on the horizon. Narda is turned away from her million-dollar view, running gingery fingers through fresh auburn highlights in a waist-length mane braided with coral beads.

"Sounds like a case of the U.S. Constitution v. the goddess Kali," Cyrus says with a British accent. Dark and elongated as an African carving, he used to be a well known set-designer for the small theaters that once prospered downtown. Now he does window displays for chain department stores, and describes himself as a recovering New Orleanian and a retired snap-queen. He'd reigned in the glittery clubs on Polk Street during the heyday of disco, which is when he moved in across the hall from Narda.

Others tenants in the building have drifted over to hear about Narda's eviction. Every time she picks up the cleaver to re-enact the encounter with Rhoda Reuters, Cyrus raises the stem of his wine glass to the light and shouts, "Tough titty."

Gavin, one of the first to arrive, is the surrealist painter on the first floor who has lived in the neighborhood since the Beat era. He claims that when the planets align and a tsunami washes over the city, Telegraph Hill will be left standing as an island in an off-shore archipelago, and won't be subject to California law. They'll be able to fish for salmon from the Bay windows and bathe with sea lions in their claw-footed bathtubs.

"I have thirty days," Narda says, cutting into his monologue. Gavin is off his meds again. He's been popping the Paxil ever since his art gallery on Grant Street was bought out and turned into another ActionPac video outlet.

Kirsten, editor of a feminist press, seems as serene as a pale blond madonna behind her wire-frames. She explains that speculation and evictions have become such an epidemic that all pro-bono tenants' rights lawyers are booked solid. All Narda can do, she reasons, is to stall for more time and money. Bob Bingle, the union organizer on the second floor, agrees.

"Barter with that bitch," he barks as if addressing the teamsters, "like you was buying a rug in Morocco." One night Bingle turned up at Narda's door stark-naked to demand she turn down Edith Piaf. Ever since, she's fled at the sight of his knit navy cap. "Then grab the moola and run."

"Run where?" Narda asks. "I belong here."

"Wherever you run, Dissolution Properties will pursue you," Gavin says, cocking an eyebrow, "and turn the place into Montmartre or Greenwich Village or the French Quarter. Artists are the avant-garde of real estate."

"But isn't this the city of brotherly love?" Narda asks.

"San Francisco was nothing until the Gold Rush, and was born from pure greed," Gavin says, lighting a Rameses cigarette with shaking hands. Then he blows a smoke ring. "Just like now."

"Honey, if I can't sell it," Cyrus sings, snapping his way across the kitchen, "I'm gonna sit back on it, sure ain't gonna give it away."

A tap on the back door announces Manuelito, a chubby Mexican with a red nose who carries three bottles of wine in a paper bag under his arm. For twenty years, he ran Fandango, a flamenco club that was forced out and made into a gourmet bakery for dogs.

"*Hijos de puta.* They can't kick you out. Who will be next? Ferlinghetti? We'll do a benefit, with all the top names from Sevilla," he says, arching his arms and stamping his heels until the pots and pans hanging on the wall rattle.

Everybody feels threatened now, Narda senses. It's a matter of time before they're evicted, too. This last haven of free spirits, where their leftover worlds have overlapped and merged, will also disappear. Soon they'll be displaced like the others, people who put the city on the map, wave after wave of pioneers and innovators and creative misfits who took refuge here and made the air fizz. After the painters and editors, union organizers and flamenco dancers wander off to bed, Narda and Cyrus clean the kitchen without saying a word.

Then she creeps up to the roof. The sky has cleared, and the soaked neighborhood is silvered in moonlight. The twin spires of Sts. Peter and Paul glow blue, and the bridge beyond twinkles and beckons as it did when she was nineteen, and everything as far as she could see was youth and possibility and hope. One at a time the cats pad up the back stairs and settle in around her djellabah in a protective circle. She gathers them in against the chill.

For once in my life, she decides, I'm going to do the sensible thing.

The next morning she rises early and phones Rhoda Reuters, a porcelain cup of jasmine tea trembling in her hand. "Call me Penny," Narda says sweetly. After some good-natured bartering, she agrees to move for seven thousand dollars, half to be paid upfront, half in thirty days after she's moved. After studying the for-rent ads in the *Chronicle*, Narda calls in sick and goes back to bed for the rest of the week.

Narda looks and looks, and the cheapest apartment she can find is in the Richmond at Geary and 44th Street, a large efficiency for $1,150 a month, which would take every cent of her temp check after taxes. It's next to a Texaco station and across from a Burger King, has aluminum windows, beige acrylic carpeting that smells like Styrofoam packaging, and a Formica pullman kitchen accented with gold specks. The realtor says the owner's mother-in-law lived there until she died last month. It's a steal.

Worn down by renter's résumés, want ads, leads that go nowhere, and the feeding-frenzy that ensues whenever a livable apartment does fall vacant, Narda ties up her hair, takes off her jewelry, and puts on the checkered shirtwaist her mother sent her ten years ago that she's never worn. And goes to the renter's interview.

"Women messy," says Betty Tzu, the owner. "Cook all the time."

Narda smiles and says she eats her meals out.

"No loud music."

Narda nods.

"Boyfriend?"

"Oh, nooo," Narda coos.

"No pets."

Narda blanches and signs the lease, handing over Rhoda Reuters' initial payment for the first and last month's rent, and deposit. She saves her tears for the Geary bus, where she's taunted by gang bangers with baggy pants falling off their butts who call her an "old hippie hag." What hurts even worse is who she really feels like: Penny Davenport from Pasadena, California.

"Shriek and say you saw a mouse," Cyrus suggests. "That way you can sneak one cat in. Then spoil the others on weekends at the SPCA. Let's see, we'll do a rose marbling, with ivory trim. One thing," he says, surveying Narda's tapestried walls and overflowing shelves, "you'll have to get rid of most of this stuff. You're such an item queen. What about a garage sale? You know, go minimal for the millennium?"

"Too much is not enough," Narda groans, pulling a Quechua poncho over her head.

For three weeks, the boxes she's salvaged from the liquor store sit empty. The cats love them, jumping in and out, and whenever Narda tries to start packing, she picks up a boxful of cat. She makes a desultory effort to sift through stuff, rereading old love letters and issues of *Rolling Stone* and *Vogue* she's saved, listening to her records and washing antique fabrics in Woolite and taking things from one shelf and putting them on another. She makes a pile of relics to sell at the garage sale—a Turkish belly-dancing belt, bags made at the Auroville ashram in India, a hammock from the Yucatan, guidebooks for trips she's never taken or countries that no longer exist. In a patchouli-scented marble box, she finds a ticket stub for a Jefferson Airplane concert at the Fillmore, an eagle feather, and at the bottom, six hits of organic turquoise mescaline.

A week before she's supposed to move, Narda tries to organize a garage sale. A biting wind whips around corners as she tapes flapping APARTMENT SALE signs to lamp posts and utility poles. The only people on the busy streets who notice her wrestling with papers and tangled curls of cellophane tape are the homeless, sitting in doorways next to their overflowing shopping carts. They follow her every move with knowing expressions. And as never before, she studies the blotchy faces squinting up from their lost worlds, wondering if the only place left for her in this city is on the sidewalk next to them.

She spends the whole afternoon plastering the neighborhood with fuchsia photocopies. Walking back from the laundromat that evening, she notices her signs have been taken down. On a few posts all that remains is a ripped lip of Scotch-taped fuchsia.

The next afternoon she tries again, and within an hour, she retraces her path to find the signs gone. Returning home, she spots the colonel on a ladder, sponging graffiti from a stop sign. A wad of fuchsia is stuffed into his back pocket. And Rhoda Reuters is walking out of the front door of her building.

"Penny, love your outfit." Narda is wearing a pink tutu and torn black lace. Rhoda has the flea collars around her ankles. "Just checking. Will you be out by Monday?"

"I'm trying to get an apartment sale together for Sunday, but somebody," Narda says, her voice breaking, "keeps taking down the notices." She points her chin at the neighbor on the ladder.

Rhoda beams. "A new ordinance says no ads on public property. Isn't that great?"

"But this is North Beach, for God's sake. That's how we communicate with each other . . . lost kitty, yard sale."

"It's not upscale to have the street filled with junky old papers," Rhoda says. "Ever tried selling things on eBay?"

The day before she's supposed to move, Narda strings pastel balloons around the light post in front of her apartment and stations Cyrus on the corner in a black beret, black leather jacket, and mirrored sunglasses to guard them. The colonel paces up and down with a pushbroom and dustbin, barely able to restrain himself. Every time he starts across the street, Cyrus shoots him a menacing glare and pumps his fist in the air.

"Power to the *people*, girlfriend," he hollers across the street.

At the corner of Grant and Green, Manuelito guards a piece of butcher paper stretching between two posts that reads: APARTMENT SALE. EVERYTHING MUST GO. 512 UNION. FREE TIBET! Anyone who tries to rip it down is immediately swept into a tango that carries him halfway down the block.

Gavin is placed in front of another apartment-sale sign and descends on those attempting to tear it down with a messianic gleam in his eye and a rather large book about Egypt. An hour later they're still there, trapped inside the vaults at Luxor with an exulting Gavin.

Narda hasn't slept in three days and wears all black. Her first customer is an elderly Russian who pants up the stairs wearing a badge that reads "Asthma."

"Apartment sale?" he asks. "How much you want apartment?"

Narda gives him a tea ball and sends him on his way. Next comes a French woman with a crochet change purse who buys a saucer for a quarter, then a painter with three pairs of glasses strung around her neck who, Narda fears, has excellent taste. Almost everything she points at is not for sale.

"How much is this?" she asks, holding up the Turkish belly-dancing belt.

"Fifteen." Narda bites her lip and looks away.

"Feel the vibrations." The painter holds out the belt for Narda to touch. "So intense."

Narda cups her hand over the silver buckle and is blinded by purple-tinged ripples of light. She can smell eucalyptus and hear a joyous cacophony of flutes and drums fading through the mist. Tattered velvet bellbottoms are twirling, twirling.

"Wow," says Narda. "Twenty-five?"

The painter leaves empty-handed. So does the young couple in matching striped bicycle suits rummaging through the basket of fabrics and handbags.

"Does this look too hippie?" the woman asks her boyfriend, modeling a mirrored bag from India.

Narda does manage to sell two plastic washtubs to an enormous Samoan, who also wants to buy her nice fat cats, and a *Sticky Fingers* album with a broken zipper to a punky art student from L.A. A stream of neighborhood friends passes through to perch on the sofa, a Greek chorus of hippie spinsters who lament the fate of the neighborhood. Each leaves the potlatch with a basket or plant, reminding Narda of those wailing crones dragging their booty out of the dead Bouboulina's house in *Zorba the Greek*.

By late afternoon Cyrus, Miguelito, and Gavin have abandoned their posts and gone to Tosca for drinks. That evening they stomp up the stairs drunk, Cyrus belting out "Don't Leave Me This Way" in falsetto.

"I spend all damn day standing off Ollie North, and you hardly sell anything." Cyrus kicks his way through a jumble of boxes. "And you haven't started packing yet?"

While Miguelito is in the kitchen uncorking a bottle of wine, Cyrus tosses books into boxes. Gavin fishes each one out, opens it, and declaims a sentence at random, cackling at the uncanny significance. Then he reverently replaces the book on a shelf.

While Miguelito serves the wine, they decide the moment has arrived to mount a rickety ladder and take down the elephants. Each wants one. Everybody in North Beach wants one.

"Not yet," Narda protests. "They're still holding each other up."

"Elephants," Gavin slurs, "are one of the few animals to have burial rituals. The herd will carry each others' bones to a communal graveyard, which they tend . . . to tend."

"But what happens," Narda asks, "if an elephant loses her way and can't find the tail of the elephant in front of her and goes off in the jungle alone?"

"Elephants," Gavin says, knitting together his bushy eyebrows and staring straight at Narda, "never forget the way home."

Two days after Narda doesn't move, Grumbel & Goodfellow mails a ten-page Notice of Unlawful Detainer, and a week later comes a Breach of Contract affidavit. She files these documents under the belly-dancing belt. One evening she takes a sleeping bag, a cup, and a teakettle on the Geary bus to the apartment she's rented on 44th Street, spends the night, and swears she'll never move in. But Betty Tzu won't refund her money.

"It's the cats," Narda tells her friends. "I can't bear to bring them to the SPCA."

She refuses to open the door to Rhoda Reuters, and takes to pretending she isn't at home for anybody. She tries affirmations: the stock market will crash, she repeats, an earthquake will strike, and Rhoda will be happy to keep her as a tenant. Narda has lived in California too long to believe in the future. But that month, the Nasdaq index almost doubles, three new Crayola joints open on Columbus, and parades of tourists continue to climb the hill in front of Narda's apartment toward a postcard-view sky.

Kirsten the editor finally buttonholes Narda on the back porch, next to the recycling bin. "What comes next is the sheriff's eviction," she says in soothing tones, emptying a bag of bottles into the bin. "That means they stick a red-lettered notice on your door that you have to be out in three days. On the morning of the third day, a sheriff comes to escort you out, puts your possessions on the street, and padlocks the place."

"I'll need a Berber caravan of shopping carts." Narda twists the ivory bracelets on her arm. "Maybe I won't have to move after all."

Kirsten opens her arms in a hug.

The morning the three-day eviction notice is posted on her door, Narda takes out the boxes again.

"Get the fuck out, Catamaran," Narda explodes, trying to empty the enormous spayed cat out of a Gallo box. The cats still think it's a wonderful game.

On the evening before the sheriff's eviction, a low fog rolls in from the Bay. Foghorns are moaning, and the hall heater is blasting as she huddles on the sofa studying the wispy silhouette of the tower, listening to Bob Dylan sing "Sad Eyed Lady of the Lowlands." Half of the stuff in the living room is jutting at odd angles out of open boxes. The rest of the apartment hasn't been touched.

On top of the heap next to her is the Italian marble box. She opens it, trying to remember how long the six tabs of mescaline have been there. Did she take it with Angel, her Puerto Rican boyfriend who she hasn't seen in eight years, or with Jean-Claude in the houseboat ten years ago? She really doesn't need psychedelics anymore. Her life is already one long flashback.

She pops a tab in her mouth. That's what she'll do, stay up all night on mescaline, packing. It makes perfect sense. When she feels nothing, she swallows another. One more ought to do it—if it still works. She is in the kitchen, emptying Catastrophe out of a box, when she feels the familiar rush, a warm tingling that begins at the base of her spine and sparks out of her finger tips like electricity. She plops down in the middle of the floor, overwhelmed by the vermilion pattern in the kilim. Has red ever been so red?

"I'm home," she says to Catastrophe, who has climbed back into the box. "This is what home feels like."

Catastrophe leaps out of the box to luxuriate in Narda's lap.

"Dissolution Properties," Narda says, starting to giggle.

Catastrophe answers with the deep engine of his purr.

"Dot-com," Narda says, holding her sides. "Dot-org. That's who I'll be next time! Dotty Org from Oregon."

Catastrophe revs up his motor to match Narda's laughter.

"Sheriff's eviction," she howls. "Showdown at the dot-com corral."

A bowlegged John Wayne lumbers past with spurs jangling on his boots. "Nice Mr. Sheriff," she says, petting the cat.

Narda feels herself expanding, filling the room. She towers to her feet, as if she could meet the sky. Waltzing through the apartment, she gathers the marble box, eviction papers, and Turkish belly-dancing belt in a basket, convinced she's packing at last. Then she throws on the Quechua poncho and carries the basket up to the rooftop, where she settles like a Peruvian market woman, spreading her wares around her on the tarpaper.

"I'm ready to barter. How much will you give me for all of this?" Narda asks, gesturing along the full expanse of the horizon. The fog is beginning to lift, and the alabaster tower is backlit against midnight blue. The pastel city emerges in focus through stray tufts of mist as Narda reaches into the marble box and swallows the last three tabs of mescaline.

"Get behind me, Satan," she hisses.

She tears the stapled pages from the Notice to Terminate Tenancy, the Unlawful Detainer, and the Breach of Contract and tosses them into the air. Fluttering in gusts of wind, they drift over the edge of the roof and down to the street. A light flashes on in the colonel's window at the corner.

Narda fastens the belly-dancing belt around her waist and curls her fingers upward in an Indian dance mudra, as if to receive manna from heaven. She is surrounded by writhing cats whose sinuous bodies expand with the contours of the night. Their faces grow noses as their heads are crowned by black-and-white striped headdresses. Suddenly they are sleek, muscular Egyptians, their fur turned into swarthy skin oiled to a sheen. And they are hoisting her on a veiled palanquin up from the tar-paper and over the rooftops. Lit windows below are diamonds in a tiara slipping from her head, lost forever. I didn't rescue the cats, she flashes. They were sent here to rescue me.

Vast stretches of fleshy-pink sand gleam beneath Narda as she approaches the head of a sphinx, whose smile cracks through millennia of stone to welcome her. It is Cyrus, changed into a massive limestone cat, eyes crinkling in merriment as she arrives on a chariot drawn by four human-shaped felines. At the feet of the sphinx, a procession of elephants sways in tandem down a winding road lined with gigantic fern trees. Flutes and drums play, and on their backs the elephants are transport-ing carved sandalwood chests filled with Narda's possessions to a new country—far away—one where she has never been before.

At dawn, joggers appear one by one huffing up Telegraph Hill. A *Chronicle* delivery truck wheezes past the corner, unloading bales of headlines, and a sheriff's car creeps by, manned by yawning officers on their round of routine evictions. The street smells of espresso, and tai-lored young executives toting briefcases and cell phones filter onto the sidewalk. The colonel is busy sweeping crumpled legal documents into his dustbin, and North Beach seems clean and in good order, ready for almost anything the morning might bring.

Under the ashen tower, a fierce North African ululation rises from a rooftop, although unlike the famous howl that shattered the peace here decades ago, few actually hear it. People don't gather on the sidewalk until the wailing ambulance arrives.

Blue lights flash, sheriffs pace, radio static crackles.

"Apartment sealed but not emptied," an officer barks into a speaker. "Hold former tenant for observation seventy-two hours in Acute—over."

Finally Narda is carried out, pallid face held high in haughty profile, perched triumphantly on the shoulders of two paramedics like a queen paraded through the streets of Thebes, followed by her retinue of temple cats.

"Put that velvet chair in the foyer," she orders, pointing through thin air at the bus stop. "And the bookcase next to the mantel. Be careful with the Chinese urn. It's already cracked."

A whiff of patchouli drifts in her wake and then, like magic, is gone. Several blocks away, the police are shaking homeless people awake in doorways, and inside the elephantine gray building where someone who called herself Narda Onyx once lived, vacant eyes are frozen behind curved windowpanes. As the ambulance disappears, Cyrus King stands staring down into the empty street below, as if imagining himself in rags, trudging toward the Bay.

THE PRIZE INSIDE

Gus dreamed of swimming in money, rolling on a beach of fifties, wading through twenties up to his thighs. In the dream, he was swimming toward an eye inside a pyramid set on top of a distant lighthouse. "In God we trust," he kept repeating as he swam on through the money, only he never reached the eye in the pyramid. And he always woke up poor. Gus was proud to be working class, but as he liked to say, you couldn't be working class if there wasn't any work left.

No matter where Gus looked, nobody needed him anymore.

How he got hooked up with the Calvary Prayer Circle was through the fan man from Chalmette. Not exactly through the fan man, but through his mother—or so Gus thought. The fan man and his nineteen-year-old white girlfriend had spent three hours at his house one sweltering June afternoon hanging two ceiling fans he'd bought on sale at Home Depot. That night the phone rang at 10:30 while Gus was sprawled in his feral nest of old magazines, unmatched socks, and empty potato chip bags.

"Excuse me, but I have Caller I.D.," a lady announced in a rich contralto. "Somebody call me from this number today?"

During the afternoon, the fan man and his girlfriend hadn't been there twenty minutes before they'd each phoned their mothers. This must be the one they called MawMaw. How Chalmette can you get? Gus had thought, offering them a beer. But the fan man said he didn't want to touch anything wet, and the girlfriend was already sucking on a Slurpee, shaking her long blond hair.

"T-Red or Angeline must have called but they finished around 7:30," Gus answered, holding a swimsuit issue at arm's length. Wire-rimmed bifocals lay bent somewhere under his bony rump.

"He's my son. Angeline was there? She precious."

A real doll, Gus thought, with a two-year-old kid she had with T-Red when she was seventeen. T-Red was slight and light-skinned, his face freckled with chocolate chips. As if he'd grabbed hold of a live wire, tufts of crinkly hair shot from his scalp and glowed with an auburn sheen. While they sat on the floor putting the fans together, T-Red laid out the details of his life along with the sockets and bolts. By thirty, he'd had six other kids with two women who had skipped out on him. His oldest son was going on fourteen.

"Bet you proud of those grandchildren," Gus told the old lady. It was late and he felt like talking. His own mother had died when he was eight.

"They'll be my ruination. I pray every day he marry that girl so those seven children I look after can have some kind of mother. I send in my seed money to the Lord, and one day it going to be multiply like fishes and loaves."

"I could use a little multiplying myself. Just lost my job, and last year I had to declare bankruptcy." Until he was laid off several months ago, he'd had a good job in prosthetics, painting porcelain eyeballs.

"Pray, child. And I'll pray for you. You the Mr. Scramuzza what with T-Red was going to hang the ceiling fans?"

"August Scramuzza. Only one in the New Orleans phone book."

"I'm Mrs. Verlena Horne. Bless you. And remember, 'as ye sow, so shall ye reap.'"

A few days later the letters started coming. Whenever the postman dropped mail through Gus's front-door slot, the noise set off the toy gorilla in the hall, which started gyrating its hairy shoulders, shaking maracas in both paws, and singing "The Macarena" in a mechanical screech while Gus tore up bills.

The first envelope announced: *Something will happen . . . that has never happened before.*

"Gus Scramuzza," the letter read, "This is no accident that I have contacted you. A prophet friend told me God woke him several times in one night with new revelations. I am led of the spirit to tell you to hold onto *the seven revelations* until 24 hours from now. Place them under your bed as you sleep. Satan does not know your future, but God does, and at times He reveals it to our elderly little prayer team."

The Macarena gorilla clicked off.

Although Gus had never finished college, he suspected this was mail fraud meant to rip off old ladies living on cat food. A picture of a black couple in front of a brick house bore the handwritten testimonial: "My husband listed 7 things he wanted God to do for him. He sent it off the same day and last Sat. God blessed us with $10,700 and Mon. he went out and bought him a car. Enclosed is our seed donation."

Gus was broke. And at fifty-five, it wasn't easy to find another job. The color and shape of the artificial eye was a delicate matter. It had to exactly duplicate the real eye, and he'd been an expert at working with individual patients. When one of his eyeballs was popped into place, nobody could tell which eye could see, and which couldn't.

Now the company used computer imaging and sent the manufacturing to South Korea. Occasionally Gus did a little sign painting, but nothing steady. He lived in the house his father had left him on Piety Street in the Ninth Ward, but couldn't even afford to run the air conditioners. So Gus slept with the Seven Spiritual Revelations under his bed and the next morning sent in seven things he wanted God to do for him, along with a couple of bucks.

Not much happened that week, except the battery in his Chevy van died and he filed for unemployment. Walking down St. Charles Avenue to the unemployment office, he was caught in the first summer thunderstorm. Lightning struck the Pan American Life Insurance building just as he was darting in front of it with a newspaper over his head, and his stringy gray ponytail and red baseball cap got sopping wet. He arrived for the interview shaking. The forms he'd filled out were soggy, and his teeth chattered so much in the air conditioning he could barely answer the lady's questions. She treated him like a bum, he thought, trudging home through puddles, ready to hang himself from a ceiling fan.

Two days later the Macarena gorilla started to sing again. The unemployment notification said he would get $180 a week in benefits, and another letter marked "Confidential" contained five miracle prayer cakes.

"Dear Gus," it said. "Amazing things happen when God speaks."

During the next month Gus started dancing along with the Macarena gorilla every time the mailman passed. First came the notice informing him that he was eligible for a federal supplement since his job had been part of an industry shipped abroad under the GATT agreement. Unemployment and the supplement came to almost a thousand dollars a month. Immediately he flicked on the two rusty air conditioners, replaced the battery in his van, bought a case of Abita Amber, and put on the Rolling Stones.

Then came the letter from Pan American about his father's disputed life insurance policy.

"Out of the blue," he told his younger brother Leo, "they decided Daddy's death wasn't 'self-inflicted' but an accident."

"Out of the blue, my ass," Leo the day-trader snarled, leaning the lawn edger against the brick pillar of his carport. "I've had an attorney on contingency fee hounding their butts ever since Daddy died. Thirty percent goes to the lawyer, so that's about $17,500 left for each of us. That, with interest, is Byron and Missy's college education. God knows what you'll do with it."

Gus and Leo's father had been a member of the pipefitters, part of a generation that had made it to the middle class through union wages. He'd bought a house, owned a fishing boat and camp, and was able to send each of his two sons to college for a while. Two years ago he died in pulmonary at East Jefferson Hospital when he snuck in a pack of Chesterfields and lit up.

"Don't forget," Gus said, "I haven't even had a checking account since you bamboozled me into declaring bankruptcy to clear the hospital's liability case. All because J.P. Morgan here didn't want to lose his 'bluechip investment portfolio,'" he quoted with a sneer.

"You got Daddy's house, free and clear, and had the least to lose on the liability deal. Let's go inside. Want the whole neighborhood to know our business?"

"I don't care what Lake Vista thinks."

"We do."

Leo had moved as far as he could from the shabby shotgun houses, weedy, potholed streets, and loud corner bars of the Ninth Ward. Gus and Leo saw each other only on Christmas and Thanksgiving. Even that was a strain. Leo called Gus a loser, and his children pronounced their uncle weird after the Christmas he gave them each a slightly flawed artifical eye in a sateen carrying case. "Turkey time again," their mother Charlene would mutter under her breath, loading the dishwasher.

"How's everything on Piety Street?" Leo boomed as they settled into the breakfast nook that opened onto a lawn smooth as a putting green, bordered by beds of flaming caladiums. "Still placing those quarter bets and drinking those dollar drafts?"

Gus squirmed, feeling small and tentative across from the former linebacker, half a foot taller and a hundred pounds heavier. "I still hang at the midnight barbecue at Vaughn's on Thursdays, and sit in on the Friday evening poker game at BJ's. But I'm doing a lot of painting and going out with a new lady," Gus lied.

He took out a cigarette, then put it back in the pack.

After his father had set the emphesema ward on fire, a doctor had given Gus Prozac to stop smoking. The pills made him so euphoric he went out and found a girlfriend. Then he quit the Prozac, kept the girlfriend, and started smoking again. It was heaven, but didn't last long. Toward the end, all she'd wanted to do was talk about what she called their "relationship." Gus had learned how to cook, vaccuum, and iron after his mother died, and could do everything else for himself but the bedroom part. If nothing was going on there, why bother? You either stick it in, he reasoned, or you don't. What's there to talk about?

"For the thousandth time, lose the art and find a real way to make money. What about landscaping?" Leo asked, surveying the velvety slope of his lawn on the other side of the sliding glass door. "That's artistic."

"Remember when I had that show at the gallery on Royal Street?" For three years now, the same gray beachscape stood unfinished on the easel in Gus's living room. Everyone swore it showed talent.

"That was twenty years ago," Leo said, leaning over with a napkin to wipe a small handprint off the glass door. "Tell you what. I'll take your cut of Daddy's money and invest it on the Internet in high-yielding tech futures. I might be able to double it in six months." Charlene swept through the room with a vase of dried hydrangeas spray-painted gold, raising her penciled eyebrows at Leo. Then a door slammed. "We're expecting company. But call me at the office in the morning."

Gus trusted his brother about only one thing: money. Even though he was resigned to die poor and alone, toking on the sugar tit of his pot pipe, in his dreams he was still swimming through money toward an eye in a pyramid on top of a far-off lighthouse.

So Leo invested his brother's windfall, and by Thanksgiving it had almost doubled. With that, Gus opened a money-market account at Whitney, then renewed his unemployment and supplement. The day the ATM and Visa cards arrived, he tossed his baseball cap into the air, untied his ponytail, and danced the Macarena out onto Piety Street, rotating his legs and thrusting his pelvis until the old lady next door called the cops.

In the same mail came another letter from the Calvary Prayer Circle, with a "financial blessing pack." "Dear Beloved Gus," it began. "The credit bureau tries to predict your future by looking at your past. But God is not interested in what you did yesterday. He is only concerned with what you are doing today."

In the bookcase under the Macarena gorilla, Gus had a shoebox filled with blessed oil, half of a Xeroxed ten thousand dollar bill, a sheet of lucky numbers, a swatch of flowered prayer cloth, a red cross keychain, and magic pennies. He'd written his name three times on the prayer cards, annointed himself with the oil, carried the prayer cloth in his wallet, and placed the magic pennies on his doorsill.

Now Calvary had delivered on its promise.

His first purchase with the credit card was a half-gallon of J & B Scotch. Then he called everyone in his address book, ranting and clinking ice cubes into the receiver until everyone in his address book hung up. Then he took his new checkbook and made one out for five hundred dollars to the Calvary Prayer Circle.

The next morning he groaned as he popped three aspirins and tore up the check. But he knew someone who deserved it more. That afternoon he mailed a check for $500 to Mrs. Verlena Horne in Chalmette.

T-Red turned up the next Sunday afternoon covered with dirt and grass clippings, a power mower hanging out the back of his pickup. When he opened Gus's screen door, the first thing he did was to reach down for the shiny new penny on the sill.

"Lucky penny," he said, calling heads and flipping it. It came up tails. Then T-Red dug a crumpled paper out of the pocket of his enormous overalls. "Mawmaw had this on the kitchen table for five days. Finally I remembered you were the guy I put up the fans for, and she say, 'You go tell that poor man I don't need his money. God bless him and I appreciate it. Tell him to use it for his kids.'"

"I don't have any kids. I sent it to her because she put my name in with the Calvary Prayer Circle. Here," Gus said, trying to hand back the check, "tell her my fishes and loaves been multiplied."

"She say she don't want your money," T-Red said, twisting on a tuft of his hair. "She all with the African Methodists, and don't belong to no other church."

"Come back in the kitchen, man, and let's have a beer." They drank a six-pack of Miller, stoked the pot pipe, then started on another six-pack.

"I been blessed and want to share my blessing. Why don't we each take $250 of this money," Gus asked slyly, "and make just a *liiittle* overnight investment?"

T-Red looked away. "I stopped dealing after my baby brother got sent up. I swore to MawMaw—"

"I don't mean dealing, I mean casino. Blackjack. One-armed bandits. I always wanted to check out those casinos on the Gulf Coast. Screw Leo and his stockmarket."

While T-Red took a shower, Gus tore up the check to Mrs. Verlena Horne, wrote another for $500, and cashed it at the liquor store. As the sun was casting shadows through the tangle of bare fig branches surrounding the house, they set off in the van, following the coast toward a place T-Red had heard of, Gold Rush Casino.

Whitecaps were breaking on the dark green water as seagulls swooped through the sunset with bloody bits of chum in their beaks.

"This so damn righteous," T-Red hooted, hanging his head out the van window to study a billboard they were speeding past. "Gold Rush Casino," he read. "More Holler for Your Dollar."

"What do you want," Gus started to sing in a little boy's singsong, "when you gotta have something, and you don't know what it is. . . ."

"But you gotta have a *lot*," T-Red joined in. "And you gotta have it *now*?" they sang off-key, in unison.

"Crackerjacks!" T-Red shouted. "Hey, the old Crackerjack commercial. You having a Crackerjack moment?"

"A Crackerjact moment. But you know what I want?" Gus asked, draining a Miller and tossing the can clattering toward the back of the van. "I want to praise the Lord for his bounty bestowed. "

"You talk like church," T-Red accused. They both fell silent for a moment, then cracked up.

"Crackerjacks," they roared.

On Sunday evening, the Gold Rush Casino was humming with the silver sound of money. As Gus ascended on the escalator, every nerve in his body felt tuned to the xylophone of slot machines set at the unrelenting pitch of high C. His life dropped away from him and seemed a distant memory, like a drawerful of last year's light bills and parking tickets. The escalator shot him forward across an orange carpet printed with cowboy hats and cacti into the nave of a temple pulsing with neon. He gazed up into the cathedral ceiling aflutter with the angels of good luck, and knew this was his moment.

He was saved.

T-Red stumbled after him wearing a sucker's grin and a plastic white cowboy hat that said VIP. "Hey pardner, let's chow down first. This fun book they gave me at the VIP booth got a coupon for free food at the Wagon Wheel Buffet."

Gus looked down at T-Red as if he suddenly ran into somebody he'd known in high-school gym class, a reminder of another world. But he allowed T-Red to grab his arm and propel him through corridors of slot machines toward a flashing "All You Can Eat" sign. Obese people in extra-extra-large T-shirts were sleepwalking past aluminum troughs of congealed food, plates piled high with porkchops and boiled shrimp. Even after the rest of their slack-jawed faces had shut down, their eyes implored *more, more.*

Gus watched T-Red load his tray, and felt he was stuck with a clueless bumpkin. Seated across from each other, Gus's gangly, pot-bellied frame towered over T-Red, whose head was bent over a mound of gooey jambalaya. His dreads were bouncing as he shovelled the food in with a fork clutched in the palm of his left hand. Seven children to feed, Gus thought, and still nickel-and-diming his way through life like a teenager, whooping it up on Saturday night, then asking his MawMaw for three bucks for gas the next morning.

Even inside the restaurant, Gus could hear the *ching-ching-ching* of the slot machines sirening from outside.

"Catch you later," Gus said, standing. "Crackerjack moment. Gotta get to those machines."

"What's your hurry?" T-Red asked. "This VIP pass says they got 24-hour slot machines, video poker, live poker, blackjack . . . and a family fun center."

"Lady luck is drawing me," Gus called, already out the door.

He immediately collided with an owl-eyed blonde, cigarette hanging off her lip, pushing a change cart. Gus got forty dollars worth of quarters, and the rest in fives and singles. Then he claimed a seat next to a skeletal old man in a frayed maroon suit whose gangrenous-looking fingers were blackened by the coins he kept feeding into the slot machine.

Something else took over.

Gus's mind leapt ahead of him, as if after that first jolt of morning coffee, a first snort of cocaine. A thin wire pulled taut between the top of his head and his toes, vibrating. His eyes twitched, and his hand couldn't scoop quarters fast enough into the slots. With every fiber flexed, he was no longer in the Gold Rush Casino but was swimming through money toward the eye in the pyramid, his whole being focused on the revolving lighthouse ahead. Vodka tonics appeared and disappeared in his hand, T-Red sailed past, his plastic cowboy hat filled with quarters, while lights oscillated, cards spun, and the silver coughed and sputtered.

Soon Gus found himself in the live polka game, then at the black-jack table. He was fifty dollars ahead, then a hundred behind. *Splurge* was the word that formed on his lips, a plump titty of a word he repeated out loud as he gripped the wads of twenties from the ATM machine in his fists. "Splurge," he repeated as he leaned over to rake in the chips, then "splurge" as he doubled his bet and pushed the chips back out. Then hundreds appeared in his hands, crisp and unreal as blue Monopoly bills, and he was signing a cash advance from his Visa card because he was so close to the lighthouse, he could see the eye wink. He could win it all back. He knew he would.

And he did. For awhile.

Then he lost it. And there was a confused transaction with a personal check, another wad of hundreds, another check, then another. He didn't care what it took, he just needed to maintain himself in that vortex, on that high, eye-to-eye with *the eye*. When he saw the eye wink, he doubled his bet, fanning fifties and hundreds out before him.

Splurge, Scramuzza, splurge, the crowd roared inside his head.

Gus followed the silvery high-C note wherever it lead, ignoring what he was drinking and how much, or droopy-faced T-Red, who occasionally sidled by with one eyebrow cocked, as if to ask, *When we going?* He followed it from room to room then back again, hoping to hit that winning streak he'd had hours ago at video poker, at the $500-minimum blackjack table. He felt like a man in a whorehouse with a permanent hard-on who wandered from girl to girl but never got off, repeating and circling back, thinking each time this is going be it.

Inside the casino it was neither day nor night, summer nor winter, and the only idea he had of time was when lady luck—that owl-eyed change girl—yawned in his face.

At dawn on Monday morning, August Scramuzza hung his head as he rode down the escalator of the Gold Rush Casino, rattling the ice cubes in his vodka tonic in one hand and a plastic cup filled with quarters in the other.

That was all he had left in the world.

Spit out of the electronic doors, he staggered past a red-faced man with a gauze eyepatch struggling to unlock his vintage Impala, one of four cars left in the parking lot. The pearl-gray sky met the oyster-gray Gulf in an impenetrable sheet of oblivion. Casino lights were still wincing through the morning mist, turning the air a sickish lime-green.

As he stepped off the curb and into the sand, Gus slipped, spewing ice cubes and quarters everywhere. Then he crawled on all fours toward the soft lapping of the waves. His father's life insurance, and months of Leo's careful investment, were gone. Gus lay flat on his back cupping handfuls of sand, then letting them run through his fingers.

"Thought you'd be hungry, so I brought you these." Gus squinted up into a cheerful face, oppressive as a searchlight, a rose T-shirt announcing itself through overall straps and auburn wisps curling under a VIP cowboy hat. T-Red was standing next to a boarded-up Sea-Ski Shack, holding a large white bag that smelled like cinnamon.

"Hit the jackpot, crackerjack?" T-Red asked. "Me, I still got $49.50, more than when I started out yesterday."

"Help me up," Gus demanded, holding out a hand that reeked of sweaty quarters. That was all he needed, breakfast with the fan man. Next Mrs. Verlena Horne and the heavenly hosts of Calvary would form a circle to pray over him.

After T-Red had hoisted him to his feet, Gus began to spin, his cyclopean bulk twirling through the sand, arms akimbo, whirling like a dervish along the horizon. Offshore lights flashed and sea gulls shrieked as he eloquently marked a string of zeros through the wet sand.

"I got to get back to New Orleans by 7:45 this morning," T-Red called to Gus, starting to stumble and fall. "My kids need me to take them to school."

Gus steadied himself, then lunged toward T-Red, nostrils flaring. "*Who* needs you?" he shouted in his face. "You barely make enough money for gas and beer."

"My kids," T-Red answered, backing away. "Mawmaw and Angeline do. Need me to be there. You a rich white man living by his own self, without a care in the world. But let me tell you something—my little eight-year-old Tamara, we took her to the eye doctor on Friday. She got a new pair of pink-colored glasses she so proud of, if she don't show up at school this morning with those glasses, she just about die."

"You have $49.50 to your name. Think anybody fucking cares whether you live or die?"

T-Red stared at the bakery bag in his hands. "You ride me, or I start hitching right now. I got nine people . . . to my name," he spit out. "Don't nobody need you to be somewhere?"

The sun rose like an aggravated red sty. Shielding his eyes, Gus stared across the water. Far out in the Gulf a rickety wooden pier was lined with fishermen. They were pulling in redfish hand over fist, filling bucket after bucket with flapping fins and tails, scales gleaming like silver in the first glint of sunlight. His father had spent every spare moment with a fishing line in his hand, and what did it amount to? Gus turned and shuffled across the empty expanse of sand, trying to come up with any real reason to drive back to Piety Street.

Nobody was waiting for him, there or anywhere, not even a cat or dog to feed.

Running hands through his pockets, he yanked out fistsful of credit-card and ATM receipts that then fluttered behind him in the breeze. He finally found the car keys, attached to a red plastic cross. Some folks were born rich, he thought, eyes narrowing with the approaching hangover, some born poor. Funny, but no matter how much money they happened to have, nothing ever changed that. Poor people worked as hard to get rid of money as rich people did to get it.

T-Red appeared at his side, sunrise illuminating his electric locks into a coppery nimbus. The VIP cowboy hat he carried was brimming with raisin buns oozing glazed sugar. He handed Gus a pastry, still as warm and fresh as morning. Everywhere people were eating thousands like it pouring from ovens, heaped in bakeries, miraculously covering dashboards and desktops and kitchen tables like sticky manna. But Gus was still scanning the horizon for the eye in the pyramid, thinking about all the money he didn't have, and when he went to eat his later, it had melted.

The Night After Christmas

Mother leaned over inside the vinyl booth, all the diamonds on her arthritic fingers glinting at once. "Think your sister's on dope?"

"Mary Ellen?" I snickered. "Come on, she's an ex-therapist on Prozac. She doesn't need anything else to make her crazy."

It was the night after Christmas and freezing-ass cold outside. Mother had picked me up at Louis Armstrong International Airport, so shrunken she could barely see over the dashboard. Through alternating gusts of sleet and rain, we inched our way down deserted suburban streets lined with the tinselly skeletons of Christmas trees tossed on their sides and plastic bags disgorging tangled red ribbons and crushed toy boxes. Now, over my dead body, we were sitting under a golden Buddha strung with blinking red and green lights at the Hao Tai-Tai restaurant in the Metairie Plaza Shopping Center. The last time I'd eaten in a Chinese restaurant, during a late-afternoon lunch with my lover Don, he hit me with his diagnosis. At that exact moment, the manager decided to drain and clean the tropical fish tank next to our table. While one waiter served our meal, another was suctioning up stinky strands of green goop as my mind reeled with Don's treatment plans.

"After that," I told Mother, "I swore I'd never set foot inside a Chinese restaurant again."

"Just because your roommate died?" Mother's eyebrows shot up. "That's no excuse."

"But for months I've been dreaming of oyster dressing and candied yams."

"Don't they know how to bake a turkey up North?"

"Not like yours."

"Well you're too late," Mother said, unwrapping her chopsticks. "I don't cook anymore. I gave all my pots and pans to Mary Ellen, who never uses them. That daughter of hers is being raised on fast food, and now only eats shrimp fried rice. So Chinese it has to be."

We were waiting on my sister and her eight-year-old daughter Brittany, an hour late and due in any minute from Lake Charles. My mother was sipping a Mai Tai with a red umbrella in it, and had a copy of my historical novel about New Orleans on the table in front of her.

"My son here wrote this book," Mother informed the Cantonese waitress in the brocade jacket as she handed us menus. "It's a story about his grandparents—my mama and daddy—and their parents, too. He's even got the Civil War in it."

"Wah, the Silver War." The young woman giggled. "Make a lot of money, I bet."

Leafing through the menu, Mother started back in on Mary Ellen. "Promise me one thing. That you'll never put anything in those story books about your sister."

"You think she's a fascinating nut case because she's your daughter," I blurted out, tired of the subject before we even started. We'd already picked over censored details of my life.

"One thing I want to know," Mother had asked the minute we sat down, "does your principal allow you to wear those gold earrings?"

"My principal? These," I said, tugging at my ear lobes, "are acceptable male dress in university teaching."

"A male dress? That's not acceptable. I don't even wear a dress anymore."

Now it was my sister's turn. "I wouldn't want it to get out what she said about your father after he died. That's something they could trace back to me." My mother straightened her frail frame with dignity. She had shriveled to the size of a fifth-grader sticking out of a baggy pink pants suit. The air around us was bubbling with hilarity. Booths were filling with elderly ladies wearing too much lipstick and plastic candy-cane corsages, escorted by jocular old gentlemen in plaid sport coats. A bovine woman with a bouffant hairdo and a name tag was wandering among tables with a clipboard.

"Mary Ellen isn't the only one," I assured Mother, "who paid some hypnotist to make up a recovered memory."

"Your father worshipped the ground she walked on," she enunciated, rapping her knuckles on the table.

According to the therapists, Daddy's whole generation liberated concentration camps, saved Europe from fascism, studied on the GI bill, bought ranch houses, and then raped their daughters. Every so often my sister would present Mother with yet another theory about why she turned out like she did, smug as a cat dragging home a dead mouse. "My life is your fault" was the jist of her line of therapy. The latest dead mouse she'd dumped in my mother's lap was that Mary Ellen broke up with her boyfriend because she was the "adult child of alcoholics."

"I'll drink to that," Mother told me she had said, lifting a tumbler of Sprite. Once every six months my parents managed to finish a fifth of discount bourbon, if that, which they kept on a kitchen top shelf along with a dusty bottle of pink champange they'd saved for over twelve years, waiting for some special occasion that never arrived. Yet Mother was bawling when she phoned to tell me that my sister had called her a drunk.

"Like they say, the statue of limitations on blaming your parents," I said, "runs out at thirty." That made Mother cackle. Then shrieks of laughter arose from the booths around us, followed by a spatter of applause.

"Mother, Franklin, Merry Christmas! Look, let me get off the phone, and I'll be with you in a sec." Mary Ellen finally made her entrance, dragging two bulging Sak's shopping bags with one hand and cradling a cell phone to her ear with the other. Scowling, her daughter Brittany lagged behind, a sweater stuffed between the shoulders under her jacket.

"Nick, listen, where I'm at now is the Hao Tai-Tai in Metairie Plaza. Why don't you come by and have a drink with us so I can reimburse you. You saved my life . . . Sure, I'd love to see you again, too . . . In a while, then. Bye."

Mary Ellen slid into the booth with an exasperated sigh and then slipped the cell phone into her purse. I barely recognized my sister from last summer. Her new hair color illuminated the booth like a klieg light.

"You'll never guess what happened to us. We ran out of gas five miles from here in a sleet storm. The car just—*ploop*—died. And all I had was seventy-eight cents. This nice man, Nick, comes along. . . ."

"He's hooor-rible!" Brittany shrieked. "Got a big thing like this on his back."

Bent over like a crone, she was scurrying between the tables with the sweater bunched up under her jacket.

"OK, when Nick was a substance abuser in the French Quarter, he was run over by a beer truck so now he's just five feet tall. Before he was six something. Anyway, his spine collapsed so he's sort of like a hunchback."

Brittany was down on all fours now, screeching, with her butt up in the air. "He drives to get us ten dollars of gas at Texaco," Mary Ellen said, "puts it in the tank, and I invited him to come have a drink with us so I can pay him back. Mother, can you lend me ten dollars? Take it out of my Christmas money, all right?" Mary Ellen lowered her eyes to arrange the shopping bags under the table with a defeated look I'd never seen before on my little sister.

"You mean to tell me," Mother shouted, gathering strength from her stomach like a Sumo wrestler, "you set out on an automobile trip from Lake Charles on these icy roads with seventy-eight cents to your name and not enough gas in your car to get to Metairie? Traveling alone with that baby? And now you've invited a dwarf to have dinner with us?"

"Care for cocktail?"

The waitress was back, placing a menu in my sister's hands and staring down with a forced smile at her little hunchback daughter. "She need special facility?"

I grabbed Brittany by the collar and placed her howling on the seat next to me. She was squirming monkey-faced as I yanked the sweater out from under her denim jacket. Mary Ellen cooed, "Go kiss Mémère hello, sweetheart," as she excused herself to the restroom with a Louis Vuitton bag slung over her shoulder. I passed the sobbing child to my mother, who assumed a familiar expression as she gathered the crumpled girl into her matchstick arms.

After she had quieted her granddaughter and was taking a comb to her matted mane, Mother looked at me with a grimace halfway between mock gravity and irrepressible laughter, and then called back the waitress.

"Might as well have a second one of these Mai Tais, hon, since my daughter thinks I'm such a big lush."

Brittany asked for some quarters and went to play the claw machine in the lobby. The piano struck up "Happy Days Are Here Again" and several couples slid out of their booths. The ladies took the gentlemen's arms as they high-stepped it into the bar, wiggling their polyester behinds.

I hadn't eaten a bite since I stuffed a croissant into my face at the Newark airport at nine that morning. Then in Atlanta I had to scamper from Concourse A to D to make the connection. Mother had promised we'd drive straight to a restaurant, but nobody seemed interested in eating. I flicked open the heavy menu, and then caught the waitress's eye.

She held up her hand, as if to say *just a moment*. The place was packed. I couldn't order a platter of scallops in black bean sauce just for myself in a family-style Chinese restaurant. That wouldn't be right.

"What's this, a convention?" I asked, looking around.

"Must be a holiday package," Mother said, "like the tour I took with your Uncle Goozy's third wife last spring. I noticed they have a piano and dance floor in the bar when we came in."

I waved the menu at another waitress as she marched straight past us. Maybe we could start with the fried calamari.

"Mary Ellen's probably in there right now, " I said, "fox-trotting with the dwarf."

"I'd rather see her fox-trotting with dwarves than sitting around the house all the livelong day steaming about how everyone else has ruined her life. I mean, she's the one who decided to take her student loan to study poor people and spend it on that nose job. Don't look at me. Now that would make a good story, don't you think?"

"We're not even Jewish. Catholic girl gets nose job to better serve the needy? Get a load of that nozzle on Mother Teresa. It wouldn't sell."

A waitress finally scurried over, pen poised.

"We'll start with an order of egg rolls." I slapped the menu down.

"Anything else?" she asked, glancing at Mother. "Want entree now?"

"Not now, honey. We'll wait until my daughter and granddaughter get back. They're off somewhere in there." She waved her hand toward the bar, then turned to face me. "Come on. That's an interesting story. Put in that part about how she had to advertise those abused twins on the TV show in Lafourche Parish."

"My sister, the incest worker. Until she realizes she forgot to have a baby, hooks an oil-platform engineer, who she divorces a few months after the child is born because. . . What was it little Brittney asked me a few years ago? 'What's a mature jaculator? Mommy says Daddy's a mature jaculator.' Mary Ellen said that in front of her five-year-old."

I fished around inside the pockets of my blazer for the packet of pretzels the stewardess had handed me with the Coke, then ripped open the cellophane with my teeth.

Mother bristled, staring straight ahead. "Talk about child abuse. Imagine having to spend half the week with one parent, half with the other. What do you call that? Shared . . . ?"

"Custody." I crammed a pretzel into my mouth, running my tongue over the salty crust. "And do you know what your darling granddaughter did in my custody last summer when I took her to the petting zoo at Audubon Park?"

"What?"

"She kicked the llama," I sputtered with a mouthful of pretzel.

"She didn't."

"She did. She said the animals on TV were much better." I balled up the cellophane, searching my pockets again.

"I know better than to expect any more grandkids," Mother said, shaking her head as she studied my receding hairline and salt-and-pepper goatee for any signs of potential lingering in her hopeless bachelor.

"Would the lovely lady care to dance?" This florid geezer in an emerald blazer was shifting from one foot to the other in front of us with a Bud Light in his hand. His tag read: "Hello! My Name's Napoleon Tatum."

"That's so sweet of you," Mother gushed, "but we're all set to have a family reunion. This is my son Franklin who flew in this evening from New Jersey, where he teaches history at the community college. And my daughter Mary Ellen just drove in from Lake Charles."

"People call me Uncle Na' Tatum, and we're senior citizens getting together after having to put up with our children all day yesterday. Just kidding. We call ourselves the Turkey Trotters, and decided to come to a Chinese place 'cause we couldn't stand to look at no leftover turkey today."

I peered over the old man's shoulder, scanning the room for my eggrolls. I could almost taste a sandwich of leftover turkey, slathered with mayonnaise and scarfed in front of an opened refrigerator the night after Christmas.

"I'm Vergie Dordain." Mother's taut face lit up as she twirled the umbrella in her Mai Tai. "Looks like y'all having a lot of fun. My son won't believe me, but we cut up more than the young folks when we go out. They're so serious these days. Everything has to be such a big deal, a 'relationship' or whatever they call it."

"We didn't have all of them communicative diseases like they got now," Mr. Tatum said.

Here was the waitress, at last. The egg rolls were charred, but I picked one up. On its way to the mustard dip, the greasy egg roll slipped out of my chopsticks and skidded onto the floor.

From the bar swelled a chorus of "Bye, Bye Black Bird." There was hooting and applause, as if some old dame had claimed the dance floor with a shimmy. I reached down to the carpeting, grabbed the egg roll between two fingers, and bit into it. Mother's eyebrows shot up to her hairline.

"Come on, Mr. Tatum." She hoisted herself up with both hands. "Let's go show them how to do it. Looks like those Mai Tais just reached my arch supports."

Two burned egg rolls did not hit the spot. As I started to peel the label off my Heineken, I was carried back to the smells of fresh pine and simmering gravy in my grandparents' shotgun house on Christmas day, a gas heater flaring under the chimney hung with chunky red stockings embroidered in green with our names. The roasting turkey would draw everyone toward the linoleum-floored kitchen, until Mémère shooed us out. After Don's funeral in November, I'd hoped Christmas at home would be . . . Christmas, but Brittany had to spend the big day with her father and his new girlfriend's family.

My luggage was still in the trunk of Mother's car. Our lives didn't fit together anymore.

I drifted through the bar, where Mother and Mr. Tatum had joined a group at the piano. "I'm dreaming of a white Christmas," they were singing, "just like the ones I used to know." Mary Ellen waved me over to where she was flirting with Quasimodo in a Santa Claus cap. I pretended to misunderstand, waved vigorously back, and rushed into the lobby, where a fat, freckled kid was playing the claw machine.

"The little girl went thataway," he said, pointing.

I found Brittany back near the kitchen door, hiding in the shadow of a plastic dieffenbachia. She was staring at the round table in the corner where the elderly owners were having dinner with their children, who did the cooking, and with their grandchildren, who were the waiters. A moon-faced baby was being bounced on laps and chopsticks were flying over round white bowls as steaming platters of shrimp, chicken, and clams revolved on a lazy-Susan at the center. They glanced around at each other as they were eating, but no one interrupted the nurturing silence of clacking chopsticks. Our waitress caught my eye and stood up, embarrassed. She said something in Cantonese to her family then rushed toward me.

"Ready to order yet?"

"As soon as everybody gets together. I'm starving. You hungry yet, Brittany?" I took her hand, smiled and winked. "Why don't you go round up Mémère and your mother so we can eat?"

"Nooooo," she whined, pulling away from me into the dieffenbachia. I gave up, leaving her to gawk at a real family sitting down to eat a meal together as if they were some rare species of crustacean masticating on the Discovery Channel.

I slipped out to the parking lot, my breath hanging in a cloud before me, leaving my family parked in the restaurant like Christmas trash on the curb. At the moment, I was toying with the idea of catching a cab to the French Quarter, where I could bite down into a shrimp po'boy or something else that tasted like home. Stepping behind the Scenicruiser that must have bused in the Turkey Trotters, I unwrapped a thin joint from my United boarding pass. Time to run away from home again, I told myself, firing it up.

When we were kids, Mary Ellen and I had run away from home. One afternoon we just packed a little red valise and skedaddled to the bus stop, just like that, then hid under an oleander bush in front of a raised double. We checked out people's shoes getting on and off the bus, but didn't have fourteen cents between us to get on. Mary Ellen was clutching the red valise, and I was doodling with a stick in the mud. The damp ground was littered with cigarette butts and gum wrappers, and we crouched there way past suppertime, streetlight filtering down through white blossoms that smelled like birthday-cake icing. We wanted every day to be our birthday, and we'd just figured out it wasn't. Somewhere down the line, we learned the luscious oleander flowers were poisonous.

Where else but home, I wondered, did we think there was to go?

Just as I yanked out the cell phone to call a taxi, a snowflake settled on the sleeve of my navy-blue blazer. I looked up, blinking, as the sky filled with fuzzy white chips fluttering down through the glaring security lights. Turning in a circle, I stood in the middle of the parking lot as the snow drifted down around me. The last time it snowed in New Orleans on Christmas had been in 1965, when I was seven. Awestruck, I'd scooped up the cold white powder from the sidewalk to make a snowball that I kept in the freezer until my mother asked what that dirty hunk of ice was doing there. She thought it would make the hamburger meat go bad.

"Oh my gawd," shrieked a woman in a black rabbit coat walking out of the restaurant. "It's snowing." Then she raced back inside.

The snow was beginning to nestle inside the gigantic cupped leaves of the elephant-ear plants next to the door. Soon everyone inside the restaurant was out in the parking lot with their cocktails, looking up at the sky and reaching out to touch snowflakes with their fingertips.

"It's snowing, Uncle Franklin." Brittany raced up to grab my legs. "I've never seen it snow in real life." Then she ran around trying to catch snowflakes on the tip of her tongue.

Of course, I was used to slugging through the yucky stuff in Newark, but to see it snow in the parking lot of a Chinese restaurant in New Orleans the night after Christmas was like witnessing it for the first time, too. Even the rowdy Turkey Trotters had fallen silent, arms tentatively outstretched, as if trying to caress a lacy wraith that had suddenly appeared among us.

Soon I was joined by Mother and a flushed Mr. Tatum, by Mary Ellen with her dwarf in a ratty Santa Claus cap. We were beaming like fools, embracing each other and jigging around on top of the crunchy tarmac.

"Wait a minute," Mother said. "Nobody is ever going to believe this." Out of her handbag came the old Brownie, then she and I and Mary Ellen and Brittany were entwining arms in a pose in front of glistening elephant ears as Mr. Tatum snapped a picture.

And let me tell you something about that photograph. Although it was the last photo ever taken of us together, believe it or not, we look like the happiest family in the world. That was why I had it enlarged and framed, and then hung it in my living room. The picture elicits a smile from everyone who sees it. "You must come from a great family," people say, or "You guys look so close-knit." The snow is flurrying around us, dusting our shoulders and heads with sparkling cut crystal as we hug in a snug mass of pink cheeks, flashing eyes, and gaping grins. If I close my eyes, I can still see the flurries of snow spiraling around in the parking lot of that Chinese restaurant. It's like the glass snow dome I used to take down off the chimney mantel at my grandparents' house on Christmas Eve, turning it upside down over and over again, mesmerized by those old-timey carolers under the street lantern, the flakes whirling and whirling as if they would never stop.

SAFELY HOME

T hat was one way to get rid of wrinkles, Adrienne thought, contemplating her aunt's waxen face. Osterhold had done a beautiful job. Silver hair was swept back from the powdered profile as if Tante Sis were entering a wind tunnel, her aquiline nose jutting forward to lead the way. Adrienne hoisted herself to her feet from the prie-dieu stationed next to the coffin. Her son Jerome, who had the nerve to ride his yellow bicycle to the funeral, was next in line to bid Tante Sis good-bye.

Like most of the women in her family, Adrienne Raby was olive-complexioned, small-boned, and probably would live too long. Tante Sis Lanoux had been ninety-seven and decided to die only after she heard a social worker at the hospital whisper "nursing home" to the doctor. That evening she sat up in bed to announce she was either going home or to heaven. The only replies were indulgent smiles and the laugh track from a sitcom. So she threw the hand cream, Kleenex box, and water glass from her nightstand to the floor, lay back, shuddered twice, and by morning, was dead.

In the hospital bed she had resembled an ancient doll wrapped in tissue paper, but dominated the room with her tart, high-pitched voice just as she had the Lanoux family house where Adrienne grew up. During the Depression, after Adrienne's father had abandoned his family rather then watch them starve, her mother took both of her children to live in Tante Sis's dilapidated shotgun house on North Miro Street in the Faubourg Tremé of New Orleans. The two sisters—one unmarried, the other eventually widowed—had lived there ever since, until Adrienne's mother died three years ago at ninety-two. That was when Tante Sis fell, broke the other hip, and had to walk balanced between both of her parents' silver-handled canes. At home she refused to use a walker, and swung her way through the house by bracing herself on one massive piece of furniture after another, chattering like a rhesus monkey to a series of sitters, none of whom lasted long.

"She so mean she wouldn't give the toilet a good shit," one of them told Adrienne the afternoon she quit. That disagreeable image stuck in Adrienne's mind as a pretty apt description of her aunt's character. It came back to her when she tried to explain to her cousin Yvette LeBlanc why Tante Sis entered Mercy Hospital to begin with. "Tante Sis," as she finally put it, "hasn't gone to the bathroom in three months. She's got blockage."

After Adrienne had settled herself in a funeral-parlor arm chair next to her blind friend, pudgy Yvette ran up red-faced, a hand cupped over her mouth.

"You'll never guess what I just did?" she giggled. Adrienne could see it coming: death made Yvette giddy. At the funeral of Adrienne's husband, something the priest said set off Yvette until she had to put her head between her legs. "I introduced Jerome as your brother . . . instead of your son. Either you're looking much younger today, or he's looking a lot older," she said with a guffaw that turned heads.

Adrienne's face froze.

Out of the corner of her eye she caught sight of her son across the room. Jerome had just come home after eight years in Italy, an up-and-coming painter whose canvasses hung in some of the best galleries in the Warehouse District. Yet he'd embarrassed her again this morning, turning up in a striped biking jacket with muddy socks and green running shoes. Even though she'd given him the money to get his teeth fixed, they still looked like day-old apple cores.

At sixteen, her brother Jerome's white teeth had flashed in his dark Creole face when he smiled. He had been artistic, too, an Eagle Scout who helped out with a paper route, supplementing Tante Sis's salary as a clerk at the Sewerage and Water Board. Jerome had been Adrienne's guiding star until that Thanksgiving evening of 1938.

"Mama," Jerome asked, appearing at her side as if silently beckoned, "how are you taking this?"

"Tante Sis is safely home at last, isn't she? You've never met Herence Summers, my brother's closest friend."

Herence rose unsteadily in the direction of Jerome's voice, and held out his hand. Then he began to feel Jerome's forty-year-old face, lingering over the scraggly beard and squeezing his shoulders, as if to measure his height and weight. Jerome stared into the blind man's mirrored glasses, as if he were studying his own image.

"You're about as tall as Jerome would have been, same build," Herence said in a hesitant croak. "I hear you're quite a painter. Jerome was creative, too." Adrienne, who had remained dry-eyed all morning, reached into her purse for a handkerchief.

"Mama not only gave me her brother's name but all of his art books and sketches. Seems my fate was sealed before I was born." While his mother dabbed at her eyes, Jerome rested his hand on the blind man's shoulder. "I did everything he'd done, slept in his bed, played with his toys. One thing I've always wanted to know. When Jerome was sixteen he was run over delivering newspapers on Thanksgiving evening. Who did it? Did the cops ever catch them?"

"Catch them?" Herence stepped back from Jerome's embrace.

"Mama never talked about—"

"Jerome, don't go bringing that up now at Tante Sis's visitation." Adrienne's eyes narrowed to pink slits.

"Nobody had to catch them," the blind man said. "They're still here, right now. Doyle Osterhold and his brothers got drunk at Thanksgiving dinner. Then Doyle, with his brand-new driver's license in his wallet, decided to take the hearse on a joyride to the Fair Grounds. The horse races started that day, and Jerome was finishing his route, riding his bike home—"

"You mean the Osterholds, the people who own this mortuary where we've come for every funeral since I can remember, killed my uncle?"

"Doyle never joined the business," Adrienne cut in. "This morning I had to deal with his brother Tilden in the office. He said Doyle never got over what he did." She stood up, tucked the handkerchief into the pocket of her black jacket, and took Herence's arm. "And I told him, 'Tilden, neither have I.'"

"Would the family now prepare for the final viewing," a matronly woman announced, "then gather in the chapel for the funeral Mass."

Adrienne recovered her composure in front of the casket, admiring Tante Sis's hairdo and makeup. As mourners filed past and left the parlor, Jerome stood alone in the April sunlight spilling in from Canal Street through the floor-to-ceiling windows. He stared as two employees with Osterhold crests on their maroon jackets closed the lid, shifted flower stands, and wheeled the casket out of the room. While men in white jumpsuits carried the flowers out, an orange-haired woman with a mole on her chin plugged in a vacuum cleaner. As the machine began to whirr, Jerome scratched his scalp, and then drifted in green running shoes across the plush carpet and into the chapel.

. . .

Adrienne rolled up Tante Sis's hooked throw rug, wondering who in the world would want that old thing. She leaned the rug in a corner next to the vacuum cleaner, then tightened the flowered kerchief around her gray curls, fresh from the beauty parlor. She still had to go through two more closets and the chifforobe she'd used as a girl. Adrienne wished when people died, their belongings disappeared with them.

She'd always hated mopping the cracked yellow linoleum in the kitchen, and wanted to fall on her hands and knees to tear it up at last, piece by piece. It had been there since the year she married, and when was that, forty-one years ago? The dining room floor was still wet, and through the sheer film of marquisette curtains, a leaden sky cast a grizzly light over the chairs stacked upside down on the dining room table. She took a root beer from the refrigerator, packed with nothing but cookies and candy, and sat in a dry patch watching dust motes dance in the air.

The upturned chairs looked as if they were kneeling in prayer. For years on Ash Wednesday Tante Sis would turn all the cane rockers and dining room chairs upside down like this. It used to frighten Adrienne how Tante Sis, Mother, and her brother would run around with ash crosses smeared on their foreheads wringing out rags and turning everything upside down. They gave up dessert during Lent, and on the first night not eating ice cream or cookies became confused in Adrienne's mind with her aunt turning the furniture over.

"Because we've sinned," Tante Sis had explained to Adrienne, "and must ask God for forgiveness."

"What's that mean?" Adrienne asked, a six-year-old asthmatic wheezing next to the sideboard, watching Tante Sis place damp rags on the underside of cane seats.

"Means we've been bad and have to pay for it. Go wet another dishrag and bring it to me."

"I haven't been bad."

"Yeah you have, bad as they come."

Adrienne was never sure if they paid for being bad by not eating dessert, or by turning the furniture upside down on Ash Wednesday. By the next morning, her fairy-princess carnival costume would be put away in a dress box, the glass beads she caught from the floats swept off her chifforobe, and the chairs and rockers set right-side up, as if the world had been cleansed of sin. She grew to dread Mardi Gras, when they would spend all day eating ham sandwiches and screaming themselves silly as parades passed in front of Krauss department store. She knew how it would end, in silence and disapproval with the chairs upside down.

A sudden gust of wind slammed the side-gallery door shut, and from the yard Adrienne could hear the patter of rain on the wash shed roof. She crossed the groaning floorboards, still not dry, and began to wrap the china from the glass cabinet in newspaper. This blue Wedgwood set, her grandparents' wedding presents, went to Yvette who, like Tante Sis, didn't marry and would never have her own. They were used only on Christmas and Thanksgiving. As a girl, Adrienne also came to dread Thanksgiving, with this china, the crystal decanter filled with sweet wine, and these chipped porcelain serving dishes. All were part of the unspoken accusation that she was responsible for what happened to her brother. Her hero and protector.

She had been watching a double feature with Claire Waguespack at the Loew's State Theater on Canal Street after that Thanksgiving dinner. When the picture show let out Jerome was supposed to meet her in front of the movie house. The surprise was that Tante Sis came for her right after the police car arrived at North Miro with the mangled bicycle. Tante Sis marched up and down the aisles until she spotted the two ten-year-olds—right in the middle of a tap dance number—then made Adrienne say good-bye to her little friend. Claire promised to tell Adrienne how the movie turned out.

Tante Sis broke the news at the Desire streetcar stop in front of Lord's Dress Shop. "Jerome has gone home to God," she whispered, then closed her eyes. Her face was as impenetrable as a Mardi Gras mask or a plaster saint.

"Why?" Adrienne asked, clutching her nickel carfare.

"Because God loves him more than we did," she replied, eyes still closed. Tante Sis said nothing more during the streetcar ride, or during the walk home under the looming live oaks along Esplanade. After the funeral at Osterhold's, Jerome's clothes were given away, his books, sketches, and toys stored in boxes in the wash shed.

And his name was never mentioned again inside the house.

Not until Adrienne married Johnny, home from the war in Europe, and then held their only child in her arms, was she able to pronounce "Jerome" again. Eventually, her son looked up and responded to that name. Jerome was home again, but not for long. It took her five years of therapy to forgive her son for running away from home at sixteen to live in an "art commune" in the French Quarter filled with half-naked dope fiends and demon worshippers. She'd seen them with her own eyes, leering at her from behind beaded curtains. After her only visit to the decrepit building, she'd sat parked on Decatur Street leaning on the horn and screaming to everyone on the sidewalk that "my son is a degenerate, a degenerate." Scratching his scraggly beard, her doctor had smiled and diagnosed the problem as a "generation gap." Tante Sis just sighed and said, "Boys will be boys." Jerome finally came to his senses, graduated from high school, and then managed to go as far away as an airplane could fly.

Adrienne jumped up as the side door behind her swung open, and the front wheel of a yellow bicycle protruded into the dining room. Then her son's face emerged from the hood of a bright yellow slicker as he shook rain out of his long, wet hair.

"Don't tell me you rode that thing in this downpour. Leave the bike outside. I just mopped this floor."

"Think it'll be safe here on the side gallery?"

"This neighborhood isn't as bad as when I had your father put up the burglar bars. Families are moving back. The phone has been ringing off the hook with agents wanting to look at the listing. I wish we could keep this house in the family, you know."

"We covered this territory after the funeral," Jerome answered from the porch, steadying against the railing a ten-speed Coppi he had shipped from Italy. "Sorry I can't take over Tante Sis's house," he said, hanging his raincoat on the door, "but I need space and light."

"You live in a warehouse filled with river rats. Sleep on a mattress on the floor. That's not a home. You've never had a real home, ever since you left. Look, there's plenty of light here," she said, flicking on the chandelier in which all but two bulbs were burned out. "And space," she said, her voice rising, gesturing around the wallpapered room cluttered with marble-topped furniture that dwarfed her. "You'd have it all to yourself, not like when all four of us lived in these rooms with no doors between them. You know how shotguns in the Tremé are for privacy. We lived right on top of each other, and—"

"Tante Sis's house always reminds me of the *pensione* I lived in for months at a time, that same mix of antiques and kitsch." Jerome picked up the pink swan filled with plastic daisies on the sideboard.

"Paint it purple for all I care, put in track lighting and a jacuzzi," Adrienne said, wrapping the decanter in want ads. "You should see how young people are fixing up these old places."

"I need my part of the money for painting," Jerome said. "I promised to help you pack." Standing next to her, he lifted a gold-rimmed candy dish. "Can I ask you something?"

"Go ahead."

"Why didn't you ever let me know the Osterholds killed your brother?"

"Listen, nobody ever told me anything when I was growing up. Children were meant to be seen and not heard. These aren't . . . secrets, they're just normal things that happen to normal people that we never understand. They get blown out of proportion, become—"

"How could they have your brother's funeral at the business of the drunken guys that ran over him? Not to mention Daddy's, Nana's, and now Tante Sis's. Talk about morbid."

"Why do you think? Because we didn't have any money, and they buried Jerome for free. And now it's like doing business with family. Tragedies bind people together, even the ones who should hate each other. In the end that's all you have, not cups and saucers," she said, jamming dishes into the box, "but people, no matter what part they played in your life."

Adrienne had grown to love Tante Sis when she found herself turning into her. She came to dote on the two old sisters in the shotgun house, scraping by on the Sewerage and Water Board pension. They refused to leave when the area became a slum, or even later, when agents started hounding them to sell. After her mother died, Adrienne invited Tante Sis to share her condo near the airport. Tante Sis wouldn't hear of it. Adrienne was relieved, hired sitters, and felt it was her fault when anything went wrong.

"The floor's dry now. Honey, would you mind setting the chairs right-side up? They make me nervous like that." After Adrienne married, Tante Sis complained one day about how much it cost to have them recaned. That was why once a year she had to moisten the seats to keep the caning from drying out and cracking. To remind herself, she made a point of doing it every Ash Wednesday after supper, to take her mind off of the dessert she was giving up.

While Adrienne finished packing the china cabinet, she could hear Jerome in the kitchen, throwing pots and pans into boxes. He'd told her after the funeral that if there was anything he knew how to do, it was pack. He should. She had three scratched-out pages in her telephone book devoted to his changes of address. But at least Jerome had been home to serve as pallbearer, along with five parishioners from St. Rose de Lima she recruited. They had a hard time getting the coffin inside the opening to the tomb. The pallbearers pushed and shoved, but something was obstructing it. Finally a man from the cemetery leaned inside to straighten some plywood that the coffin was supposed to slide along. Adrienne was standing there, thinking Tante Sis just refuses to go until she explains one last secret, gives one last order, one last warning.

Shutting the china cabinet door, Adrienne wondered what warning Tante Sis had wanted to give her during her final moment in the sun.

Adrienne and her son worked all afternoon, emptying drawers and stacking boxes, listening to rain gurgling through gutter pipes and to their own footsteps echoing through the musty rooms. At the bottom of the chifforobe she discovered her faded blue baby pillow embroidered in pink curlicues with the names *Adrienne & Jerome*. She came across a shoe box of her brother's Indian arrowheads, and a sheaf of her son's grade-school drawings that said in uneven block letters "FOR TANT SISE." When she found him, Jerome was sprawled on the front-porch steps next to his bicycle, gazing at the profuse yellow fruit nestled among the dark dripping leaves of the Japanese plum tree.

"What's that bicycle doing out here?" Adrienne asked. "You're not leaving, are you?"

"I was just thinking how when I was little and got in the way in the kitchen, Tante Sis would say, 'Go to the front gallery and see if you're there.' And I'd run out here as fast as my legs could carry me, then race back to the kitchen to tell her, 'I'm there!'"

"She pulled that on me, too, when I was a little girl."

"Then she'd say, 'No you're not, you're here. Now go see if you're there.' So I'd run to the porch and scream all the way through the house, 'Quick, come see, here I am!'

"You always preferred there to here." The bearded psychiatrist had pointed out that Adrienne's son left her at the same age as her brother did. Until recently, she pictured them both frozen at sixteen. But time had resumed now that Jerome was back.

Her son stood up to leave.

"Look at these." Adrienne unfolded the yellowed tablet paper, trying to detain him. "Drawings you made for Tante Sis in grammar school. I'm sure art historians will be interested in them one day."

Jerome rolled his eyes, slipped the bundle into his backpack, and then put on the slicker. "The rain's slacked off now," he said, "and I have an appointment with a collector at 4:30 at a gallery near City Park. I'll be back tomorrow to help you load Yvette's van."

"Only one more closet to clean out, then I'll give you a lift. I'm driving that way. Wait," she said, grabbing the handlebars, her features suddenly fierce. "I want you to stay here with me. Jerome, do you hear me?"

"Can't, Mother. I'll be late," Jerome said, lifting the bicycle from her grasp. "I need to sell something."

"We still have so many things to go through together. Don't you dare—"

"Tomorrow. I promise. *Ciao, bella.*"

Adrienne crossed her arms as he carried the light-weight bike with one hand to the street and mounted it, then turned to wave. The bearded face smiled sweetly as a jack-o'-lantern, framed by a blur of yellow against the slick cement, one foot on the ground, one poised on a pedal. Where had she seen a black-and-white photograph just like this? Then the other foot rose, his back arched, and he veered onto Esplanade to vanish under the live oaks.

Adrienne stomped into the house and began throwing everything within reach into boxes. She stripped clothes from hangers in the bedroom closet, separating them into three piles, one for Goodwill, one for Yvette, and one for herself. She paced restlessly through the house, low heels clacking along bare floorboards. A dog was howling next door, and then whimpered as if it wanted to be let in. A man shouted, a screen door slammed. The dog kept howling.

She began to pack the framed family photographs lined up along the living-room mantel, the eyes in each picture searing her with accusations until she placed it face down in a box. If only she could have five, maybe ten minutes more with each of them, just to say how sorry she was. In these rooms she had managed to extend childhood well past middle age. And now, for the first time, she felt like an old woman. In her daydream, Jerome would take over the house, and then, oh no, such-and-such would happen and she'd be forced to move back in. They would while away afternoons reading the paper on the side gallery and laughing at a scruffy stray that would have puppies under the steps, causing so much commotion she'd have to lie down on the daybed with a cold washrag over her forehead just to contain her happiness that everything was together again.

Adrienne & Jerome.

Wait a minute, she thought. This wasn't who her son was at all. He drank espresso all day and stayed up all night listening to pounding, mechanical music as he swirled paint around on huge canvasses. The fumes alone made her dizzy. Did he have any love in his life? Did Sunday morning make him feel blue, too? She'd never really gotten to know him but soon would, after all this dying business was finally over.

Adrienne stepped back to observe the half-emptied room. The house seemed smaller and shabbier, not like the imposing stage set where she'd grown up, but like a place strangers would gut and remodel. A unit they'd say had potential. A fixer-upper. She took Tante Sis's flannel housecoat from a hook in the bathroom and held it to her face. It still smelled like her, of lilac talcum and coffee and Vap-O-Rub. In the pocket she found a Walgreens receipt for $4.29 dated two weeks ago, and then folded the housecoat into the Goodwill pile.

The last time Tante Sis had worn it, she had no idea she would never be back home.

Police sirens wailed in the distance, growing louder and louder. Adrienne didn't want to be walking to her car in the dark, not alone in this neighborhood. She fastened the doors and windows, and at the last minute stuffed the embroidered baby pillow into the pocket of her rose-colored raincoat.

When she stepped onto the front gallery, it was drizzling, slowly, endlessly, every drop in the sky being wrung out like a dishrag. She hesitated in the yellow porchlight, looking out over leafy North Miro, as if she knew this was the last moment she'd ever see the world right-side up. "There you are, Jerome," Adrienne muttered to herself, locking the empty house behind her. "And here I am."

The windshield wipers squeaked as she drove her Datsun along Esplanade, hugging the steering wheel to squint with hooded eyes through the rain. Her hair was sopping wet from the run to the car, sticking in damp strands across her forehead. By the time she reached Broad Street, traffic had slowed to a crawl. In the distance strobes were pulsing in overhead branches, and cars creeping in the right-hand lane past the Fair Grounds and St. Louis Cemetery toward City Park.

She still had to ring Yvette about tomorrow, talk with the estate-sale people and the tombstone engravers. If that wasn't enough, now there must have been some awful accident. There always was when you didn't have a moment to spare. A policeman was directing cars past an ambulance with a revolving red light that cast an infernal glow over the rain-slickened street. At the same instant she felt in her raincoat pocket, she spotted the twisted yellow metal on the neutral ground. In the eerie light, her son's contorted bicycle wheel was pointing upward between two black tree trunks like a medieval crucifixion.

She leaned on her horn, braking the car.

Her expression froze, and then melted like pink Crayola into the blotchy face of a little girl who had been punished for life. And never knew why.

Rain dribbled through her hair and down her cheeks. She found herself on the street clutching the baby pillow, as if this were the perfect place for an old lady to take a nap, next to the shrouded gurney with green running shoes poking out. She wanted to show the pillow to the policeman, tracing the names with her finger, as if this were her I.D. and would explain everything: *Adrienne & Jerome.* You see, officer, she was Adrienne and needed to ask where Jerome was, to make sure the policeman told her brother she was waiting for him and loved him more than God did and not to keep leaving her alone like this, again and again.

The double feature was over, and it was getting late.

WHAT FLOATS

"**S**he's lying down."

That's what I told Miss Viola from down the block when she stopped by to see my mother. Miss Viola straightened the strap on her flowered sundress, peering through the half-opened screen door into our messy kitchen. She held a pack of Kools in one hand and looked like she expected coffee.

"Jonathan," asked Miss Viola, squinting her mascaraed eyes, "is your mother sick?"

"No. I mean, yes. A little."

"One of those headaches?" Miss Viola wrinkled her brow, waiting for a response. I said nothing. "Well, tell her to ring me when she feels better."

I closed and locked the door, and went back to washing dishes. This was the first Wednesday after it happened, and I'd never cooked for myself before. I didn't even know you had to defrost hamburgers from the freezer before you fried them. The charred lump of meat that I gobbled took an hour to cook. I put a lot of mustard on it. There was no bread.

I still had homework to do. I tiptoed into Mother's room and turned up the air conditioner. I don't know why I tiptoed, but it was awfully quiet in there. I flicked on the lamp next to the bed and tried to tug the covers out from under her, but they were tucked tight and wouldn't budge. So I ripped the pages out of my fifth-grade arithmetic workbook and spread them on top of her in case she was chilly. She looked so peaceful in the blue rayon dress she'd been wearing when she rushed home from work on Monday evening.

"Just need to lie down for a few minutes," she'd said, sweeping past me into her bedroom. Lately she'd had a lot of headaches, so I knew how to take care of myself while she rested. I peeked into her room every half hour. Usually she asked for a glass of water, but now she wasn't asking for any water. I brought her a glass anyway.

She was still lying down.

I shook her. She moaned.

Then I shook her again. She didn't moan.

Her eyes were wide open, staring straight at the ceiling.

I let the phone ring and ring, and latched the doors. She was afraid of burglars and murderers in Gentilly, our neighborhood of raised wooden bungalows behind the racetrack in New Orleans. Mostly there were just kids like me with moms like her, except the other houses had daddies. We lived in my grandparents' house, where my mother had grown up. After my father left us, MawMaw and PawPaw moved to Jackson, Mississippi, and let us live there. But my grandparents thought I was a big mistake.

"Look how that boy is growing up." MawMaw would shake her head. "A nine-year-old needs a father and brothers and sisters. He can't live alone with a woman who works in a drugstore all day. And kids shouldn't be raised around a man with a temper like that. Should have known that before you started."

Whenever I sassed or wouldn't go to bed on time, my mother would say she couldn't do a thing with me.

"I'll have to send you to live with your father. He could make you listen."

That was my worst fear, that I'd have to go live with my father in California. When he left, he busted up everything. It took us a week to pick the broken glass out of the carpet. He didn't remember my birthday, and when he called he was gruff and grouchy and didn't ask to talk with me. "Put your mother on," he'd say when I answered. I was just a nuisance in the way.

I climbed into bed and tried to read the chapter in *Faraway Lands and Peoples* about the Egyptian pyramids, but I couldn't keep my eyes on the page. So I slid under the bed where no bad thoughts or murderers could get me. Late at night I would often lie there listening to clicks and thumps and footsteps echoing through the four-room house. Closet doors creaked open and closed, drawers slammed shut. Shoe shadows shuffled past the slit of light under the bedroom door. Sometimes I heard a suitcase being packed. I was convinced my parents were stealing away to leave me alone under the bed. But in the morning they were both at the breakfast table.

Except for the morning after my father left. It looked like a hurricane had hit. There wasn't a single unbroken dish in the house.

I lay there under the dusty box springs for the longest time, wondering what was going to happen to me. When I spotted daylight creeping across the carpet, I crawled out, ate some Coca Puffs, and got ready for school. I still had clean clothes in the chifforobe, only I wasn't used to picking out what to wear. I climbed on a chair and stuck my hand into the big pickle jar on top of the refrigerator, taking whatever money I would need for busfare and lunch at school.

I checked on mother. Her hand was stiff as a baseball mitt, but I needed to hold it while I talked with her. I told her I'd see her at 3:30. Then I kissed her on the forehead.

Before I left, I switched the overhead light on and off about a hundred times. Darkness, light, darkness, light. The light was never gone for good. I could always get it back when I wanted it.

Then I amped up the air conditioner to high.

The room was already starting to smell.

"What's that you're fooling with, Jonathan?"

"A mosquito hawk." I was petting its crackly head while fussy Miss Avery was telling us how Egyptians buried Pharaohs in the pyramids.

"But it's dead," she said, staring into my hands.

"How do you know?" When I picked it up off the playground, it was twitching.

"Go put that thing in the trash."

I walked to the garbage can, but tucked the brittle wings inside my shirt's breast pocket.

"Now, class. After the Pharaoh was mummified, he was placed into a sarcophagus." Miss Avery wrote "sarcophagus" on the blackboard. I wrote "mommyfi" in my notebook. This was starting to make some sense. "Then food and water were placed in bowls to give him something to eat and drink during the long journey to the underworld."

"What's the underworld?" Eileen Gusman asked.

"Hell," shouted the redheaded kid from the back of the room.

"He cussed," Eileen said. Everybody exploded. Only I wasn't laughing. I was almost crying. I had to excuse myself to the bathroom to think this over. Where is hell? I wondered, and how do you know if you're there?

After school I walked the six blocks to City Park. Mother wouldn't miss me. I perched on a big gnarled root under a live oak and studied the mosquito hawk. How could a mother or a mosquito hawk or a Pharaoh be alive one minute, and not alive the next? What was the spark inside something that made it alive? Was it like the on/off switch for a light bulb or air conditioner? If you turned it off, couldn't you turn it back on again? Forever was the part I couldn't get. How long did forever last? Did it go on and on and on and then stop somewhere in the middle of the sky?

Was a star the end of forever?

I'd never really known anybody who just stopped. I'd seen sparrows rotting in the back yard, but mother said don't touch them, they had diseases. I wondered if the mosquito hawk had a disease now that it was dead. Was disease what you got when you stopped moving, like Mother?

When I arrived home, Miss Viola was standing in front of the kitchen door with her arms crossed.

"Your mother doesn't answer the phone or my knocking. Where is she?"

"She's at work."

"But you said she was sick."

"She felt better today, and went to work."

Miss Viola looked me straight in the eye. "Tell her to call me as soon as she gets home."

"Sure."

"Promise?"

As soon as I got inside, I put the mosquito hawk next to my school books on the kitchen table. I didn't promise Miss Viola anything. Mother never really liked her anyway.

The key to keeping our secret was not answering the telephone, and some nights it rang and rang. I knew the minute I spoke with MawMaw or PawPaw they would insist on talking to Mother. I couldn't just say she was lying down. I couldn't just say she was still at work. I couldn't even say she was in the bathroom. I needed to wait until Mother got to the end of forever and came back. I hoped it didn't last past the weekend.

I was running out of everything.

I took whatever money was left and bought milk, cereal, Cokes, and cookies at the corner store. I put a Coke and cookies on Mother's night table, like the Egyptians did for the Pharaoh's mommies to eat and drink on their trips to forever. Mother didn't eat or drink much, but once a bite of Oreo was nibbled away. Maybe she was hungry and ready to come back.

At night I would stare at the stars and wonder if she'd gotten there yet. The mosquito hawk was flaking to pieces, and I really had to take a deep breath every time I stepped into Mother's room. I pictured it as her pyramid, and her bed as a boat that the dog god Anubis rowed to the other side.

I wanted her back so bad. But when I looked up in the sky, forever was far away.

Miss Avery said I smelled, so I had to remember to take a bath. And comb my hair. I tried to avoid my friends at school, afraid I would burst out crying. I told them I had a disease, and they shouldn't get near me. During recess I walked along the outside walls of the building with a pencil in one hand, marking a continuous line in the gray cement of Jean Gordon Grammar School that got darker and darker every time I circled around.

That was my map to forever.

My grandparents raised me in Jackson, and never took me back to New Orleans except once, to visit my mother's tomb. They said the city was too dangerous. The story of the boy who stayed with his mother's corpse for ten days after she died of a stroke made the newspapers, but my grandparents never showed me the clippings. I found them stuffed in a yellowed envelope with my mother's death certificate after my grandparents passed on, when I was already in college in Massachusetts. Not once did MawMaw and PawPaw ever mention my mother or father in front of me. My childhood split into two separate hemispheres, like an peeled orange.

The first half, the nine years I spent in New Orleans with my mother, eventually shriveled and dried up. I seldom thought of it. Soon after I arrived in Mississippi, my grandparents treated me as if I'd been born yesterday. Their only therapy was complete erasure, and it worked. The second half of my childhood I ate up greedily, sucking out every last drop of juice. I was an honors student and star athlete. To this day I speak with the hint of a Mississippi drawl. I haven't talked with my father in twenty years, since the first time he was sent to jail. I've never felt the slightest curiosity to look him up. I'm an agnostic, a Democrat, and an architect, divorced and with two kids of my own. Up here in the North, I'm considered a colorful character, a self-styled Mississippi redneck, a personality I exaggerate whenever possible. Except for my ex-wife, I've never told anyone about my origins in New Orleans, or about my mother. In my white-wine circles, I'm already considered enough of a lunatic because I eat boiled peanuts and listen to country western.

Why go overboard by telling people the truth?

Like everyone up here, I was riveted to the TV coverage of the hurricane that just devastated the Gulf Coast. I watched it day and night for two weeks, and became a source of firsthand commentary among friends. I was even interviewed on the radio as a Mississippian. I paid special attention to the details about New Orleans. I studied the city floodmaps posted neighborhood by neighborhood on the Internet, and finally located the block where I used to live on Gardena Drive. My grandparents had sold the house years ago, after my mother died. I tried to picture it flooded up to the roof.

I recognized familiar landmarks in TV footage of the rescue boats patrolling the neighborhood. People died on nearby rooftops or suffocated in attics. I stopped eating and began to lose sleep. When I did manage to sleep, I'd often sleepwalk, and once woke up at three in the morning behind the wheel of my truck in the garage. I dreamed of my mother's house, of Miss Viola and Miss Avery. My mother was floating down the street on her bed holding a pyramid. She kept calling and calling for me, warning me not to let anyone in. I waded through water up to my waist looking for her but could never find her bedroom.

Her death took New Orleans away from me for the first time. But all these years a nine-year-old boy had been waiting there inside a sealed room for his mother to return. Then the hurricane washed that room away. Strange, but when a tragedy strikes once, you think what tough luck. But when the same tragedy is repeated, you crumble, reliving both at once. I couldn't concentrate on blueprints and spoke out of turn at meetings. I'd wake up dazed and confused. Nobody could understand why I took what was happening in New Orleans so hard.

My ex-wife suggested therapy.

I said "naw."

As soon as I stepped out of the doors of Louis Armstrong International Airport, the blanket of heat and humidity wrapped me from head to foot. At first I couldn't breath, and then I sank into air as familiar as old bedclothes. My long-sleeved Oxford shirt was soaked with sweat. Immediately I began to sneeze and cough, and the cough followed me during the next three days I spent in New Orleans.

I had booked my seat at the last minute, on impulse. It was Easter week in April, eight months after the storm. I justified the trip at the office with some architectural gobbledegook about studying "paradigms of restoration in flood-impacted urban centers." There was nothing I could do for the city. I knew that. But I hadn't even gone to my mother's funeral, if she had one, and I was being eaten alive by a sense of loss. I planned to visit my mother's tomb, walk around, scarf up some jambalaya, and then hightail it home.

And maybe drive down the street where I once lived.

"Where you from?" The man from the airport car rental agency was the first to greet me with that unnerving question.

"Originally from here," I shot back without thinking.

"How did y'all do?" That was the other question I heard everywhere. It didn't mean how was I feeling but how much of my life the storm had destroyed. I blinked my eyes.

"Where abouts in the city your people from?" he asked.

"Gentilly."

He shook his graying afro as he filled out the form. "Eight foot of water. Nothing left, baby. My mama stayed by there. Nothing left. Sign here. And welcome home."

It was late afternoon when I pulled up in front of 1327 Gardena Drive. I'd been circling the ashen streets of the ghost-town city all day. Even with the windows rolled up, I kept coughing. For mile after mile I'd been tracing the brown flood lines on houses: up to my knees in this block, up to my waist a few blocks down, over my head closer to Lake Pontchartrain. Most houses stood empty or boarded up. Others showed signs of gutting, with crusty belongings heaped in piles at the curb. Here and there I spotted a white FEMA trailer parked in a driveway, with masked people dragging Sheetrock across dead gray lawns. But in most neighborhoods, the houses sat abandoned, doors opened, windows askew, with ominous red Xs painted on the outside. In the crux of the X was the number of dead bodies discovered inside.

I felt as if I were encased in a submarine bell, floating through the amber shadows of a submerged world. A giant horned toad looming on the horizon, or a python twined around a rusted swing set, wouldn't have surprised me more.

"If you get out the car," the gas station attendant had warned, "be careful of gators. They taking over."

I hadn't been to my mother's tomb yet, but I carried her photograph in the breast pocket of my shirt. Now I was seeing the city through her eyes. When I drove past the cemetery, a Holy Friday procession had been winding its way between the rows of little white houses. The entire city was my mother's tomb. I thought I'd spotted her once from the back, until the woman turned around, skull teeth bared, laughing.

A corroded tricycle sat in the walkway to my mother's front door.

The splintered door stood ajar. The X spray-painted on the side of the house indicated one body had been found inside.

I kicked open the door and stood on the threshold. Great splotches of mold blackened the walls, and the furniture was upside down, strewn across the floor. The curtains were shreds of rotting fabric hanging translucent in late afternoon sunlight. I swabbed my face with a handkerchief and stepped into the oven-like heat, kicking my way through a fetid nest of buckled books and broken crockery. This was how the room had felt the morning after my father left. I could see my mother and me on our knees, picking through the debris.

I walked into the kitchen. In a cleared area smelling of Clorox, Miss Viola was seated at the table. She was still young, younger than I appeared, wearing a flowered sundress. A white rose in a bud vase stood at the center of the table, next to two coffee cups. She smiled and beckoned me to sit down.

"You probably don't recognize me. I'm Jonathan."

"Your mother told me you were coming."

The blood drained from my face.

"She said you'd be tired and to fix up your room."

"Where is she?"

"She's lying down."

"Do you live here?"

"I look after all these places now."

"Miss Viola, I—"

"Hush. You've been gone a long time. You'll get used to it. We'll all still here, just the way you left us. You take cream in your coffee?"

While I drank the coffee, she smoked a cigarette and then touched up her lipstick. The refrigerator was on its side, and the stove on top of it, the oven door hanging open like a panting tongue.

"Is Mother in her room?

"You remember where it is?"

I reached for the light switch when I stepped into the room. Off, on. Off, on. Nothing. Both windows were open, and a huge chunk of the wall was missing. The outside had moved inside. Leafy mirliton vines were climbing up the mildewed walls, and green garden lizards scampered through overturned furniture.

The irridescent wings of a blue mosquito hawk were vibrating on the bed post.

But the bed was empty. Fern fronds were sprouting out of the sodden mattress, the spiny kind that grew between the bricks of tombs.

"Good night," I told the bed. "Good night."

In my room I pictured where each piece of furniture had been. This still must have been a boy's room, I thought, stepping around a moldy catcher's mitt and plastic action figures strewn across the floor. The bed was in the same place mine had been, made up with fresh white sheets.

I slid under the bed. The carpet stank, but I felt safe. Next to me I found a red rubber ball and a vinyl children's book, an inflated bathtub book called *What Floats*. I paged through it.

It was amazing what floats and what sinks.

I wondered if I'd be arrested for trespassing. Did New Orleans even have a police force anymore? Sometime during the second week I had remained inside the house with my mother's body, a police car pulled up out front, and two officers banged on the door. I opened it just a sliver.

"You Jonathan?" they asked.

I nodded through the crack.

"Your grandma called a few days ago from Jackson to place a missing person's report. She can't reach y'all. Why's that?"

"The phone is broken."

"They had Bellsouth send a lineman out here yesterday. Said the line is clear. We need to speak with your mother, young man."

"She's at work."

"She hasn't been to work in ten days." The officer adjusted his belt with the holster on it. "Your grandma checked."

"She's lying down."

"Look, son—" The policemen pushed through the screen door, and I ran into my room, sliding in here, under the bed.

One policeman let out a slow whistle as he entered my mother's bedroom. "Hey, come look at this," he said, coughing.

The next thing I knew, a long flashlight was aimed at me under the bed. I kicked at it, and the policemen dragged me out by the feet, screaming. One of them held a fistful of crumpled workbook pages.

"You don't understand," I was shouting red-faced as they carried me squirming between them. "She's coming back. She said to wait here for her. She told me to *stay*."

But I didn't stay.

And here I was, a thirty-five-year-old man with a family of my own, hiding under the bed and sniveling like a nine-year-old.

I eased myself out from under the bed, stood up, and dusted myself off. In the kitchen the three-legged table was upside down, with no hint of Miss Viola or her ghostly coffee klatsch. I staggered from the house, eyes stinging, and stumbled onto the eerily silent street. Even the crickets were quiet.

Everything was poised, as if waiting for someone to return.

At dusk on my street in Massachusetts, boys would be playing softball in the street, toddlers careening up driveways on tricycles, and gravy smells wafting from kitchen windows. Men would be hosing lawns,